Witnessing Christ
in Diverse Contexts

Papers from the 17th Annual Consultation of the Centre
for Mission Studies of Union Biblical Seminary,
held at Union Biblical Seminary
from 12th to 14th January, 2011

Witnessing Christ in Diverse Contexts

Papers from the 17th Annual Consultation of the Centre for Mission Studies of Union Biblical Seminary, held at Union Biblical Seminary from 12th to 14th January, 2011

Editors
Sungjemmeren Kijong Imchen
Asangla Lemtur

2019

Witnessing Christ in Diverse Contexts - Jointly published by the Rev. Dr. Ashish Amos of the Indian Society for Promoting Christian Knowledge (ISPCK), Post Box 1585, Kashmere Gate, Delhi-110006 and Union Biblical Seminary (UBS), Pune, Maharashtra-411037.

© CMS-UBS, 2019

ISBN: 978-93-88945-09-7

Laser typeset by

ISPCK, Post Box 1585, 1654, Madarsa Road, Kashmere Gate, Delhi-110006 • *Tel:* 23866323

e-mail: ashish@ispck.org.in • ella@ispck.org.in
website: www.ispck.org.in

Contents

Preface

The Church is often a two-party system. This divided house is sometimes framed in terms of Ecumenical and Evangelical segments. Some try to bridge the gap between the two groups. While we all long for a united brotherhood, the reality remains that people think and theologize differently in different camps of Christian belief and practice. While working for unity, we need to minister in the reality of who we are speaking to. This edition of the Centre for Mission Studies publication provides a *shibboleth* by pointing to the common practice of redefinition of yet another precious concept. This has typically occurred in the case of terms such as: evangelical, inerrancy, and mission. One further term that has fallen into redefinition is 'Witness.' The way one uses witness can be an indicator of where they stand theologically.

It was my privilege to represent UBS at the Centenary of the 1910 World Mission Conference in Edinburgh and to promote our CMS publications there. The concept of 'Witness' was a hot topic at that gathering and formed the title concept for the second volume of that consulation's conference publication. This prompted me to encourage the next CMS consultation to focus on the theme "Witness to Christ in Diverse Contexts." As evangelicals how do we understand and practice witness in a manner that is consistent with a high view of Scripture, a high level of compassion for the needy, and an acute sensitivity to the cultural context in which we serve?

As Union Biblical Seminary celebrates the 25th anniversary of the Centre for Mission Studies, this collection of articles draws attention to this crucial concept of witness. What makes this such an appropriate focus is the background biblical term *marturion*, which reminds us that the martyrs of scripture suffered and lost their lives to demonstrate their faith in a hostile environment. This attitude of costly discipleship is central to the purposes of the CMS in its endeavor to promote and centralize mission in the vision of UBS. The theme of the 17th Annual CMS Consultation was "Witness Christ in Diverse Contexts." This theme echoes the history of UBS and the intention to biblically train disciples to live and share their Christian faith boldly in the various settings of India and beyond.

We wish well to those who find ways of using the concept of witness that do not reflect the costly discipleship of the New Testament martyrs nor of the estimated 100,000 worldwide that give their lives each year as they take up their cross of suffering discipleship. At the same time, by speaking out on a biblical perspective, we can remind all involved that there is an original intent of Scripture that it is essential to remember. Through this theme we hope to give evangelical voices an opportunity to speak out clearly on what witness should look like in this era of mission in India and beyond.

Frank Fox, Ph.D.
Professor of Global Studies,
Liberty University, Lynchburg, Virginia

Introduction

Witnessing Christ in Diverse Contexts consists of ten papers only out of twelve essays that were presented and two devotional messages that were delivered at the 17th Annual Centre for Mission Consultation which was held at Union Biblical Seminary, Pune from 12th till 14th January 2011. This is due to the unavailability of materials. This essay introduces the essays briefly.

In "Taking Our Cue from Isaiah on How to Witness Today" Charles Echols explains the four dimensions of the meaning of "witness" in Isaiah 40-55, namely, witness as testimony that Yahweh exists, is sovereign, is the only God, and that it is praxis. He then compares it to the idea in Acts 1:8. He concludes that, "the selected passages reveal a dual dimension of the witness – internal and external, or stative and proselytizing" and that [i]ronically, even the internal dimensions have evangelistic potential."

In "Becoming All Things to Everyone: Witnessing to Christ in India Today" V. J. John presents the Indian context in terms of plurality. He then describes the Corinthians setting in terms of political subjugation, economic inequality, and cultural alienation. After which he gives a biblico-theological analysis of 1 Corinthians 9:19-23. Finally, he derives a formula of witnessing relevant for Indian context.

In "A Macarian-Wesleyan Theology of Mission" Matt Friedman explores the idea of *theosis* focusing on the works of Macarius Symeon and how it permeated into the teachings in early Pietism and early Methodism and derives "a theology of mission in which this union with God is meant to be lived out individually and in community in a manner in which the *missio Dei* is extended in witness to the entire world."

In "Christian Witness as *With-Ness* in the Context of the 'Conversion' Controversy in India" Rufus Peniel "conceives of witness in the Indian context as 'with-ness' - as radical accompaniment and not abandonment - of those who have opted to convert, especially the subalterns, the term subaltern in this case implying those who have been rendered the 'Others' in the human story of exclusion, marginalization and oppression."

In "Witnessing Christ to a Community in Chaos," A. Selvaraj describes the reality of chaos in India. He then exposes the biblical view on chaos. He prescribes that, "[t]he church has to play a liberative role to work for equality and justice to free people from the bondages of chaos, discrimination, poverty, and exploitation. That way we can offer through Christ a new life and meaning to them."

In "Witnessing to Christ in a Pluralistic Context: Five Models from the Madras Christian College" Joshua Kalapati brings out five models of witnessing from the lives of five former principals of Madras Christian College, namely, Rev. John Anderson, Rev. William Miller, Rev. Alfred George Hogg, Rev. Alexander John Boyd, and Dr Chandran D. S. Devanesen. He concludes that, "there can be no ONE way of presenting Christ and His message in the Indian context. We need to employ culture-specific, context-specific, people-specific models of Christian witness."

In "Witnessing to Christ among Intellectuals" Joshua Iyadurai presents a conviction that "the focus of Mission in 21st century needs to be shifted towards intellectuals in campuses and corporate world." He describes Jesus' style of reaching individuals; he then describes postmodernism; and exposes that the mindsets of Indian intellectuals are religiously inclined. He prescribes that in our strategizing, "[w]e need to keep in mind that our intellectual presentation is not going to win a person to Christ; but it can clear the philosophical barriers in understanding the gospel intellectually."

In "The Early Mizo Mission School Teachers' Role in Witnessing to Christ" Marina Ngursangzeli discusses "witness" in historical perspective" especially describing the role played by early Mizo Christians who brought about transformation of the Mizo society.

In "The Missional Church in a Secular Age with Special Focus on the 'Homo Areligious'" Martin Reppenhagen describes "a secular age" as context for a missional church with special reference to Germans whom he considers as homo areligious. He describes conditions of spirituality and church membership in Germany and prescribes a missional church as one of the best responses to the secular age.

In "Mission to the Digital World" J. N. Manokaran describes the digital world and the impact of information technology and concludes that "the digital world has opened up new opportunities and open doors for innovative mission. The digital natives could not be reached out through traditional methods and strategies." And prescribes "the Church to look at this as a new frontier and allot resources for reaching this world effectively."

Editors

Sungjemmeren Kijong Imchen and Asangla Lemtur

1
Taking Our Cue From Second Isaiah on How to Be Witnesses Today

Charles L. Echols

Although it may seem counterintuitive, Isaiah is very relevant to the theme of this year's consultation, "Witnessing to Christ in Diverse Contexts." Regarding the witness component, Augustine of Hippo is said to have remarked that if you want to lead someone to Jesus, have them read Isaiah. Indeed, in Acts 1:8, Jesus quotes Isaiah 43:10, 12 and 44:8. Regarding diversity, like the primitive and modern churches, the Israelites of Isaiah's day lived in a heterogeneous world. Sandwiched between Egypt and Mesopotamia, Israel was well informed of the cultures and religions of these empires. Moreover, located in Canaan, its immediate socio-religious neighbors included several other northwest Semitic peoples who worshiped deities other than Yahweh. Isaiah was thus well placed as a witness amongst diversity. Given the subtext of this year's consultation, "You will be my witnesses" (Acts 1:8), Isaiah 43:10, 12; and 44:8 offer a germane and economic focus by which to explore this year's theme from the perspective of one section of the Old Testament as well as its nexus to the New Testament and to the contemporary church. [2] This exercise demonstrates that, in these verses in Isaiah 40-55, any proclamatory role is predicated upon an internal, reflexive role.[3] That is, one must first be a witness to oneself before one can be a witness outside of the faith community.

It is possible to substantiate this proposition, first, by establishing the meaning of "witness" in the Old Testament in general and then, second, in Isaiah 40-55, where it comprises at least four dimensions. These findings can then be compared fruitfully with the meaning of witness in Acts 1:8, and, finally, serve as the basis for some conclusions for the contemporary church.

The Basic Meaning of "Witness" in the Old Testament

Although the English noun, "witness," is rendered by more than one Hebrew term in the Old Testament, the principal expression is the noun עֵד, *ēd*; and, indeed, it is the term which is used in Isaiah 40-55.[4] Semantic relatives include the denominative verb, II *ûd*. Occurring only in the Hiphil and Hophal stems, it means "to testify, bear witness (for or against); cause to testify, take as witness; call as witness, invoke; protest, affirm solemnly, warn; exhort solemnly, charge; enjoin solemnly."[5] The capacity of testifying can occur in legal or covenantal contexts.[6]

The present focus, however, is on the noun *ēd*, which means "a witness," "testimony," or "evidence."[7] Moreover, a witness could include people, deities, or even inanimate objects such as mountains or the heavens. Joshua, for example, appoints the Israelites as witnesses against themselves (Josh 24:22), and Yahweh calls for songs, the book of the law, and even "heaven and earth" to be used as witnesses on his behalf (respectively, Deut 31:19, 26, 28). The capacity of humans to function as witnesses is particularly important in the legal or covenantal context, which occurs nominally as well as verbally. Here also, witnesses can be animate or inanimate. For instance, Abraham offers sheep to Abimelech (Gen 21:30), Jacob and Laban construct a stone heap as a witness to their agreement (Gen 31:48, 52), and Samuel calls Yahweh as witness before the people of his innocence.[8] In the Old Testament, then, a witness is someone (or something) who verifies an assertion by a claimant. Typically, three parties are involved: the claimant, the audience of the claimant, and the witness who verifies the authenticity of the claimant's assertion.

The Meaning of Witness in Isaiah 40-55

Before considering what Isaiah has in mind by "witness," it is necessary to identify where the term occurs in the book of Isaiah, and then to explain why attention will be restricted to four occurrences. A brief discussion of the literary unit, Isaiah 40-55, and its historical setting will contribute to the meaning of "witness" in the four occurrences and in Acts 1:8. The final preliminary task is to delimit the units in which the four occur and to provide a brief exegesis of both. This effort will yield four dimensions of "witness" in the selected passages.

In the book of Isaiah, the term *'ēd*, "witness," occurs eight times: 8:2; 19:20; 43:9, 10, 12; 44:8, 9; 55:4.[9] The first two are almost certainly from the eighth-century Isaiah ben Amoz. The rest occur in what is routinely referred to as Deutero or Second Isaiah. Of these, 55:4 is concerned with David; and 44:9 occurs in what is arguably a prose polemic against idolatry, and is thus form-critically distinct from 44:8. Moreover, the "witnesses" in v. 9 are Gentiles, and the Jewish witnesses are out of the picture. For these reasons I will exclude 44:9 and 55:4 from consideration and focus on the remaining four, viz. 43:9, 10, 12; and 44:8.

As mentioned the four remaining verses occur in Second Isaiah, a corpus that is dated to the exile, or ca. 587-538 B.C. While some scholars continue to argue for a unified Isaiah – which would place the entire book in the 8th century B.C. – it is a minority view. The overwhelming consensus is on cps. 40-55 as hailing from the exilic era.[10] Regarding the geographical setting, Duhm suggested Phoenicia, and Marti favored Egypt; but most scholars locate the prophet in Babylonia. A minority, however, argues for Judea.[11] Blenkinsopp thinks that one cannot settle the issue with certainty, but on balance it is probably Babylonia.[12] It is possible, however, that the prophet was addressing his people both in Palestine and Babylonia – that he was supporting a two-fold effort, viz., witnessing in Judea and Babylonia, or, evangelism and mission, respectively. This has tantalizing heuristic possibilities for Acts 1:8, but first things first. It remains simply to observe that the destruction of the Jerusalem temple and the exile to Babylonia called into question the very existence of Yahweh, his sovereignty (and thus his capacity to deliver vis-à-vis the other gods), and the status of the covenant.

Isaiah 43:8-13

The four occurrences of "witness" can be grouped into two units, the first being 43:8-13. Form critically it is the trial genre, and thus initiates a break from 43:1-7, which can be classified as an oracle of salvation that describes the restoration of the Jews.[13] Once restored, however, Yahweh has a point to make, for which the prophet uses the trial genre. There are also rhetorical grounds for making a division between v. 7 and v. 8, including the imperative in v. 8 and the series of rhetorical questions in v. 9b, both of which are followed by jussives

(vv. 9a, 9c). The next unit, 43:14-21, returns to the oracle of salvation, with creation and restoration accented.

The first unit features three parties: Yahweh (speaking through the prophet), the blind and deaf people, and the nations. The second group is somewhat ambiguous, but its identity as the exiles is reasonably clear from references such as Isa 6:6-10, where the iniquitous Israelites are condemned by Yahweh in the pre-exilic era, and Isa 35:5, which occurs in an oracle of salvation. More significantly, in Isa 42:18-19 Yahweh distinguishes (disparagingly) blind, deaf Israel from his servant. The servant is also blind and deaf, nevertheless he is able to perceive Yahweh's will and follows it accordingly. In 43:8-13, the blind and deaf exiles are redeemed (43:1) and thus akin to the servant in that despite their disabilities they will serve as Yahweh's witnesses (v. 10).[14] Since the lawsuit is over the question of who is god, Yahweh summons the nations to settle the dispute of divinity, which essentially amounts to the ability to prognosticate.[15] The court being prepared, Yahweh makes his first charge to the nations: can they declare the former things (v. 9)? The former things are not specified, but probably refer to past events in history in general and in the history of Israel in particular. Their declarations must be verified by their witnesses, but neither claims nor verifications are mentioned. Hence, the nations, and by implication, their gods, cannot even state what happened in the past – a fairly low-level ability. The matter is thus settled, and the nations fade from view. Yahweh makes a second statement: the exiles are his witnesses and his chosen servant (v. 10). The shame of the past blindness and deafness (42:18-25) is gone or in the process of passing. The conferral of the exiles to the status of witness and servant is, however, less to settle a dispute between Yahweh and the nations than for the benefit of the exiles themselves. The conferral is so that they will come to the realization and faith that Yahweh is the only god (43:10b-13). Unmistakable is the four-fold occurrence of the clause, "I am": "I am he" (אֲנִי הוּא, 'ănî huʾ, vv. 10, 13), I am Yahweh" (אָנֹכִי יהוה, "ānōḵî yhwh, v. 11), and "I am God" (אֲנִי־אֵל, 'ănî-'ēl, v. 12). These "I am" declarations echo Yahweh's first self-revelation to the Israelites: אֶהְיֶה אֲשֶׁר אֶהְיֶה, 'ehyeh 'ăšer 'ehyeh, "I am who I am" (Exod 3:14).[16] The point is that as Yahweh revealed himself at the beginning of the covenant, so he does now to signify both that the covenant continues and that he is God.[17] Unlike the first self-revelation, however, here Yahweh raises the ontological stakes by claiming that he is not simply the most powerful god, but the only god (v. 10c).[18] Moreover, deliverance may be found only through him (v. 11). Then follows a related claim, particular to Israel, that Yahweh revealed himself and delivered Israel early in its past. The proof is to be supplied by Israel's own witness (v. 12). His past capacities as deity and deliverer are the warrants for the final claim of the unit, which has a present and perhaps even future orientation: Yahweh still exists as does his might and capacity to save (v. 13).

The first unit thus uses the trial genre, in which Yahweh summons the nations and the exiles to court. The unit is unusual in for its silence on the part of the nations and the exiles, so that the six verses are essentially a divine soliloquy. The deity who was presumed dead for some seventy years now speaks with uncontested authority. He has two opponents, the first being the nations, and, by implication, their gods. Yahweh challenges them simply to recount the past, and their inability to do so is striking. Things are not always as they seem. The

exiles are also defendants. They should learn from the nations'
failure to reply that Yahweh not only did not suffer defeat from
his Babylonian opposite number, Marduk, he has reemerged
victoriously and alone in the heavenly sphere. Israel is not,
however, to remain passive. It is Yahweh's servant. It is also a
witness for the prosecution. The latter role is, oddly, reflexive –
at least initially. Yahweh does not charge the exiles to proclaim
his sole divinity to the nations, although that role is implied.[19]
Rather the immediate need is for Israel to witness to itself that
Yahweh is alive, the only god that exists, and, therefore, the
sole source of salvation.[20]

Isaiah 44:6-8
The second unit, 44:6-8, is preceded by an oracle of assurance.
Therein Yahweh effectively reaffirms his covenant with the
Israelites, as indicated, for example, twice through the line,
"my servant . . . whom I have chosen" (vv 1, 2). The messenger
formula marks a break at v. 6, and introduces what may be
regarded generically as a divine boast or a dispute, or a trial.[21]
Again, Yahweh has a claim to make about his singularity. Even
if the next unit (vv. 9-20) is regarded as verse rather than
prose, the shift of attention in v. 9 to a sustained polemic on
the absurdity of idols warrants delimiting vv. 6-8 as a unit (cf.
the same from Elijah to the prophets of Baal in 1 Kgs 18:27).

The messenger formula (v. 6a) proclaims Yahweh as Israel's
ruler and redeemer as well as conveying his sovereignty through
the use of the martial term, "hosts." These acclamations
distinguish Yahweh from Marduk as Israel's god and from
Cyrus as the source of Israel's impending liberation – both of
which are possible because Yahweh is a god of war. Verse 6b
ups the ante through the first-last merism. It clarifies for the
exiles that though Cyrus is the visible deliverer, his success

is attributable entirely to Yahweh. Verse 6 thus lays the basis for the unanswerable challenge in v. 7a. Given his unique ontological status, who can rival Yahweh? The identity of the "ancient people" (v. 7b) is somewhat ambiguous, but probably refers to Israel. The appointment came initially in the covenant with Abraham, but was finalized with Moses. The covenant relationship means that Israel has always known at least some of what was to come: a people, an appointed land, kings, and the blessing of the nations. The exiles have seen most of these promises fulfilled, albeit only to be abrogated over pre-exilic apostasy. Still, Yahweh is about to re-fulfill those same covenantal promises as some of his "new things" (Isa 42:9; 48:6). But to whom are the exiles to declare? The addressee of v. 7a is unstated, and v. 7b offers little light. It seems that two referents are possible: the unnamed nations and the exiles themselves, whose testimony would thus, again, be reflexive.[22] Verse 8 lends some support to the idea that the testimony is directed outwards. Although the content of what was told "of old" is open to many interpretations, the affirmation that the exiles are Yahweh's witnesses makes more sense if the testimony is intended to be directed outwards, to the nations. The content of the message is not explicit, but that it is monotheistic follows naturally from v. 8c.[23] Any doubt that the question, "Is there a god besides me?", is rhetorical disappears from the ensuing statement which uses the metaphor of a rock to compare the stable, unending nature of Yahweh alone.[24] The charge not to fear at the beginning of the verse thus makes sense in a Babylonian setting, especially given the monotheistic message of the testimony.[25]

Looking at the two units together, a few observations follow. Common to both is the trial or dispute genre. Yahweh has a case to prosecute. In the first unit, he summons the nations and the exiles, whereas in the second unit only Israel is summoned (although it is possible that the nations are summoned implicitly). In neither unit do the nations or the exiles speak. It is as though the prosecutor's case is so unshakable as to leave the defendants speechless (cf. Job 40:4). Also, monotheism is central to both passages, which is a clear theological development from the henotheism of the pre-exilic era. The exiles are, furthermore, Yahweh's witnesses, but about what, and to whom? The content of the testimony and its intended recipients are not stated. By drawing on the previous exegesis and by considering the historical context of Second Isaiah, it is possible to delineate four dimensions of being a witness.

Four Dimensions of Witness in Isaiah 43:8-13; 44:6-8

Ego Sum Ergo Deus Est: *Witness as Testimony that Yahweh Exists*

For Descartes the only unequivocal proof of existence was thought, famously expressed in his dictum *cogito ergo sum* ("I think, therefore I am"). The fact that he could think meant that he must necessarily exist. To make a Cartesian pun, *ego sum ergo deus est* ("I am, therefore God is") expresses something of the reverse, viz. the Jews could have reasoned that since they still existed after the destruction of and deportation from Judah, then so must their god, Yahweh.[26] This is because in the ancient Near East the belief was that two nations did not wage war by themselves. Rather their respective deities were engaged simultaneously in battle in the heavenly sphere. In fact, the thinking was that the defeat of a nation signaled the defeat of its god by the opposing god. At this point, Babylonia was still the dominant power, so the exiles would have reckoned

Yahweh as dead. "You are my witnesses" is thus testimony to the ongoing existence of Yahweh.

Witness as Testimony that Yahweh is Sovereign

One corollary of the first dimension is that Yahweh does not simply exist, but is sovereign. How did Israel move from Yahweh's existence to his sovereignty over Marduk? Isaiah 37:12-13 is salutary: Sennacherib of Assyria had not defeated Hezekiah, and, indeed, Assyria succumbed to Babylonia ca. 612 B.C., and Babylonia in turn fell to Persia only 73 years later. Scripture records no speech by the Babylonian king, Nebuchadnezzar, akin to that of Sennacherib, but 2 Chr 36:6 (Septuagint) reports that Yahweh sent him to destroy Judah. Also, 2 Chr 36:23 has Cyrus attributing his victory over Babylonia to Yahweh, and Yahweh orders him to rebuild the Jerusalem temple. Although the exiles were still under Babylonian control, it was possible to infer from the fall of Assyria that Babylonia too would fall from power. Again, the ancients would have accounted such a fall not simply to a change in political fortunes, but as the result of warfare in the heavenly sphere. Since Yahweh continued after the Mesopotamian deities, Assur, Ishtar, and Marduk (et. al), the exiles were witnesses that Yahweh was sovereign over other gods.

Witness as Testimony that Yahweh is the Only God

A more striking corollary is that Yahweh was not simply equal to, or predominant over, all competing deities, but was in fact the sole god.[27] Yahweh's challenge is to "show the former things" (43:9) and the "things to come" (44:7). Anyone with a memory can do former! It is the latter – prescience – which is difficult. Therefore, the inability of the gods simply to articulate past events was damning evidence against their ontological status as deities. The two passages under consideration are part of one of Second Isaiah's most important theological messages, viz. the message (progressive revelation) that moved the exiles' faith from henotheism to monotheism. Israel's witness thus also included the message that there is only one god. The others are simply pretenders, mute, and constructs from earthly materials (e.g., Isa 44:9-20).

What Flavor Witness: Anglican, Baptist?

The three previous dimensions have to do with the content of the testimony, but the fourth concerns the proclamatory nature. In neither of the units does Yahweh command unequivocally the exiles to testify to the Gentiles. To anachronize: were the exiles to function as Anglicans or Baptists? In other words was there an imperative to the exiles to sit tight with the "good news" (the Anglicans), or to bear witness "among the nations" (the Baptists)? For Goldingay the purpose of the trial in 43:8-13 is to "build up the convictions" of the exiles rather than a charge to them to "convince other peoples."[28] From the jury box of the first unit, the exiles had observed the inability of the nations to make a response to Yahweh's charges, and in the second unit, no one makes a rejoinder. It seems, then, that the exiles were to witness to themselves - that "You are my witnesses" carries a reflexive purpose. Yahweh's revelation in the two units was to bolster the faith of the devastated exiles. But was that it? Exiled Israel was not in a vacuum, but in the midst of its captor.[29] Moreover, recalling the basic meaning of "witness" in the Old Testament as someone who verifies an assertion by a claimant, the implication gains strength that there is an "evangelistic" role for the exiles. The appositional mention of "my servant" in 43:10b supports Yahweh's commission as including an external witness.[30] We have seen, furthermore, other points in Isaiah

40-55 which indicate similarly.[31] Goldingay is thus incorrect
– at least at the implicit level – that the role of witnessing is
entirely reflexive. The selected passages evince that being a
witness has internal and external dimensions.

The Meaning of Witness in Acts 1:8

Although the focus of this paper is on Isa 43:8-13 and 44:6-8,
it is fitting to give attention, if only briefly, to the meaning of
"witness" in Acts 1:8. Linguistically, the English term, "witness,"
derives from the noun μάρτυς, *martus*, and, excepting Gen
31:47, this is the word that the Septuagint uses for *'ēd*.[32]
Assuming that Jesus quotes from Isa 43:10, 12; 43:8, he is
consistent with the use of *martus* for *'ēd*. In the New Testament,
martus has a range of meanings, including, literally, a witness
in the legal sense and, figuratively, anyone (including God)
who is able or obliged to bear testimony about something (the
figurative sense also includes the English, "martyr").[33] It is the
second meaning, one who is able to bear testimony, that is at
hand in Acts 1:8.[34]

Dibelius regards Acts 1:8 as the "main theme" and
"programme for the book," an opinion which has support.[35]
Given such significance, it is especially important to understand
the meaning of "witness" in v. 8. Many New Testament
scholars understand it in its external dimension, or mission
as praxis. Strathmann, for example, observes that Luke uses
the term in a particular way, viz. it is not simply attesting to
a historical fact (i.e. the death, resurrection, and ascension
of Jesus), but an explanation of the importance of that fact,
which can only be conveyed by those who know the fact by
experience and by faith.[36] Bruce faults Second Isaiah's audience
for failing to engage as "God's witnesses in the world."[37] Barrett

understands Jesus in v. 8 as commissioning the Apostles "to bear oral testimony, to perform miracles, and in general act with authority."[38] Similarly, Bock regards witnessing in v. 8 as the Spirit-empowered capability to "speak boldly by testifying to the message of God's work through Jesus."[39] Thus the common New Testament scholarly understanding of "witness" in Acts 1:8 has either not recognized the reflexive dimension of witnessing or has not given it adequate attention. Indeed, as mentioned, Bruce chides the exiles for not engaging in witnessing, despite, ironically, citing the very lines, "you are" and "you will be." To be fair, in Acts 1:8, Jesus prophesies that the Apostles would become his witnesses without giving direction as to the shape of that witness. It is only elsewhere – most notably Matt 28:19-20 – that he provides clarity on *what* to do, but even there the "how" is not terribly specific. Did Jesus quote from Isa 43:8-13 and 44:6-8 simply for a coda that would have been both familiar to his Apostles and a slogan for outreach?

Witness as Reflexive and Proclamatory

By now it should be clear that the selected passages communicate primarily that being a witness is internal, or reflexive. For the exiles one result of such witness was to revive their faith in the God of the covenant. The Jews were a minority community that was dominated by a polytheistic people. If those Jews were to be a witness to their neighbors, they needed first to discover that Yahweh existed and to know that he was omnipotent and the sole deity. Similarly, before the ascension, the Apostles were a minority community in fear of the dominant powers (Jews and Romans), living in the larger, polytheistic culture of Hellenism. They were beginning to understand that their recently-resurrected Rabbi-God would ascend to sit at the Father's right hand, and, subsequently, return in uncontested power. But it was all rather much! They needed to digest the magnitude of recent events and the impact of those events on themselves. That is, they needed to be witnesses reflexively before they could be effective witnesses externally in their Greco-Roman context.

If proclamation was implicit in the concept of witnessing in the selected passages, how was it to be proclaimed to those outside of the covenant? The average Babylonian might have surmised at least one of the dimensions of Israel's witness, viz., that Yahweh did exist, but Israel's witness would have piqued greater curiosity among its captors. Traditionally, Moses is said to have given not simply Ten Commandments, but 613. Still, it would have required far fewer than this latter number for a Gentile to recognize that Jews were unique. They did not make images of their god, and refused to work on the seventh day. They strapped strange little boxes to their foreheads and arms. Once a year they killed a lamb and then splashed its blood on their lintels and door posts, but they did not eat meat with its blood in it. A strange bunch indeed! If that Babylonian had thought further, she would have realized that this insignificant people had survived destruction and deportation (indeed many were well-off). Perhaps this might have been enough to move her to strike up a conversation with one of the Jews. If so, she would have heard an incredible story about a mighty god, who chose an obscure people to be a light to the Babylonians – to point her away from false gods to the living god, who gives wise direction for blessed living. In other words, the very character of the Jews would have pointed to the greatness of their god.

Conclusion

Does our exilic prophet contribute to what it means to be a witness in diversity in our day as well? In some ways not much has changed. As Christians in India, we are a minority community in the larger Hindu culture which is both polytheistic and, in the best of times, indifferent towards us. One difference is the arrival of a new, hitherto unknown god, secular humanism, whom many believe has dealt the death blow to God. Thus, even Christians may occasionally wonder if there really is anything or anyone beyond the universe.

Perhaps, then, we also should take our cue on witnessing from Second Isaiah. The selected passages reveal a dual dimension of the witness – internal and external, or reflexive and proclamatory. The latter is implicit in mandate and indefinite in praxis. In Isaiah it is conveyed most clearly in the connection with the servant. The greater emphasis lies on the internal, reflexive dimension. That is, the primary emphasis in these passages is the importance of *being* witnesses. The exiles do not need to *do* anything. They are witnesses to Yahweh by simply *being*.[40] Israel's existence was a witness – silent testimony – to Yahweh (especially after Babylonia fell to Persia). "You are my witnesses" thus refracts through the message, "I am Yahweh," to produce a spectrum of several self-missional "colors." The first is that self-witness re-stokes the fires of our own faith, which, in a world of even more gods than in antiquity, our god, Jesus, does indeed exist. Given the elapse of two-thousand years and the scientific barrage that all that exists is contained within the universe, one can find oneself beginning to question the existence of Jesus. Self-witness reassures such doubts. To borrow a line from the writer to the Hebrews, "Jesus Christ is the same, yesterday and today and forever." Second, our self-witness must also include the testimony that Jesus is sovereign. The Lord competes now against millions of traditional and new deities as well as worldviews such as postmodernism. The

prevailing culture in which we live promulgates the gospels of
its gods (e.g., health, wealth, comfort, salvation). Self-witness
goes further, third, by responding to the statement, "I am
Yahweh," by rejecting the competing deities and acclaiming
the existence of only one god, Jesus. Finally, it is an essential
prerequisite for effective outreach; because if we do not believe
"the story," how can we expect to convince others?

Much can be said about the external, evangelistic dimension
of witness in the selected passages and in Acts 1:8. That
dimension is, however, relatively well-rehearsed. I have chosen
to accent the internal dimension, because it receives little if any
attention, and, again, if it is not in place, the external aspect
will probably have limited impact. Thus, ironically, even the
internal dimension has evangelistic potential. Francis of Assisi is
said to have advised, "Preach the Gospel at all times, and when
necessary use words." That is, there is something inherently
attractive about the Christian whose internal witness is robust.

Endnotes

[1] I am grateful to Dr. Donald Stanley and the Rev. David Pileggi, both
of CMJ Israel, who made possible my stay in Jerusalem, where I wrote
this paper, and to the Rev. Timothy Lowe, Rector of Tantur Ecumenical
Institute, Jerusalem, who provided access to the institute's library and
an office.

[2] For the issue of mission in the book of Isaiah as a whole, see, e.g.,
Elmer A. Martens, "Impulses to Global Mission in Isaiah," *Direction* 35
(2006): 59-69, *idem*, "Impulses to Mission in Isaiah: An Intertextual
Exploration," *Bulletin for Biblical Research* 17 (2007): 215-39.

[3] By "reflexive" I draw from grammar to the type of verb in which the
subject acts upon itself or with respect to itself, as in the Hebrew Niphal
and Hithpael stems, or the Greek middle voice.

[4] One alternative is עָנָה, *ānāh*, the basic meaning of which in the Qal
is "to answer, respond" (F. Brown, et al., *A Hebrew and English Lexicon of
the Old Testament* [Boston: Houghton Mifflin, 1907]), hereafter, BDB; so,

essentially, L. Koehler, et al., *The Hebrew and Aramaic Lexicon of the Old Testament*, trans. and ed. under the supervision of M. E. J. Richardson, 2 vols., (Leiden: Brill, 2001), 1: 851-52; hereafter, *HALOT*. It can mean, "to respond [as a witness], testify," as in Gen 30:33, but the precise, juridical use of the term is absent in Isaiah 40-55. Another term is שָׁמֵעַ, *šōmēa* , but there are no unambiguous instances of "witness" associated with it in BDB or *HALOT*. The NAU and NRSV translate the Qal participial form of it as "witness" in Judg 11:10, which comports with the idea of witnessing, but "hearing" is equally suitable. Moreover, the occurrence of both √עֵד and √שׁמע (Hiphil) in Isa 43:9, 12; and 44:8, "witness" and "make known," respectively, shows a distinction between the two meanings – at least in these units. There are, furthermore, instances in which English translations use "witness" as a dynamic equivalent of אֹת, *'ōt*, "sign," as in Exod 4:8, where the Hebrew is literally "voice of the first sign . . . voice of the second sign" (KJV, NASB).

⁵ BDB; cf. *HALOT*, "to call as witness, require as witness, witness, be a witness, admonish."

⁶ Robert B. Chisholm, "עוד," in *New International Dictionary of Old Testament Theology and Exegesis*, vol. 3, ed. Willem A. VanGemeren (Carlisle, Cumbria: Paternoster, 1996), 336.

⁷ BDB; cf. *HALOT*. *'ēd*, is masculine, and the feminine form,עֵדָה, *ēdāh*, may be included as well. The form עַד, *ad*, occurs in the textually problematic Isa 30:8, where one should read עֵד, *ēd*, with the two Hebrew manuscripts and the versions. The same pointing occurs in Zeph 3:8, which should also be read as עֵד, *ēd*, even this follows the Septuagint over against the Masoretic text. Both occurrences are probably due to scribes mistaking *ṣērê* for *páṭaḥ*.

⁸ Robert B. Chisholm, "עוד," 337-39.

⁹ To this Isa 30:8 should possibly be added. The Masoretic Text reads עַד, *ad*, "to, until," whereas two Hebrew manuscripts haveעֵד, *ēd*, "witness," which is followed by Aquila, Symmachus, Theodotion, the Syriac, the Targums, and the Vulgate. The Masoretic Text is probably the strongest of the Hebrew texts and is the *lectio difficilior*, both of which favor it; but the context supports the variants (so RSV, NRSV, NIV, NAS, ESV).

¹⁰ The consensus includes confessional scholars such as B. S. Childs and evangelical scholars such as C. R. Seitz.

¹¹ E.g., Michael Goulder, "Deutero-Isaiah of Jerusalem," *JSOT* 28 (2004): 351-62. See also the older studies of Mowinckel and Torrey.

[12] Joseph Blenkinsopp, *Isaiah 40-55: A New Translation with Introduction and Commentary*, vol. 19B of The Anchor Bible (New York: Doubleday, 2005), 104.

[13] On 43:8-13 as a trial genre, see also James Muilenburg, *The Book of Isaiah: Chapters 40-66 (Introduction and Exegesis)*, in vol. 5 of The Interpreter's Bible, ed. George A. Buttrick (New York: Abingdon, 1956), 485, Christopher R. North, *The Second Isaiah: Introduction, Translation, and Commentary to Chapters XL-LV* (Oxford: Clarendon, 1964), 121, Claus Westermann, *Isaiah 40-66: A Commentary* (OTL; Philadelphia: Westminster, 1969), 120, John D. W. Watts, *Isaiah 34-66*, eds. Bruce M. Metzger, et al., vol. 25 of Word Biblical Commentary (Waco: Word, 1987), 128; Daniel J. Muthunayagom, *The Relationship between Election and Israel's Attitude towards the Nations in the Book of Isaiah* (Delhi: ISPCK, 2000), 48, Klaus Baltzer, *Deutero-Isaiah: A Commentary on Isaiah 40-55*, Hermeneia, trans. Margaret Kohl (Minneapolis: Fortress, 2001), 161; John Goldingay, *The Message of Isaiah 40-55: A Literary-Theological Commentary* (London: T&T Clark, 2005), 197.

[14] How can redeemed Israel be blind and deaf? For Muilenburg, *Isaiah 40-66*, 486, the ears and eyes of the people to Yahweh's past events make them witnesses, though they do not understand the full meaning. Similarly, for Henry S. Coffin, *The Book of Isaiah: Chapters 40-66 (Exposition)*, vol. 5 of The Interpreter's Bible, ed. George Arthur Buttrick (New York: Abingdon, 1956), 486; Israel witnessed Yahweh's pre-exilic deeds, and was witnessing his current ones, but not recognizing that Yahweh was the author of both. Westermann, *Isaiah 40-66*, 121, relates the disabilities to Israel's failure to heed Yahweh's instruction in the pre-exilic era, yet he can still use them. Watts, *Isaiah 34-66*, 130, understands the witnesses as the "heavens and the earth." The explanation of Baltzer, *Deutero-Isaiah*, 163, is not altogether clear. Blindness and deafness undermine the ability of one to witness, yet somehow Israel was able to testify to the fulfillment of earlier predictions. For Goldingay, *Isaiah 40-55*, 199, Israel remains blind and deaf in 43:8-13, making Yahweh's pronouncement of them as his witnesses "an implausible affirmation."

[15] Cf. Muilenburg, *Isaiah 40-66*, 487, North, *Second Isaiah 40-66*, 121. For Westermann, *Isaiah 40-66*, 121-22 the matter is that "a god conducts his people through history on a way which it can tread with confidence." Similarly, Muthunayagom, *Relationship*, 48, sees the dispute as over which deity "is able to interpret the historical process taking place in the past, present and the future" and which deity can "control history." In addition

to prescience, Baltzer, *Deutero-Isaiah*, 163, sees a god's intervention in history as part of the trial and Blenkinsopp, *Isaiah 40-55*, 224-25, includes the prediction and execution of events, including the advent of Cyrus. These nuanced interpretations are correct but are derivative from and subordinate to the main point of prescience.

[16] Cf. Blenskinsopp, *Isaiah 40-55*, 224. The Hebrew admits other English translations.

[17] Muthunayagom, *Relationship*, 49, also sees in this section the affirmation that the covenant remains.

[18] Muilenburg, *Isaiah 40-66*, 485, regards the "I am statements" as "the classical expression of Hebrew monotheism," and Baltzer, *Deutero-Isaiah*, 166, appraises v. 13 as a "monotheistic formulation in succinct form."

[19] Cf. 42:4, 6; 49:6; 51:5; 52:10. On the external role, see also C. Van Leeuwen, " *'ēd* witness," in *Theological Lexicon of the Old Testament*, vol. 2. חֶסֶד *ḥesed*– צִיּוֹן *ṣiyyôn*, eds. Ernst Jenni and Claus Westermann, trans. Mark E. Biddle (Peabody, MA: Hendrickson, 1997), 842.

[20] Many commentators have recognized the need for Israel to witness to itself, e.g., Muilenburg, *Isaiah 40-66*, 488, North, *Second Isaiah 40-66*, 122, Westermann, *Isaiah 40-66*, 122-23, Baltzer, *Deutero-Isaiah*, 163, Goldingay, *Isaiah 40-55*, 201.

[21] On the unit as a trial genre, see also North, *Second Isaiah 40-66*, 136, Westermann, *Isaiah 40-66*, 139-40 (for whom the trial genre begins specifically with v. 6b), Goldingay, *Isaiah 40-55*, 234; cf. Baltzer, *Deutero-Isaiah*, 188.

[22] Goldingay, *Isaiah 40-55*, 234, maintains that the only parties present are Yahweh and Israel.

[23] Westermann, *Isaiah 40-66*, 140, comments that "abstract monotheism, in the sense of the existence of one God and one only," was impossible for Second Isaiah (so Goldingay, *Isaiah 40-55*, 203, for whom Yahweh's monotheism is of "saving power"). Abstract or philosophical monotheism is not, however, an especially abstruse concept, and one which would seem to be well within the intellectual capacity of the ancients.

[24] Goldingay, *Isaiah 40-55*, 237 observes in v. 8 the unusual use of the theonym אֱלוֹהַ, *'ĕlôha*, "god," remarking that it underscores "the singularity of Yhwh."

[25] "The theme of witnessing and the exhortation not to fear come together 'because being witness to Yahweh in the hostile environment of Babylonian ideology is a scary thing'. It is scary not only because it may

provoke reaction from Babylon but also because the community itself is afraid that its witness may not be true" (Goldingay, *Isaiah 40-55*, 236, citing W. Brueggemann, *Isaiah* [Louisville: Westminster John Knox, 1998], presumably vol. 2, but without the page number(s). It may be more the case that the exiles were not certain that they even had a witness rather than that they were uncertain about it.).

[26] The theology of this interpretation has a grammatical basis. The expression, "you are my witnesses" (אַתֶּם עֵדַי, *'attem 'ēday*) is the same in Isa 43:10, 12; 44:8. As a nominal clause, the verb must be supplied, and past, present, or future tenses are all possible. The rule of thumb, however, is that the verb follows the action that has been established by the context. In support of the present tense ("you *are* my witnesses"), cp. 43 begins in present action with the conjunction-plus-adverb,וְעַתָּה, *w'attāh*, "and now," and, following the messenger formula, with the imperative to refrain from fearing,אַל־תִּירָא, *al-tîrā'* (v. 1aα, bα, respectively). Similarly, the unit (vv. 8-13) begins with the imperative, הוֹצִיא, *hôṣi'*, "bring out," and v. 9 also continues this time, which carries into the second occurrence in v. 12.

[27] So Martens, "Impulses to Global Mission," 60-61.

[28] Goldingay, *Isaiah 40-55*, 197. Perhaps Christians in Orissa and other areas, who have suffered acute persecution, feel similarly "shell-shocked" and are also in need of such reassurance.

[29] Cf. Martens, "Impulses to Global Mission," 63: "given the sheer proximity of other peoples, Israel cannot but relate to them in some way."

[30] So, e.g., Muilenburg, *Isaiah 40-66*, 488, in general. Blenskinsopp, *Isaiah 40-55*, 237, connects witnessing in 44:6-8 with the role or the servant in v. 21, who is to verify the past and present acts of Yahweh.

[31] See note 18. Baltzer, *Deutero-Isaiah*, 165, recognizes in the role of witness an outward role, but does not indicate specifically what it entails beyond Yahweh's acts in history.

[32] H. Strathmann, "μᾳρτυς, μαρτυρσω, μαρτυρωα, μαρτυρωον, πιμαρτυρσω, συμμαρτυρσω, συνεπιμαρτυρσω, καταμαρτυρσω, μαρτ{ρομαι, διαμαρτ{ρομαι, προμαρτ{ρομαι, ψευδψμαρτυς, ψευδομαρτυρσω, ψευδομαρτυρωα," in *Theological Dictionary of the New Testament*, vol. IV, Λ-N, ed. Gerhard Kittel, trans. G. W. Bromiley (Grand Rapids: Eerdmans, 1967), 482.

[33] H. Bauer, et al., *A Greek-English Lexicon of the New Testament and Other Early Christian Literature*, 2nd ed. (Chicago: University Press, 1979), 494 (hereafter, BAGD); cf. Henry George Liddell, et al., *A Greek-English Lexicon with a Revised Supplement* (Oxford: Clarendon, 1968), 1082.

[34] BAGD, 494; cf. Strathmann, "μqρτυς," 492-93. Darrell L. Bock, *Acts*, Baker Exegetical Commentary of the New Testament (Grand Rapids: Baker Academic, 2007), 64; however, understands Acts 1:8 as expressing the legal nuance, viz. "someone who helps establish facts objectively through verifiable observation." This is why it applies to disciples: they saw Jesus' death and resurrection and are thus qualified to witness. Bock seems to overlook that the context in Acts 1:8 is not forensic, therefore, technically, the legal sense is less persuasive. His explanation, however, of its use compares with the figurative sense.

[35] Martin Dibelius, *Studies in the Acts of the Apostles* (ed. Heinrich Greeven; London: SCM, 1956), 3, 193; cf. Richard N. Longenecker, *The Acts of the Apostles* (EBC; Grand Rapids: Zondervan, 1981), 256.

[36] Strathmann, "μqρτυς," 492-93.

[37] F. F. Bruce, *The Book of the Acts*, rev. ed. (Grand Rapids: Eerdmans, 1988), 36.

[38] C. K. Barrett, *Acts: A Shorter Commentary* (London: T&T Clark, 2002), 6.

[39] Bock, *Acts*, 63. Other commentators do not state explicitly what is meant by witnessing, but imply a similar understanding, e.g., Johannes Munck, *The Acts of the Apostles: Introduction, Translation and Notes*, vol. 31 of The Anchor Bible, rev. W. F. Albright and C. S. Mann (New York: Doubleday, 1967), 7-8, Longenecker, *Acts*, 256, Ben Witherington III, *The Acts of the Apostles: A Socio-Rhetorical Commentary* (Grand Rapids: Eerdmans, 1998), 111. The analysis of J. Beutler, "μqρτυς, υρος, A *martys* witness*," in *Exegetical Dictionary of the New Testament*, vol. 2, ἐξ-ὀψώνιον, eds. Horst Balz and Gerhard Schneider (Grand Rapids: Eerdmans, 1991), 395, perhaps comes the closest to an internal dimension; but since his discussion involves Luke's understanding in general, rather than Acts 1:8 specifically, it is not altogether clear.

[40] Martens, "Impulses to Global Mission," 63-65, makes this point (if somewhat equivocally) from Isa 42:1-6; 49:1-13. For Emmanuel Suhard being "means to live in such a way that one's life would not make sense if God did not exist" (cited in Stanley Hauerwas, *Theology Without Foundations*, ed. idem, et al. (Nashville: Abingdon, 1994], 327, in Goldingay, *Isaiah 40-55*, 200).

Bibliography

Baltzer, Klaus. *Deutero-Isaiah: A Commentary on Isaiah 40-55*. Hermeneia. Translated by Margaret Kohl. Minneapolis: Fortress, 2001.

Barrett, C. K. *Acts: A Shorter Commentary*. London: T&T Clark, 2002.

Bauer, H., W. F. Arndt, F. W. Gingrich, and F. W. Danker. *A Greek-English Lexicon of the New Testament and Other Early Christian Literature*. 2nd ed. Chicago: University Press, 1979.

Beutler, J. "μαρτυς, υρος, A *martys* witness*." In *Exegetical Dictionary of the New Testament*. Vol. 2. ἐξ-ὀψώνιον. Edited by Horst Balz and Gerhard Schneider, 393-95. Grand Rapids: Eerdmans, 1991.

Blenkinsopp, Joseph. *Isaiah 40-55: A New Translation with Introduction and Commentary*. Vol. 19B of The Anchor Bible. New York: Doubleday, 2005.

Bock, Darrell L. *Acts*. Bakers Exegetical Commentary of the New Testament. Grand Rapids: Baker Academic, 2007.

Brown, F., S. R. Driver, and C. A. Briggs. *A Hebrew and English Lexicon of the Old Testament*. Boston: Houghton Mifflin, 1907.

Bruce, F. F. *The Book of the Acts*. Revised ed. Grand Rapids: Eerdmans, 1988.

Brueggemann, W. *Isaiah*. 2 vols. Louisville: Westminster John Knox, 1998.

Chisholm, Robert B. "עוד." In *New International Dictionary of Old Testament Theology and Exegesis*. Vol. 3. Edited by Willem A. VanGemeren, 335-40. Carlisle, Cumbria: Paternoster, 1996.

Coffin, Henry S. "The Book of Isaiah: Chapters 40-66 (Exposition)." Vol. 5 of The Interpreter's Bible. New York: Abingdon, 1956.

Dibelius, Martin. *Studies in the Acts of the Apostles*. Edited by Heinrich Greeven. London: SCM, 1956.

Goldingay, John. *The Message of Isaiah 40-55: A Literary-Theological Commentary*. London: T&T Clark, 2005.

Goulder, Michael. "Deutero-Isaiah of Jerusalem." *JSOT* 28 (2004): 351-62.

Koehler, L., W. Baumgartner, and J. J. Stamm. *The Hebrew and Aramaic Lexicon of the Old Testament*. Translated and edited under the supervision of M. E. J. Richardson. 2 vols. Leiden: Brill, 2001.

Liddell, Henry George, R. Scott, and H. S. Jones. *A Greek-English Lexicon with a Revised Supplement*. Oxford: Clarendon, 1968.

Longenecker, Richard N. *The Acts of the Apostles*. Expositor's Bible Commentary. Grand Rapids: Zondervan, 1981.

Martens, Elmer A. "Impulses to Global Mission in Isaiah." *Direction* 35 (2006): 59-69.

—————. "Impulses to Mission in Isaiah: An Intertextual Exploration." *Bulletin for Biblical Research* 17 (2007): 215-39.

Muilenburg, James. "The Book of Isaiah: Chapters 40-66 (Introduction and Exegesis)." Vol. 5. of The Interpreter's Bible. New York: Abingdon, 1956.

Munck, Johannes. *The Acts of the Apostles: Introduction, Translation and Notes.* Revised by W. F. Albright and C. S. Mann. AB. New York: Doubleday, 1967.

Muthunayagom, Daniel J. *The Relationship between Election and Israel's Attitude towards the Nations in the Book of Isaiah.* Delhi: ISPCK, 2000.

North, Christopher R. *The Second Isaiah: Introduction, Translation, and Commentary to Chapters XL-LV.* Oxford: Clarendon, 1964.

Strathmann, H. "μqρτυς, μαρτυρσω, μαρτυρwα, μαρτυρwον, πιμαρτυρσω, συμμαρτυρσω, συνεπιμαρτυρσω, καταμαρτυρσω, μαρτ{ρομαι, διαμαρτ{ρομαι, προμαρτ{ρομαι, ψευδυμαρτυς, ψευδομαρτυρσω, ψευδομαρτυρwα." In *Theological Dictionary of the New Testament.* Vol. IV. Λ-Ν. Edited by Gerhard Kittel. Translated by G. W. Bromiley, 474-514. Grand Rapids: Eerdmans, 1967.

Van Leeuwen, C. "עֵד *'ēd* witness." In *Theological Lexicon of the Old Testament.* Vol. 2. חֶסֶד *hesed* –צִיּוֹן *ṣiyyôn.* Edited by Ernst Jenni and Claus Westermann. Translated by Mark E. Biddle, 838-46. Peabody, MA: Hendrickson, 1997.

Watts, John D. W. *Isaiah 34-66.* Vol. 25 of Word Biblical Commentary. Waco: Word, 1987.

Westermann, Claus. *Isaiah 40-66: A Commentary.* The Old Testament Library. Philadelphia: Westminster, 1969.

Witherington III, Ben. *The Acts of the Apostles: A Socio-Rhetorical Commentary.* Grand Rapids: Eerdmans, 1998.

2
Becoming All Things to Everyone: Witnessing to Christ in India Today

V. J. John

I have become all things to all people that I might by all means save some.

1 Cor. 9:22b

Introduction

The year long celebrations of Churches and mission agencies around the world in connection with the centenary of the Mission Conference of Edinburgh 1910 brought into sharper focus the need to reinterpret earlier understandings of the mission of the Church in the light of realities faced by the contemporary world. While the task of mission was understood with diverse emphasis over the last 100 years, the spotlight leading to Edinburgh 2010 was on "Witnessing to Christ Today" with focus on "Witnessing" as the task of mission and "Today" as the context of mission. In this paper we shall attempt to look at witnessing to Christ in the Indian context today, centered on the Pauline statement, "I have become all things to all people…" (1 Cor. 9:22). This we propose to do, firstly, by briefly highlighting the present Indian setting; secondly, the social context of the Pauline statement, thirdly, a biblical-theological analysis of 1 Corinthians 9:19–23 where the Pauline statement appears. The paper shall end drawing up some insights that may be relevant for witnessing to Christ in the contemporary Indian context.

The Present Indian Context

The Indian context has always been complex with its varieties and extremes. What is true to one part of India may not be relevant in the same measure to another part. In another words, the Indian setting is very diverse depending upon where one comes from, or situated. It can be a tribal setting, a Dalit context, a predominantly Hindu religious setting, a rural or urban setting, an affluent up market locality in one of the metropolitan cities or a slum setting. While the context is diverse, for convenience sake we may look at them as plurality of religions and cultures, social deprivation, unequal economic opportunities as well as moral and ethical depravity.

Plurality of Religions and Cultures

India is home to almost every major religion of the world. The adherents of different religious philosophies and faith traditions have harmoniously lived in the Indian soil for long periods of time. Each of these traditions carries its own understanding of reality and practices its faith, in varying, and at times, conflicting ways. Some of these philosophical systems differ from one another and sometimes within themselves. For instance, in Hinduism, the most prominent is the Vedantic philosophy with its advaitic school of Sankara and the dualistic school of Ramanuja. We also have varieties of philosophical systems within the broader Hindu tradition.[1] Among the followers of

Islam, we have the Shias and the Sunni traditions.[2] Buddhists
– Theravada (also called Hinayana) and -2- Mahayana,[3] Sikhs
and Jains[4] - all have divergent schools of thought. Besides, there
are Parsis, Christians and even some who trace their ancestry to
Judaism. There are varieties of cultures[5] that are represented in
India with its manifold riches of music, rhythms and festivals.
The songs, art forms, dance, dress, food habits are all determined
by the language and culture to which one belongs.

While the varieties of philosophies and cultures can help
enrich one another through mutual interaction and appreciation,
it can also be the cause of conflict and division. In recent times
India has been witnessing increasing fundamentalism and
lack of tolerance towards minority religious faith.[6] The rise of
militant Hinduism with its ideology of Hindutva and Islamic
extremism has only aggravated the situation. Fundamentalism by
its very nature fanatically and exclusively sticks to one religious
tradition, ideology, culture, or value system. In the name of God
and religion even violence is unleashed on those who profess a
different faith. Among other things, it is the lack of tolerance
towards other religions that has been responsible for the rise of
terrorism. Incidents like the attack on the Indian Parliament
and recent bomb blasts in various Indian cities are examples
of this. In this context there should be renewed commitment
to cultural pluralism[7] and religious dialogue.

Glaring Social Deprivation

Indian society is perhaps the most complex with regard to its
composition and social setting among societies found anywhere
in the world. Indian society is divided on the basis of caste
with the upper castes holding powerful positions in the social
hierarchy while those on the lower rung of the order do not
share the same power and privilege.[8] Role and status in society

very often is determined by the hierarchical structure in which one was privileged to be born.[9] Hence the mere accident of ones birth in a given caste or clan could determine the privilege and role one would enjoy within her/his social setting, while others are deprived of the privileges and even basic rights. This has given rise to demands for separate states, and in certain cases even independence. Those who work for the social upliftment of the poor and the marginalized sections of society, as Dr. Vinayak Sen is considered a threat to the state.

Unequal Economic Opportunities

Although India is rich in its natural resources, the wealth of the country is owned by a small percentage of its populace consisting mainly of a few industrial houses and political leaders. Economic liberalisation with its Market driven economy accompanied by globalisation has helped the rich to increase their wealth. This has opened up more opportunities for wealth accumulation for the well-to-do. The increase in the number of wealthy Indian industrialists among the richest of the world is an indication of the same. This has caused increased ecological destruction with unbridled attempts to create more wealth at all cost disregarding their effect on the environment. Therefore, there is an ever growing gulf between the few rich people and the poor masses, creating economic inequality.[10]

The majority of the Indian population consist of the Dalits, tribals and the other marginalized groups who with their hard labour largely contribute towards the generation of wealth, yet remain poor[11] as they do not enjoy the fruit of their labour. For most of these people life is a burden. They do not have the basic means of survival. Many of them live on in depilated houses in the urban slum areas, public places or even on footpaths. They cannot afford the luxury of sending their children to school. Hence their children remain uneducated.[12] Ecological degradation has only further added more victims to the already deteriorating scenario. Even the commons, such as the forest land and rivers, are no longer available to them. Struggles for economic advancement has given rise to conflicts at times as witnessed among the Gujjars of Rajasthan recently, or even armed struggles such as by the Maoists or among some of the tribes of the North Eastern states.

Moral and Ethical Deficit

The increase in wealth and power of the few and the craving to catch up with the powerful and famous on the part of others have led to a situation wherein all means are used for achieving the goal. Corruption at high places within society and centres of power both at the government level and even in the churches and other religious institutions is a cause for concern. There is a drop in commitment to morality and ethics while there is manifold increase in corrupt practices at all level. Issues of justice and fair play have become mere slogans for politicking and are seldom practiced in actual daily behaviour. Crave for power politics has become a bane of church life in recent times. The *aam aadmi* has to bear the burnt of all such erosions in morality and values. Witnessing in the Indian context cannot therefore ignore the poverty of the masses and issues of justice from the preview of its engagement.

The Corinthian Social Setting

Sometime in 50 C.E., accompanied by Silvanus and Timothy (2 Cor. 1:19), Paul arrived in Corinth. He found work and lodging with Prisca and Aquila, who came from Rome in 41 C.E. under the emperorship of Claudius (Acts 18:1-3). With them he worked as a tentmaker. While working as a manual labourer, he proclaimed the gospel. Paul's first converts were decidedly upper-class (1 Cor. 1:14-16). They assisted Paul in his preaching efforts, and opened their house for the community to assemble (Rom. 16:23). The names of members of the community are mentioned (Acts 18:1-18; 1 Cor. 1:14-16; 16:15-17; and Romans 16:21-24). Many of them were of gentile origin, but associated with Jewish synagogue.[13]

Socio-Political Subjugation

The ministry of Jesus and his disciples were centered on the villages and hinter lands of Palestine whereas Paul ministered in the urban centers of the Roman world. Jesus' audience was conservative and resistant to change, but Paul preached to those who were more open and receptive to the gospel. Those whose roots in the city probably may not have been too strong could find security and support within the communities.[14] The cities were centers of trade and relatively prosperous. Paul preached in Antioch, a thriving commercial center. Laodicea together with Hierapolis and Colossae, was a center of the wool trade.. Philippi was a center of agriculture while Ephesus was well known for its harbour and temple of Artemis. Galatia was a Roman colony while Corinth and Thessalonica were important trading centers.[15] As Theissen notes, "The Hellenistic mission was operative almost exclusively in cities with a republican constitution, subordinate to Rome's imperial power but also benefiting from it."[16]

In terms of power, influence and money, the population of Roman world was divided into two main grouping which was also true for Corinth: those with influence and those without it, the "honourable" and the "humble," the governing and the governed, those with property and those without. The upper category, though small, were fabulously wealthy and controlled the power. At the lower level were the local aristocracies who were land owners, merchants and traders. Dionysius of Athens (Acts 18:12-17) and Erastus in Corinth (Rom. 16:23) belonged to the local aristocrats who were Christian converts.[17] Many suffered from "status inconsistency."[18] Prisca and Aquila, though were successful business people, as outsider Jews, resided in the city on sufferance. Erastus (Rom. 16:23) who held a most important post in the administration of Corinth was still considered as the son of a slave. Below these merchants and crafts workers were the really poor. They owned no property and supported themselves by doing odd jobs at the docks, in construction, or on farms. The slave was on the lowest rung of the social ladder. With no legal status, slaves worked as chattel gangs on ships, farms, road construction, or mining and were treated as nothing but a commodity.[19] While the aristocrats were politically and socially powerful, the poor were under their subjugation. Corinthian community generally represented the different social strata in the city.[20] Christianity offered to them a social context in which they would be accepted for what they were as persons.

Economic Inequality

The economy is "that complex of activities and institutions through which a society manages the production and allocation of goods and services, and organizes and maintains its workers."[21] In the ancient economic context, the management of these affairs was more or less determined by the upper classes of the social structure. It is their quantum of consumption that decided much of the economic activities. The wealthy people though resided in the urban centers, their supply of the essential items, such as food grains, came from the country side.[22] Hence, as Lenski notes, "The urban economy depended on the rural economy and its ability to produce a surplus that could support the urban population."[23]

The cities consisted of ten percent of the total population, of which, two percent belonged to the elite or higher class. They were literates who held positions in the administrative and religious institutions of the society along with the absentee landlords. They were characterized by "innate superiority, conspicuous conception and disdain for manual labor."[24] The remaining eight percent, as Malina notes, "were engaged in handicraft manufacturing, for the most part, and clustered in guilds which inhabited their own sections of the city. The urban house was the workplace, and the producer sold directly to his customer."[25] "In most agrarian societies" writes Lenski, "the artisan class was originally recruited from the ranks of the dispossessed peasantry and their noninheriting sons and was continually replenished from these sources."[26] Their status was similar to that of the village peasants. "In their section", continues Malina, "the small merchant or craftsmen, the day laborers or teamsters, were not much different from the villagers, since the life of the urban elite was normally quite closed off from that of the low-class urbanite."[27] Professional traders and artisans were always looked upon with disdain throughout the Roman history. Slaves and dispossessed peasants, who needed to be fed, clothed and housed, kept pushing up the population of the city.[28] There was no middle class although below the low class urbanites were the marginal group of beggars and slaves. The society was characterized by a patron-client relationship.[29]

Cultural Alienation

In the mission to the Gentiles, there was a change in the social location of the Christians from an earlier rural and agrarian context to a more urban setting, bringing with it a shift in its cultural horizon.[30] The value systems of the ancient societies were not conducive towards commercial interests. The norms of the cities were guided by the consumption interest of the well-to-do rather than the economic interest of the entrepreneur. In the decision making process those of the lower class had no role. The peasant and those of the lower class sought to establish some kind of client relationship with the ruling class as insurance for their own security.[31] The authoritarian form of human relationship has prevailed. Emphasis was placed on sterner virtues and earnest espousal of moral regeneration as against social changes. This also meant a change of language from one of Aramaic to Greek. There were new philosophical schools and religions, new traditions, norms and values. Rich Jewish heritages of monotheism, lofty ethic, the acuteness of prophetic criticism, a universalistic view of history which the missionaries were inheritors of had to encounter with divergent claims and counter-claims of the Hellenistic cities.[32] Many of the Christians were still not fully socialized into their new moral community as 1 Corinthians shows. Many still were doing what they had always done: visiting prostitutes, practicing law suits against one another, eating food offered to idols, following social stratification at meals in homes, even if it included the Lord's Supper ceremony. There was a disjunction between belief and behaviour.[33] Hence, there were greater challenges and opportunities in the urban setting.

A Biblico-Theological Analysis of 1 Corinthians 9:19-23

The Corinthian Church was perhaps the most problematic church among the churches established in the Pauline mission. The Corinthian letters were written to deal with issues arising out of the complex socio-cultural and political situation under which the church was to practice its faith. It is in the wider context of these issues that Paul addresses in 1 Corinthians that the present passage is to be located. The letter begins with an introduction (1:1-9) and ends with a conclusion (16:1-24). The central section of the letter concerns the problems associated with Christian living in the Corinthian context. The first issue dealt is that of the Division within the Corinthian Community (1:10-4:21).

Secondly, the Role and Importance of the Community as the Body is addressed (5:1-6:20). In dealing with the questions raised by the Corinthians, Paul devotes attention to the issue of social status (7:1-40) and living in a gentile setting (8:1-11:10). He then takes up the problems associated with public worship and liturgical practices (11:2-14:40). Question on Resurrection is the last issue focused upon (15:1-58).[34]

In the practice of faith in a Gentile environment, the Corinthians were instructed on eating food offered to idols (8:1-13; 10:16-30) and the exercise of apostolic rights (9:1-27; 10:31-11:1). The Exodus history serves both as a warning and a challenge (10:1-15). The exercise of the apostolic rights concerns the apostolic freedom (9:1-6), right to support (9:7-14); waiver of the apostolic rights (9:15-23) and the need to concentrate on the goal (9:24-27) of ministry. Paul spoke of the waiver of the apostolic rights on two grounds: (1) The compulsion to preach the gospel free of cost, and (2) The willingness to adapt oneself for the sake of the gospel.[35]

Paul's Damascus Road experience and the resultant theological conviction that God was offering his salvation to all people now and that he was called to preach salvation to the Gentiles.[36] A Mission theology developed out of that experience[37] which served as the basis for Paul's mission endeavours. The motivating factor for all Paul's activity, including his urge to evangelize at all costs, was his profound conviction of who Jesus was.[38] Paul therefore, claimed that he became "all things to all people." The statement of Paul has been looked up from at least two dominant perspectives: firstly, emphasizing Paul's principle of accommodation or adaptability[39] as a pioneer missionary among Gentiles and secondly, the pastoral principle[40] that Paul followed in his ministry.

The verb in "I have enslaved" myself is a past aorist like "I have become" in the following verses. The Greek emphasizes the change that took place, but the *Aktionsart* requires the perfect in English.[41] This is an exercise of freedom with concern of love. "All people" used in the sense of having specific relationships with persons.[42] He has enslaved himself to all people. Paul was never the same person in two contexts. But "all things to everyone" was a recipe for catastrophe. Immediately it raised the question of inconsistency in his behaviour. Was he not guided by any principles of conduct? Why was it that while he accepted support from the Philippian Church he declined any such support from the Corinthian community? Was it that he loved the Philippians and detested Corinthians? How could he be true to himself? Did he not have any integrity? Paul took the question seriously and reformulated it. O'Connor rephrases them as: "What is integrity for ministers of the gospel? Is it external or internal consistency? Is it related to their vision of themselves or to their effectiveness in their ministry?"[43] Not subject to the constraints of the financially dependent, as he assured his own livelihood working with his own hands, Paul was free to decide his conduct at different circumstances.[44] Having probably received support as a Pharisee from the redistribution of revenues collected from the villagers in the tributary system, prior to his "calling," he now refused to live on the support of the poor and chose to support himself.

"I have become a Jew to the Jews in order to win the Jews. I have become as one under the law to win those under the law (v. 20). I have become as one not under the law to those outside the law (v. 21)" In the course of discharging his apostolic commission for the gentiles, he frequently used synagogues, aiming his gospel message at the God-fearers as well as at the Jews there (cf. 1 Cor. 9:19-23).[45] Gentiles referred to the inhabitants of Greece and pagans in general. Since the issue was his differing behaviour toward the two groups, Jews were redefined as "those under the Law" and "those outside the Law" meaning "the Law-less", pagans to whom the Mosaic Law had not been given.[46] In as much as Paul considered himself freed from the enslavement of the law, he was "law-less". Paul has repudiated the validity of the Law (Gal. 2:11-14) for a Christian community as law could lead to legalism. Binding commandments was replaced with "the law of Christ" wherein one is led by the self-sacrificing love of Christ.[47]

When in the midst of Jews who considered themselves under the law Paul behaved like any other Jew. It was hard on Paul's readers who felt they were being manipulated. It appeared that Paul had no hesitation accepting the social conventions of pagans, in order to interest them in the gospel. This also underlines the extent to which Paul had distanced himself from his Jewish past. Even the Jewish markers of circumcision and the food laws had become irrelevant for Paul. What became important was the imitation of Christ. Paul could therefore act as a Jew or a Gentile as it suited him.[48] However, looking from the context, Pathrapankal feels Paul's attitude to Gentiles and Gentile religion was one of the limitations of Paul.[49]

Those outside the law refers primarily to the Gentiles, but could also refer to the "strong" in Corinth. Now under the law of Christ, not a new law code but the law of love exemplified by Christ. Paul submits himself to the conscience of the weak to win the weak. Then he talks about "the weak." "I have become weak to those who are weak in order to win the weak" (v. 22) "Weak" probably referred to those who opposed the eating of idol meat (cf. 8:10-13), but could also allude to all who were socially and economically powerless. O'Connor considers, "Paul was weak in this sense and nothing could change it. Paul was always the vulnerable outsider."[50]

I might win more of them (v. 19) to win the Jews... I might win those under the law (v. 20), I might win those outside the law (v. 21), I might win the weak... that I might by all means save some (v. 22) I do it all for the sake of the gospel, so that I may share in its blessings. Paul has become all things to every one so that by all means he might save some. He is here concerned to relate people to the gospel in a saving way. Paul tries to win "the other." The purpose of mission for Paul was to proclaim the gospel among the Gentiles (Rom. 11:13; 15:16). He has received this call for a Gentile mission directly from the risen Lord on the road to Damascus (Gal. 1:15-16; Acts 26: 16-18) probably having the mission of the Ebed (servant) (Is. 42:6,7; 49:1,6)[51] However, this does not preclude his continued desire for the salvation of the covenant people, Israel (cf. Rom. 10:1). In fact, wherever Paul went first he proclaimed the gospel to the Jews in the synagogue. When they have rejected, he moved on to the Gentiles (Acts 13:46).[52] He proclaimed the gospel by accommodating his practice to that of the people to whom he was preaching. There was a relativization of the cultural values to the absolute value of the gospel. Paul was ready to renounce citizenship, legal attachments and customs. This did not take the form of flaunting his independence, but changing his conformity according to the people with whom he was witnessing to. As Orr and Walter reminds us

> Paul's policy is determined by the fact that he is under the compulsion of God and has a message that must be directed to people of all nationalities, customs and characteristics. A believer in this gospel does not belong particularly to any group but can belong to all; so that he is at home wherever he is and at the same time is a stranger even when he is at home. Paul's overriding allegiance is as a *partner with the gospel*.[53]

Paul was not a mere crowd pleaser whom the Aristocratic thinkers despised as "slaves." Paul borrowed the offending language of the defenders of the aristocratic element in Corinth to express his missionary status.[54] The basis of Paul's integrity is his love for individuals, whatever their religious or social situation. He has done it all for the sake of the gospel that by all means he might save some and so doing he too might share the blessings of the gospel. Discrepancy between word and action was to be met in the Christian service offered to neighbour as the service to Christ.[55] As an apostle, Paul can share in the blessings of the gospel as a joint-partaker only by bringing it to others.[56] The nature of the gospel is to live it out. It is by standing in loving solidarity with them, by showing practical, love, care and respect[57] that others may be won to Christ.

Becoming All Things to Everyone as an Indian Mission Agenda

Our brief enquiry into the mission agenda of Paul has highlighted some important points that may be of relevance in our endeavour of witnessing to Christ in the present Indian context. We might note the following points:

Commitment to Christ and People

Paul as a witness had an unwavering commitment to Christ and the people to whom he was called to be a missionary. The core of all witnessing is the conviction regarding the person of Christ. One can only be a true witness to Christ, if only one were truly convinced of the claims of Christ. Any wavering in this regard will not make one an effective witness. This should be accompanied by a genuine commitment to the people amongst whom one is called to be a witness. This can come only from a real conviction of a special call to live and work amidst them. When this happens one will be ready to undertake the necessary sacrifices and flexibilities required in the witnessing process. The Witness should be willing to be in solidarity with the people which is to be expressed by way of love, care and support to them and their genuine cause.

Integrity and Credibility of Character

One of the hindrances to witnessing to Christ in the contemporary Indian context is probably the lack of integrity of the witness. It is not seldom that the missionary or witness is found wanting in integrity and credibility. When things are done secretly and in suspicious contexts, the power of witness is lost. Integrity and credibility of the witness of Paul was his openness and transparency in conduct. It is very important in the context of corruption that is experienced at all levels in society today. Unfortunately, church leaders and mission workers are not exempt from the maladies that we see all around us.

Spirit of Accommodation and Flexibility

Paul was a man who learnt to accommodate himself to different peoples and cultures for the sake of the witness that he was entrusted with. This not simply compromising ones morals and values and by accepting anything and everything. Paul had a commitment to Christ and the message that was entrusted to him which he never compromised. But in the modern Indian context with many claims and counter claims seeking our allegiance a witness should be open and willing to accommodate and appropriate that which is good and valuable, even though what we believe and practice. There should be openness towards the other and willingness to listen and make changes if required. Above all a witness should not have a fixed mind with regard to his/her task and the mode of its carrying out. This should also involve ones keenness to be contextual in the manner in which witness is carried out.

Do Not Condone Evil

A witness is some one whose life style is always under watch. Hence he/she should be one character and conduct should be above reproach. The witness or mission worker should not be one who closes his/her eyes to evil practices. Churches have come forward to condemn evil only when it is committed against it, otherwise conveniently we keep a blind eye to the practices around be it in society or within the church. Prophetic protest and condemnation of evil practices and the upholding of justice and fair play are important if the witness were to be any effective. Paul refused to condone evil and spoke against evil practices. One is to carry out witness as Paul did. Witness is to be carried out in community as.Paul practiced.

Agents of Harmony and Reconciliation

In a context in which violence and estrangement characterize life at all levels, whether in family, society or church conflict, distrust and destruction mark experiences in life every day. Witnessing should lead one to bring about healing and reconciliation in such a context. The effort of Paul was to bring reconciliation between Jews and Gentile communities that they will all experience healing from hurt, mistrust and violence.

Vulnerability

One can be a witness to the gospel only from a point of weakness, never from the point of strength. Paul had to become weak by identifying with the weak so that he might witness to Christ. Vulnerability for the sake of the gospel for Paul included his suffering and persecution and rejection at several points of his missionary task. The witness should be ready to "Bear one another's burdens and so fulfill the law which is Christ." (Gal. 6:2). "The Church must learn to do mission, as Paul did, from a position of weakness and humility, through negotiation, communication and compromise."[58] This might also require suffering persecution for the sake of the gospel and being found in solidarity with the vulnerable people whether Dalits, tribals, people with disabilities or those with HIV/AIDS.

Endnotes

[1] The Hindu philosophical systems are Nyaya, Vaisesika, Samkhya, Yoga, Mimamsa, and Vedanta. See, Rajmani Tigunait, *Seven Systems of Indian Philosophy* (Himalayan Institute Press, 1983), 27-28.

[2] Edward Geoffrey Parrinder, *The World's Living Religions*, rev. ed. (London: Pan Books, 1977).

[3] Sunyavada (or Madhyamika), Vijnanavada (or Yogacara), Sautrantika, and Vaibhasika; Tigunait, *Seven Systems of Indian Philosophy*.

[4] Amulya Ranjan Mohapatra, *Philosophy of Religion: An Approach to World Religions*, 2nd ed.; rev. ed. (New Delhi, New York: Sterling Publisher Private Ltd., 1990).

[5] For an analysis of the diverse cultures of India see, Erick J. Lott, "Religious Faith and the Diversity of Cultural Life in India," in *Christian Faith and Multiform Culture in India*, ed. Somen Das (Bangalore: UTC Publications, 1987), 48–84.

[6] See, M. T. Cherian, *Hindutva Agenda and Minority Rights: A Christian Response: Study of Hindu Fundamentalism and Its Impact on Secularism in India from 1947-1997* (Bangalore: Centre for Contemporary Christianity, 2007).

[7] See for instance in this context the recent study of Lucien Legrand, *The Bible on Culture: Belonging or Dissenting?* (Bangalore: TPI, 2000).

[8] Maureen Patterson, "Caste and Political Leadership in Maharashtra," *Economic Weekly*, September 1954, 1065–67.

[9] Mysore Narasimhachar Srinivas, *Social Change in Modern India*, (1972; repr., Orient Longman, 2001); M. N. Srinivas, *Caste in Modern India, and Other Essays* (Bombay: Asia Publishing House, 1962).

[10] For a detailed analysis see, Amartya Sen and James E. Foster, *On Economic Inequality: Enlarged Edition with a Substantial Annexe "On Economic Inequality after a Quarter Century"* (Oxford: Clarendon Press, 1997).

[11] R. N. Malhotra, "India's Development Story," in *Manaroma Year Book 1997* (Kottayam: Malayala Manorama Press, 1997); Amartya Sen, *Poverty and Famines: An Essay on Entitlement and Deprivation* (Oxford University Press, 1999).

[12] Amartya Sen, *Development as Freedom* (Oxford University Press, 2001).

[13] Jerome Murphy O'Connor, *1 Corinthians: Doubleday Bible Commentary* (New York: Bantam Doubleday Dell Publishing Group Inc., 1998), x & xi.

[14] Gerd Theissen, *Sociology of Early Palestinian Christianity*, trans., John Bowden (Philadelphia: Fortress Press, 1978), 117.

[15] D. J. Tidball, "Social Settings of Mission Churches," in *Dictionary of Paul and His Letters*, eds. Gerald F. Hawthorne, Ralph P. Martin, and Daniel G. Reid (Downer Grove, Illinois: InterVarsity Press, 1993); Wayne A. Meeks, *The First Urban Christians: The Social World of the Apostle Paul*, 2nd ed. (New Haven London: Yale University Press, 2003); Ronald F. Hock, *The Social Context of Paul's Ministry: Tentmaking and Apostleship* (Philadelphia: Fortress Press, 1980).

[16] Gerd Theissen, *The Social Setting of Pauline Christianity: Essays on Corinth*, trans. John H. Scutz (Edinburgh: T&T Clark, 1982), 36.

[17] John E. Stambaugh and David L. Balch, *The New Testament in its Social Environment*, ed. Wayne A. Meeks (Philadelphia: Westminster Press, 1986), 110-13.

[18] Theissen, *The Social Setting of Pauline Christianity*.

[19] Stambaugh and Balch, *The New Testament in its Social Environment*.

[20] O'Connor, *Corinthians*.

[21] Thomas F. Carney, *The Shape of the Past: Models and Antiquity* (Lawrence, Kansas: Coronado Press, 1975), 140.

[22] M. I. Finley, *The Ancient Economy* (London: Chatto & Windus, 1973), 123f. Also, Peter Garnsey and Richard P. Saller, *The Roman Empire: Economy, Society and Culture* (Duckworth, 1987), 48-49.

[23] Gerhard Emmanuel Lenski and Jean Lenski, *Human Societies: An Introduction to Macrosociology*, 2nd ed. (McGraw-Hill Book Company, 1974).

[24] Carney, *The Shape of the Past*.

[25] Bruce J. Malina, *The New Testament World: Insights from Cultural Anthropology* (SCM Press Ltd., 1981), 72-73.

[26] Gerhard Emmanuel Lenski, *Power and Privilege: A Theory of Social Stratification* (McGraw-Hill Book Company, 1966).

[27] Malina, *The New Testament World*.

[28] Finley, *The Ancient Economy*.

[29] John K. Chow, "Patronage in Roman Corinth," in *Paul and Empire: Religion and Power in Roman Imperial Society*, ed. Richard A. Horsley (Harrisburg, Pennsylvania: Trinity Press International, 1997), 104-125.

[30] Stambaugh and Balch, *The New Testament in its Social Environment*.

[31] Carney, *The Shape of the Past*.

[32] Theissen, *Sociology of Early Palestinian Christianity*.

[33] Ben Witherington III, *The Paul Quest: The Renewed Search for the Jew of Tarsus* (Downers Grove, Illinois: InterVarsity Press, 2001).

[34] O'Connor, *Corinthians*.

[35] William F. Orr and James Arthur Walther, *I Corinthians: A New Translation*, vol. 32 of The Anchor Bible (Garden City: Doubleday & Co, 1995), 227-43.

[36] Donald Senior and Carroll Stuhlmueller, *The Biblical Foundations for Mission* (Orbis Books, 1991).

[37] Lucien Legrand, *The God who Comes: Mission in the Bible* (Quenzon City Philippines: Claretian Publications, 1991).

[38] John Patrick Brennan, *Christian Mission in a Pluralistic World* (Middlegreen, England: St Paul Publications, 1990).

[39] H. Chadwick, "'All Things to all Men' (1 Corinthians 9:22)," *New Testament Studies* (1954-1955): 261-75.

[40] S. C. Barton, "'All Things to All People': Paul and the Law in the Light of 1 Corinthians 9: 19-23," in *Paul and the Mosaic Law*, ed. James D. G. Dunn (Tubingen: Mohr Siebeck, 1996), 271-85.

[41] Orr and Walther, *I Corinthians*.

[42] Orr and Walther.

[43] O'Connor, *Corinthians*; Richard A. Horsley, "1 Corinthians: A Case Study of Paul's Assembly as an Alternative Society," in *Paul and Empire: Religion and Power in Roman Imperial Society*, ed. Richard A. Horsley (Harrisburg, Pennsylvannia: Trinity Press International, 1997), 240-50.

[44] Chow, "Patronage in Roman Corinth," 104-125.

[45] Seyoon Kim, *Paul and the New Perspective: Second Thoughts on the Origin of Paul's Gospel* (Grand Rapids, Michigan/Cambridge, U.K.: Wm. B. Eerdmans Publishing Company, 2002), 31.

[46] O'Connor, *Corinthians*.

[47] O'Connor, *Corinthians*.

[48] O'Connor, *Corinthians*.

[49] Joseph Pathrapankal, *Critical and Creative: Studies in Bible and Theology* (Bangalore: Dharmaram Publications, 1986).

[50] O'Connor, *Corinthians*.

[51] Kim, *Paul and the New Perspective*.

[52] Jey J. Kanagaraj, "The Strategies of Paul the Missionary," in *Integral Mission: The Way Forward/ : Essays in Honour of Dr. Saphir P. Athyal*, ed. C.V. Mathew (Tiruvalla: Christava Sahitya Samithi, 2006).

[53] Orr and Walther, *I Corinthians*.

[54] Craig S. Keener, *The IVP Bible Background Commentary: New Testament* (InterVarsity Press, 1993).

[55] Bruce J. Malina, "Service," in *Biblical Social Values and their Meaning: A Handbook*, eds. John J. Pilch and Bruce J. Malina (Hendrickson Publishers, 1993).

[56] Jerome Murphy O'Connor, "First Letter to the Corinthians," in *The New Jerome Biblical Commentary*, eds. Raymond Edward Brown, Joseph A. Fitzmyer, and Roland Edmund Murphy (Bangalore: T.P.I., 1994).

[57] Anthony C. Thiselton, *1 Corinthians: A Shorter Exegetical and Pastoral Commentary* (Grand Rapids, Michigan/Cambridge, U.K.: Wm. B. Eerdmans Publishing, 2006).

[58] J. Patmury, "Concepts and Strategies of Paul's Mission," in *Bible and Mission in India Today*, eds. Jacob Kavunkal and F. Hrangkhuma (Bombay: St Pauls, 1993).

Bibliography

Barton, S. C. "'All Things to All People': Paul and the Law in the Light of 1 Corinthians 9:19-23." In *Paul and the Mosaic Law*. Edited by James D. G. Dunn, 271-85. Tubingen: Mohr Siebeck, 1996.

Brennan, John Patrick. *Christian Mission in a Pluralistic World*. Middlegreen, England: St Paul Publications, 1990.

Carney, Thomas F. *The Shape of the Past: Models and Antiquity*. Lawrence, Kansas: Coronado Press, 1975.

Chadwick, H. "'All Things to all Men' (1 Corinthians 9:22)." *New Testament Studies* (1954-1955).

Cherian, M. T. *Hindutva Agenda and Minority Rights: A Christian Response: Study of Hindu Fundamentalism and Its Impact on Secularism in India from 1947-1997*. Bangalore: Centre for Contemporary Christianity, 2007.

Chow, John K. "Patronage in Roman Corinth." In *Paul and Empire: Religion and Power in Roman Imperial Society*. Edited by Richard A. Horsley, 104-125. Harrisburg, Pennsylvania: Trinity Press International, 1997.

Finley, M. I. *The Ancient Economy*. London: Chatto & Windus, 1973.

Garnsey, Peter and Richard P. Saller. *The Roman Empire: Economy, Society and Culture*. Duckworth, 1987.

Hock, Ronald F. *The Social Context of Paul's Ministry: Tentmaking and Apostleship*. Philadelphia: Fortress Press, 1980.

Horsley, Richard A. "1 Corinthians: A Case Study of Paul's Assembly as an Alternative Society." In *Paul and Empire: Religion and Power in Roman Imperial Society*. Edited by Richard A. Horsley. Harrisburg, Pennsylvania: Trinity Press International, 1997.

III, Ben Witherington. *The Paul Quest: The Renewed Search for the Jew of Tarsus*. Downers Grove, Illinois: InterVarsity Press, 2001.

Kanagaraj, Jey J. "The Strategies of Paul the Missionary." In *Integral Mission: The Way Forward: Essays in Honour of Dr. Saphir P. Athyal*. Edited by C.V. Mathew. Tiruvalla: Christava Sahitya Samithi, 2006.

Keener, Craig S. *The IVP Bible Background Commentary: New Testament*. InterVarsity Press, 1993.

Kim, Seyoon. *Paul and the New Perspective: Second Thoughts on The Origin of Paul's Gospel*. Grand Rapids, Michigan/Cambridge, U.K.: Wm. B. Eerdmans Publishing Company, 2002.

Legrand, Lucien. *The Bible on Culture: Belonging or Dissenting?* Bangalore: TPI, 2000.

—————. *The God who Comes: Mission in the Bible*. Quenzon City Philippines: Claretian Publications, 1991.

Lenski, Gerhard Emmanuel. *Power and Privilege: A Theory of Social Stratification*. McGraw-Hill Book Company, 1966.

Lenski, Gerhard Emmanuel, and Jean Lenski. *Human Societies: An Introduction to Macrosociology*. 2nd ed. McGraw-Hill Book Company, 1974.

Lott, Erick J. "Religious Faith and the Diversity of Cultural Life in India." In *Christian Faith and Multiform Culture in India*. Edited by Somen Das, 48-84. Bangalore: UTC Publications, 1987.

Malhotra, R. N. "India's Development Story." In *Manaroma Year Book 1997*. Kottayam: Malayala Manorama Press, 1997.

Malina, Bruce J. "Service." In *Biblical Social Values and their Meaning: A Handbook*. Edited by John J. Pilch and Bruce J. Malina. Hendrickson Publishers, 1993.

—————. *The New Testament World: Insights from Cultural Anthropology*. S.C.M Press Ltd., 1981.

Meeks, Wayne A. *The First Urban Christians: The Social World of the Apostle Paul*. 2nd ed. New Haven London: Yale University Press, 2003.

Mohapatra, Amulya Ranjan. *Philosophy of Religion: An Approach to World Religions*. 2nd ed.; Revised and enlarged. New Delhi, New York: Sterling Publisher Private Ltd., 1990.

O'Connor, Jerome Murphy. *1 Corinthians: Doubleday Bible Commentary*. New York: Bantam Doubleday Dell Publishing Group Inc., 1998.

——————. "First Letter to the Corinthians." In *The New Jerome Biblical Commentary*. Edited by Raymond Edward Brown, Joseph A. Fitzmyer, and Roland Edmund Murphy. Bangalore: TPI, 1994.

Orr, William F., and James Arthur Walther. *I Corinthians: A New Translation*. Vol. 32 of The Anchor Bible. Garden City: Doubleday & Co., 1995.

Parrinder, Edward Geoffrey. *The World's Living Religions*. Revised. London: Pan Books, 1977.

Pathrapankal, Joseph. *Critical and Creative: Studies in Bible and Theology*. Bangalore: Dharmaram Publications, 1986.

Patmury, J. "Concepts and Strategies of Paul's Mission." In *Bible and Mission in India Today*. Edited by Jacob Kavunkal and F. Hrangkhuma. Bombay: St Pauls, 1993.

Patterson, Maureen. "Caste and Political Leadership in Maharashtra." *Economic Weekly*, June 5, 2015.

Sen, Amartya. *Development as Freedom*. Oxford University Press, 2001.

———. *Poverty and Famines: An Essay on Entitlement and Deprivation*. Oxford University Press, 1999.

Sen, Amartya, and James E. Foster. *On Economic Inequality: Enlarged Edition with a Substantial Annexe "On Economic Inequality after a Quarter Century."* Oxford: Clarendon Press, 1997.

Senior, Donald, and Carroll Stuhlmueller. *The Biblical Foundations for Mission*. Orbis Books, 1991.

Srinivas, M. N. *Caste in Modern India, and Other Essays*. 1st ed. Bombay: Asia Publishing House, 1962.

Srinivas, Mysore Narasimhachar. *Social Change in Modern India*. 1972, Reprint, New Delhi: Orient Longman, 2001.

Stambaugh, John E., and David L. Balch. *The New Testament in Its Social Environment*. Edited by Wayne A. Meeks. Philadelphia: Westminster Press, 1986.

Theissen, Gerd. *Sociology of Early Palestinian Christianity*. Translated by John Bowden. Philadelphia: Fortress Press, 1978.

————. *The Social Setting of Pauline Christianity: Essays on Corinth*. Translated by John H. Scutz. Edinburgh: T&T Clark, 1982.

Thiselton, Anthony C. *1 Corinthians: A Shorter Exegetical and Pastoral Commentary*. Grand Rapids, Michigan/Cambridge, U.K.: Wm. B. Eerdmans Publishing, 2006.

Tidball, D. J. "Social Settings of Mission Churches." In *Dictionary of Paul and His Letters*. Edited by Gerald F. Hawthorne, Ralph P. Martin, and Daniel G. Reid, 883-92. Downer Grove, Illinois: InterVarsity Press, 1993.

Tigunait, Rajmani. *Seven Systems of Indian Philosophy*. Himalayan Institute Press, 1983.

3
A Macarian-Wesleyan
Theology of Mission

*Matt Friedman**

> And we all, with unveiled face, beholding the glory of the Lord, are being transformed into the same image from one degree of glory into another. For this comes from the Lord who is the Spirit.
>
> 2 Corinthians 3:18 (ESV)

Introduction

In this paper, I will begin by providing an outline of the development of the theology of union with God, or *theosis*. I will have a particular focus on fourth-century Syrian monk Macarius-Symeon, whose *Fifty Spiritual Homilies* had an influence on early Pietism and early Methodism. From there, I will seek to demonstrate how John and Charles Wesley, as well as their colleagues such as John Fletcher in the first generation of Methodist leadership, sought to critically fold this understanding into their own teaching regarding justification, sanctification and the ultimate goal of those who walk in union with God in Christ. Finally, this is integrated into a theology of mission in which this union with God is meant to be lived out individually and in community in a manner in which the *missio Dei* is extended in witness to the entire world.[1]

Theosis in the Patristic Period

In his landmark work, *On the Incarnation of the Word of God,* Athanasius of Alexandria famously wrote that, "through the Incarnation of the Word the Mind whence all things proceed has been declared, and its Agent and Ordainer, the Word of God Himself. He, indeed, assumed humanity that we might become God."[2] Although it sounds somewhat startling to many modern Christians, the doctrine of *theosis* to which this refers was rather widespread in particularly (though not exclusively) the Eastern Church,[3] and such ideas are found expressed clearly in post-biblical Christianity as early as the late second century. Writing in his *Against Heresies,* Irenaeus declares, "following the only true and steadfast Teacher, the Word of God, our Lord Jesus Christ, who did, through His transcendent love, become what we are, that He might bring us to be even what He is Himself."[4]

Based upon texts such as 2 Peter 1:4, at its heart it is meant to express a transformational relationship with God in which the believer is inhabited and empowered by God in a relationship of love. In addition to the 2 Peter passage cited above, other Scripture passages often referred to in connection with *theosis* include Galatians 2:20, Psalm 82:1 (along with the connected passage in John 10:34-35, where Jesus is quoting this), 2 Corinthians 3:7-4:6 and 1 John 3:2. Indeed, one of the strengths of a properly understood concept of *theosis* is that it is rooted in the Scriptures.

The image in the passage above quoted from 2 Corinthians, part of the broader passage in 2 Corinthians 3:7-4:6, has had powerfully moved many, in particular a Syrian monk who scholars now refer to as Macarius-Symeon.[5] Alexander Golitzen goes so far as to suggest that the "whole Macarian corpus is like an extended meditation on this scriptural passage," bringing together "all the essentials of what he wants to say to his monks."[6] Golitzen goes on to demonstrate how this passage contains so many of the classic contrasts relating to themes of "change, alteration, or transfiguration...which occurs in the Christian soul through the indwelling Spirit, and of the glory (*doxa*) of God in which the soul and ultimately the body are called to share."[7]

In the eighteenth of his *Homilies*, addressing those who have "this treasure in earthen vessels" in 2 Cor. 4:7, he speaks of "the treasure which they were deemed worthy to possess in this material life within themselves, the sanctifying power of the Spirit," and going on to exclaim that this is "in order that we may be empowered to walk in all of his commands without blame."[8] The homily continues with increasing vitality with each section, until it reaches a crescendo of sorts towards the end, describing one who has been enveloped in God in the fulfillment of *theosis*,

> Finally, when a person reaches the perfection of the Spirit, completely purified of all passions and united to and interpenetrated by the Paraclete Spirit in an ineffable communion, and is deemed worthy to become spirit in a mutual interpenetration with the Spirit, then it becomes all light, all eye, all spirit, all joy, all repose, all happiness, all love, all compassion, all goodness and kindness. As in the bottom of the sea, a stone is everywhere surrounded by water, so such persons as these are totally penetrated by the Holy Spirit. They become like to Christ, putting on the virtues of the power of the Spirit with a constancy. They interiorly become faultless and spotless and pure.[9]

Especially for many Western Christians, the most surprising language in this passage is that of *interpenetration* (*perichoriosis*), which is most frequently used to describe the relationship between the *hypostastes* within the Godhead one with another[10] as well as of Christ's human and divine natures.[11] This is *participation* in God; not a confusion or intermingling of natures, but rather the "human nature is transfigured by being permeated with the loving, self-giving action of God."[12]

Another enlightening aspect of Golitzen's essay is the connection between the idea of *theosis* not only with Hellenic Christian faith, as is usually emphasized, but also to traditions and emphases which point to Syrian and Jewish influences in the development of understanding of *theosis* generally, and in particular in the writing and thought of Macarius-Symeon.[13]

Golitzen is not the first scholar to notice this, however. A century ago one scholar noted the similarities in Macarius-Symeon and that of the mystical tradition of the *Merkabah* speculation on Ezekiel's vision,[14] describing how the first of Macarius-Symeon's *Homilies* opens with a description of Ezekiel's vision and "reads like a programme of his mystical faith."[15] Following the overview of Ezekiel's vision, Macarius-Symeon begins seeking to explain it in the language of *theosis* which one finds again and again throughout the *Homilies*. Here he says,

> For the prophet was viewing the mystery of the human soul that would receive its Lord and would become his throne of glory. For the soul that is deemed to be judged worthy to participate in the light of the Holy Spirit by becoming his throne and habitation, and is covered with the beauty of ineffable glory of the Spirit, becomes all light, all face, all eye. There is no part of his soul that is not full of the spiritual eyes of light. For the soul has no imperfect part but is in every part on all sides facing forward and covered with the beauty of the light of Christ...
>
> Thus the soul is completely illumined with the unspeakable beauty of the glory of the light of the face of Christ and is perfectly made a participator of the Holy Spirit. (Pseudo-Macarius 1992, 37-38).[16]

Notice here how Macarius-Symeon is connecting the *Merkabah* tradition with an explanatory principle of sorts in the form of the aforementioned passage in 2 Corinthians, in this case particularly 4:6. Indeed, the connections are strong enough that Golitzen feels confident enough to write that, "the soteriology of deification also emerges in a light at once more "Jewish," and so more in obvious continuity with the revelation accorded Israel."[17]

I want to continue with Golitzen's explanation of the Semitic elements in the Macarian *Homilies*, as an understanding of this background deepens an already rich vault of spiritual insight. Golitzen continues to pursue the theme of God's glorious presence, and which has echoes in other Patristic writers of the era:

> I should like, though, to underline what I take to be the *Homilies'* particular emphasis on the Old Testamental motifs of the promised land and holy city, Jerusalem, and of the tabernacle and temple as the place of God's abiding. Christ is the reality of these images. He is the heavenly fatherland and the celestial city, the place of God's presence and -- to borrow an expression from the *Targumim*, since I think the traditions the latter represent are close to Macarius' own heart -- the "glory of the *Shekinah*" which dwells there and fills all with light. This presence or abiding, the literal sense of *Shekinah*, which comes to the Christian through baptism and the gift of the Holy Spirit, renders the soul in its turn the city and temple of God, at least in potential.[18]

This *Shekinah* imagery of God's glorious presence is a concept which began in the Jewish *Targumim* and rabbinic writings, and, Golitzen says, was absorbed into Christian writing in Syriac, such as in Ephrem the Syrian's *Paradise Hymns*, in which the *Shekinah* is "identified with the Presence enthroned at the Tree of Life and visible atop Sinai."[19] Though he was not unique among early Christian writers in this, Golitzen finds particular significance in Macarius-Symeon's use of the word *doxa* to express this "glory" of God: "What is surely more significant about Macarius' use of *doxa* is that term's long-standing use in Greek-speaking Jewish and Christian traditions as the translation of the Hebrew *kavod* YHWH... *Kavod* and its Greek equivalent are, put simply, the biblical terms of choice for theophany. What is at work in Macarius' use of *doxa* is therefore a persistent and conscious interiorization of the biblical glory tradition, of theophany,"[20] in a manner similar to what was observed in Macarius-Symeon's use of 2 Corinthians 3:7-4:6 as an interpretive passage of sorts for the *Merkabah* passage in Ezekiel.

How can this rich heritage be integrated into an Evangelical understanding of the *mission Dei*? One example of how this tradition was critically utilized can be found in the writing and ministry of John Wesley and the early Methodist tradition. The degree and manner to which some of the distinctive teaching of the early Methodist tradition have been influenced by the theology of the early Church, and in particular its teaching of *theosis*, has been a topic of sometimes heated discussion in the past 45 years, and it is to the practical elements of this discussion that I will now turn.

Theosis and Sanctification in the Writings of the Early Methodist

It has been noted that, in common with many Christian leaders of their own day, both John and Charles Wesley were both conversant with and influenced by the writings of early Christianity.[21] There are a innumerable other more contemporary sources, too, including Anglican, Catholic and Pietist writings, which also seem to had an influence on these developments, and through which the Wesley's and John Fletcher often received many of the same ideas regarding *theosis* in second-hand form.[22] These and many others are included among those whose writings transmitted teaching regarding *theosis* which will also be touched on as secondary sources of the early Methodist ideas of sanctification.

Beginning with Albert C. Outler, a number of writers in the past forty-five years have sought to examine how the writings of some of these ancient figures in antiquity may have had an influence on the views of the leaders of early Methodism on this topic, and how the concept of *theosis* may have contributed to the Wesleyan idea of sanctification.[23] In addition to receiving the influence of these writers, however, it will be important to note how, in line with the prevailing view in England at the time, they sought to cite these ancient writers as a source of validation of their own teaching. I will also briefly examine how the Wesley's and John Fletcher interacted critically with this material.

Outler wrote in the introduction to his *John Wesley* that he believed that Wesley had acquired his concept of devotion and perfection from Gregory of Nyssa by way of "Macarius the Egyptian."[24] As Ted Campbell has traced the conversation,[25] it began slowly, but gained momentum as more scholars joined the discussion, including Campbell himself. Outler, Campbell's friend and mentor, hoped that Campbell would be able to "confirm his suspicion that Wesley's doctrine of sanctification was in essence that of ancient Eastern Christian asceticism."[26] Campbell confessed his inability to do so, concluding that, "What I discovered about Wesley's use of Christian antiquity (it should have come as no surprise) was the selectivity *he* employed in choosing (and editing) historical materials as he saw their relevance to the eighteenth-century Revival."[27] Perhaps this is a case in which Wesley was correctly engaging in the work of discernment in sifting the "gold from the dross" of ancient traditions,[28] attempting to extract what he considered to be helpful to his people while taking care as to what got passed on. Randy Maddox also notes that as positive as Wesley's view was regarding these early writers, he was not naïve, and became "increasingly aware that there were problems in both doctrine and life from almost the beginning of the Church."[29]

Perhaps what Howard Snyder offers is a balanced perspective on Wesley's interaction with Macarius-Symeon, one that takes into account the other influences in Wesley's own studies:

> I do not claim that Wesley simply "took over" this set of ideas from Macarius. Some of them he encountered elsewhere; some undoubtedly came to him through his own extensive study of Scripture; some were already present in the Anglican tradition; some were points of emphasis in the Pietist writings Wesley read (e.g., Arndt's *True Christianity* with its emphasis on the restoration of the image of God and the priority of love). But it is clear that the complex ideas on perfection Wesley taught were at key points strikingly similar to those taught by[...] Macarius and that these ideas had a particularly strong appeal to Wesley and therefore made a distinctive contribution to his doctrine of perfection.[30]

In fact, there are some strong streams of thought on this theme of union with God in John Wesley's writings, in the hymnology of his brother Charles, and as well in the writings of Wesley's influential colleague John Fletcher. It is particularly interesting that, although Campbell suggested that Wesley actually omitted "references to the ascetic life and the notion of *theosis*,"[31] when we read Wesley's own edition of Homily XIX in the Macarian corpus, we can observe that here, at least, he retained a rather clear reference to it:

> It behooveth- therefore the soul that truly believeth in CHRIST,
> *to be changed from her present nature into another nature, which is*
> *Divine,* and to be wrought new herself through the power of the
> Holy Spirit. And to obtain this, will be allowed to us who believe
> and love him in truth, and walk in all his holy commandments.[32]

Significantly, another area which has relevance for applying the understanding of *theosis* as sanctification and perfection to the work of discipleship is the idea of salvation having a soul-healing, therapeutic dimension.[33] Randy Maddox points out that the dominant understanding of salvation in the Christian East is therapeutic rather than juridical, but, importantly, Wesley seems to have been able to *integrate* these in his own approach.[34] Wesley understood grace as referring to *both* the deifying, empowering, uncreated presence of the Holy Spirit *and* pardon from sin and justification.[35]

This theme of Christ as the healer of the soul is also found in Macarius-Symeon. In fact, he integrates the Incarnation, the Crucifixion and Christ as healer at once in at least one place,

> The Lord Himself, who is the Way and is God, after he came not
> on his own behalf but for you so that he might be an example
> for you of everything good, see, he came in such humility, taking
> the "form of a slave" (Phil. 2:7), he, who is God, the Son of God,
> King, the Son of the King. He himself gave healing medicines
> and he healed all the wounded when he appeared externally as
> one among "the wounded" (Is. 53:5).[36]

Wesley and his colleagues read and interacted with the fathers' writings critically, correcting concepts where they felt they were unclear, and using terminology which was less likely to lead to confusion. When Wesley read in Clement of Alexandria's *Stromata* regarding *theosis* and the character of a "true gnostic" (in the sense that Clement was seeking to speak to *his* Alexandrian context), Wesley adjusted that which he was interacting in Clement. We see that,

For Wesley, we are justified and sanctified by "faith filled with the energy of love" (not by works nor by gnosis). We enjoy *communion* with God as creatures, but not *union* with God as equals. We may become *like* God, Wesley hopes and prays, but we do not become divine! Thus, when Wesley appropriates Clement's gnostic vision, he "corrects" the assertion of *gnosis* as the means to perfection.[37]

These ideas were contributed to the distinctly Wesleyan teaching of sanctification. Christensen notes that "what Wesley envisioned as Christian perfection, holiness, or entire sanctification is theologically dependent upon earlier versions of *theosis.*"[38]

In the same manner, John Wesley and his colleagues sought to distinguish between a healthy, Scripturally-based idea of union with God and an unhealthy, speculative mysticism. John Fletcher, considered John Wesley's heir apparent until his untimely death from tuberculosis, wrote in an essay entitled, "An Evangelical Mysticism," in which he draws a contrast between what he calls a "wise mysticism" and an "extravagant" or "frivolous" mysticism.

> Of the former he writes that it is a mysticism glowing with Divine wisdom, and shedding luminous rays on the most profound truths, a mysticism having more light and energy than all the subtle arguments of the schoolmen; in fine, a mysticism which lays the most sublime truths on a level with simple and unlearned people...that which cautiously penetrates the bark or veil of religion to sound its depths, and discover in the sacred oracles a spiritual and heavenly sense.[39]

Of the latter, speculative variety of mysticism, he noted that there is also "an extravagant mysticism, by which violence is done to sound criticism, in quitting, without reason, the literal sense of the Scriptures, and running into ridiculous and forced allegories."[40]

While we can and should take seriously the refinements made to the tradition of *theosis* by John Wesley and John Fletcher, I believe that Christensen is correct when he exhorts us (in an echo of Outler) to "read Wesley *with his sources*, and not simply read back into ancient sources Wesley's distinctive eighteenth-century vision of perfection or programmatic agenda of reform."[41] Christensen goes beyond this, however, and exhorts his reader to seek to interact with these sources in a manner which will be effective in our modern context,

> Such a reformulation would incorporate the best of John Wesley's theological refinements and improvements on the ancient doctrine of *theosis* (i.e., appropriation by faith not by works or knowledge, inward assurance over perpetual seeking, accessibility in this earthly life), while fully appreciating the Eastern emphasis on "therapeutic" soteriology with its biblical affirmation of original humanity and original blessing. In so doing, we may arrive at a progressive Wesleyan Orthodox vision of *theosis* as part of the essential quest for human wholeness and completion of the new creation in Christ.[42]

One of Wesley's important contributions to the discussion was his ability to hold in tension issues such as the importance of sanctification and a healing model of salvation without abandoning the reality of justification by grace through faith which is so clearly rooted in the Scriptural witness.

On *Theosis* and Mission

> We, lastly, have daily opportunities of knowing, if Christianity be of God, then of how glorious a privilege are they thought worthy who persuade others to accept its benefits. Seeing when the author of it 'cometh in the clouds of heaven', they who have saved others from sin and its attendant death 'shall shine as the brightness of the firmament'; they who have *reprinted the image of God on many souls* 'as the stars for ever'![43]

How can this understanding of *theosis* contribute to a robust theology of *mission*? I believe it is here as well that John Wesley offers some wisdom in terms of his theological emphases, as well as in the manner in which these emphases are meant to have an impact not only on the individual believer and the believing community, but on the world.

Howard Snyder, in a presentation on what he termed a "Wesleyan Theology of Mission," focused on four particular elements which he observed in Wesley that he understood as being related to mission. These were the image of God in humankind, reflected less directly throughout creation, a therapeutic view of salvation as healing (though without denying other elements of justification), God's prevenient grace which draws all people to himself, and the Holy Spirit empowered process of Christian perfecting, also referred to as sanctification.[44] All of these elements spill over into one another, and all can ultimately be related to the theme of *theosis*. Thus, the therapeutic theme is frequently expressed in terms of the healing and restoration of the image of God, empowered by his grace, and ultimately moving towards further realization in the process of Holy Spirit-empowered perfecting.

Wesley (and Fletcher) clearly believed that there would be an effect on the evangelization of humankind based on the state of Christians' lives and communities. If the nations were going to be impacted by the Gospel, it would be because they saw it being lived out and could observe the *glory* of God among Christian people—that is to say, if they could see a God-empowered *theosis* bringing healing and restoration to those who claimed to follow Jesus, walking in the fullness of the image of God, they would respond to the drawing of the prevenient grace of God and joyfully come to faith in Jesus.

Thus, in his sermon on "The General Spread of the Gospel," Wesley begins with what is essentially an account of the lost state of the peoples and nations of the world, beginning with those he considers to be the farthest from God, the exemplified for him among the tribal people of the South Seas.[45] From there he moves on to the Muslims, and from there to the state of the Christian community in non-Western lands,[46] to describe even the failings of those who consider themselves Christian in the West among both Roman Catholics as well as Protestants.[47]

Wesley describes what he sees as the "problem" of the unevangelized, and, crucially, made it clear that a key element of the problem is the terrible example of the lives of those who claim to be Christians. For example, he refers to the complaints of the Hindu people from the Malabar coast, who he quotes as listing the sins of the Christians in their area, concluding with "*Devil-Christian!* Me no Christian" (*sic!*).[48]

He then begins to set out the solution, which Wesley sees as the global spread of the revival of the gospel which has occurred under the course of Methodism – that as the revival spreads across the Christian world, and as those who have been "Christian" for generations actually begin to live out the faith which they claim, it will have an effect on others.[49] Interestingly, he presents this spread in precisely the reverse order in which he had earlier discussed the state of the world. Wesley perceives that the *primary* element preventing Muslims, "heathens" and others from coming to Christ is the corrupt lifestyle of Christians. Thus, as Christians begin actually to embrace and live as Christ meant for them to live, Muslims and others will begin coming to faith in Jesus. Wesley writes,

> The grand stumbling-block being thus happily removed out of the way, namely, the lives of the Christians, the Mahometans (*sic*)

will look upon them with other eyes, and begin to give attention to their words. And as their words will be clothed with divine energy, attended with the demonstration of the Spirit and of power, those of them that fear God will soon take knowledge of the Spirit whereby Christians speak. They will "receive with meekness the engrafted word," and will bring forth fruit with patience.[50]

He goes on to express a hope in the gospel's spread to those he refers to as "heathen,"[51] and finally, ultimately one might say, to the Jewish people, who must wait until the "fullness of the Gentiles be come in."[52] For Wesley, then, the evangelization of the nations of the world depends upon Christian holiness and sanctification. If Christians are living as they are meant to, and indeed, scripturally speaking, empowered to, those outside the community of Christ will be drawn in.

John Fletcher clearly also saw the light which had been received by, for example, the Muslims, to be preparatory for them, as well as perhaps for others in the lands of other religious traditions in which Islam had spread. For example, having described some of the exalted statements in the Qur'ān and Sunnah, he goes on to assert that, in spite of the distortions of the Qur'ān concerning Christian faith,

> yet it admits enough of our doctrines to overthrow idolatry, and the external empire of Satan upon earth; insomuch that in Africa and India, Mohammedanism prepares idolaters for the reception of Christianity: and secondly to nourish our hope, that the Mohammedans, who have already such exalted notions of Jesus Christ, will embrace the Gospel, when the great scandals of the Christian Churches shall be done away... (sic)[53]

Thus Fletcher seems ultimately to lean in the direction of seeing the light which the nations have as yet received as being *preparatory* to their receiving the gospel in its fullness, and echoes Wesley's sentiments in "The General Spread of the Gospel" that this may be connected with the spread of the revival in the churches, that is, that they would be demonstratively walking in the fullness of what is relationship with God.

It is in the second of Fletcher's essays on this topic, "Remarks on the Trinity," that this seems to touch more directly on several of the themes of Wesleyan theology of mission which I am examining here. The main thrust of the essay was in answering some of the arguments of Deism. An important eighteenth-century Deist spokesman, Joseph Priestly, had questioned the practical benefits of the doctrine of the Trinity. How did this understanding help to promote "morality and piety"?[54] Fletcher's response here connects the doctrine of the Trinity with some of the very hallmarks of Wesleyan theology of mission:

> But things are soon changed, when the creating God reveals himself as Immanuel in believers; as soon as God, by the manifestation of his sanctifying Spirit, has re-established his image in their souls. Then the Trinity being clearly revealed, God is adored in spirit and in truth, with a zeal like that which burned in the bosoms of the primitive Christians; then men begin to love and help each other with a charity which the world never saw before....
>
> [...] the sacred doctrine of Father, Son and Holy Spirit, which includes repentance toward God the Father, faith in our Lord Jesus Christ, and love shed abroad in the heart by the Holy Spirit: love the mother of good works, and the distinguishing badge of true Christians. From hence it follows, that Christian virtues flourish or decay, in proportion as the doctrine of the Trinity is rendered clear or obscured among men; for it is the foundation that the Gospel becomes the power of God to salvation to all who believe. And it should be remembered, that faith in the Father, Son and Holy Spirit, of which we speak, is the gift of God, Eph. ii, 8, and not the word of a nurse, or the dictate of a catechist. It is a Divine energy, which is "the substance of things hoped for, a cordial demonstration of things not seen;" for we believe with the heart unto righteousness, before we can make confession with the mouth unto salvation.[55]

John Fletcher took Wesley's understanding of the Trinity[56] and expanded upon it, extrapolating it into the practical application of life in connection with God in Christ, and empowered by the Holy Spirit. Here we see the themes of the image of God in humans, the path of Christian perfection, and prevenient grace integrated with one of what Wesley described in his related sermon as an essential of the faith.[57] This connection between renewal in the image of God and Christian perfection, or sanctification, was also expressed more concisely in Wesley's *Plain Account of Christian Perfection*, when the answer to the catechetical question, "What does it mean to be *sanctified?*" is given as "To be renewed in the image of God, in "righteousness and true holiness.""[58]

For Wesley and his colleagues, mission, then, is connected with this idea of *theosis,* and this, in turn, has a Trinitarian expression to it in its more fully developed sense. The incarnation itself, including the death and resurrection of Jesus as the Word and Son of God, are understood as bringing us into the life of the Trinity as we are brought to faith, and he fills us with the life of the Holy Spirit. Thus empowered, we are free to be united to one another, empowered to go out into the world, and to enter truly into an incarnational *missio Dei* in which the incarnation is not merely our model, but our empowering and unifying life.

Endnotes

* Matt Friedman is a PhD student in Intercultural Studies at Asbury Theological Seminary in Wilmore, KY. He is the book notes subeditor for mission and evangelism for *Religious Studies Review*. His current research is focused on a comparative study of Patristic and Wesleyan spirituality and that of Sufism.

[1] Other recent writings which have explored a Patristic and/or Wesleyan approach utilizing the theme of union with God include Peter J. Bellini,

Participation: Epistemology and Mission Theology (Lexington, KY: Emeth Press, 2010), focused more on a philosophical level and dealing with the postmodern context, and James Greear, "*Theosis* and Muslim Evangelism: How the Recovery of a Patristic Understanding of Salvation Can Aid Evangelical Missionaries in the Evangelization of Islamic Peoples" (PhD diss., Southeastern Baptist Theological Seminary, 2003), focused on using *theosis* as the focus of an evangelistic presentation.

[2] St Athanasius, *On the Incarnation of the Word of God.* trans. Penelope Lawson (1944, repr; Crestwood, NY: St Vladamir's Seminary Press, 1996), 93. Daniel Clendenin rather beautifully paraphrased Athanasius on this point, interpreting his words as, "when God descended, assumed humanity, and was 'incarnated,' he opened the way for people to ascend to him, assume divinity, and become 'in-godded'" (Daniel B. Clendenin, "Partakers of Divinity: The Orthodox Doctrine of Theosis," *Journal of the Evangelical Theological Society* 37, no. 3 [September 1994]: 366).

[3] Robert V. Rakestraw, "Becoming Like God: An Evangelical Doctrine of *Theosis*," *Journal of the Evangelical Theological Society* 40, no. 2 (June 1997): 257.

[4] Irenaeus, "Against Heresies," in *The Apostolic Fathers, With Justin Martyr and Irenaeus*, The Ante-Nicene Fathers 1, trans. Alexander Roberts and James Donaldson (Buffalo: The Christian Literature Publishing Company, 1885), 526.

[5] As his writings were circulated pseudonymously under the name of the desert Father Macarius of Egypt, and the most likely identity of the author is considered to be Symeon of Mesopotamia. See Marcus Plested, *The Macarian Legacy: The Place of Macarius-Symeon in the Eastern Christian Tradition* (Oxford: Oxford University Press, 2004), 12-16.

[6] Alexander Golitzen, "A Testimony to Christianity as Transfiguration: The Macarian Homilies and Orthodox Spirituality," in *Orthodox and Wesleyan Spirituality*, ed. S. T. Kimbrough, Jr. (Crestwood, NY: St Vladamir's Seminary Press, 2002), 133.

[7] Golitzen, "Christianity as Transfiguration," 133.

[8] Pseudo-Macarius, *The Fifty Spiritual Homilies and the Great Letter*, trans. George A. Maloney (Mahwah, NJ: Paulist Press, 1992), 142.

[9] Pseudo-Macarius, *Homilies*, 145.

[10] Vladamir Losskey, *Mystical Theology of the Eastern Church* (London: James Clarke & Co., Ltd., 1957), 53-54.

[11] Lossky, *Mystical Theology*, 145-46.

[12] Rowan Williams, "Deification," *The Westminster Dictionary of Christian Spirituality*, ed. G. S. Wakefeld (Philadelphia: Westminster, 1983), 107; quoted in Rakestraw, "Becoming Like God," 260.

[13] Marcus Plested has, however, suggested that Macarius-Symeon demonstrates what he refers to as a "double-inheritance," drawing from both Semitic and Hellenic wells; he notes that in the passage on Ezekiel's vision described above, apart from the "obvious link with the Jewish *Merkabah* tradition," Macarius-Symeon also "draws on the chariot image from Plato's *Phaedrus*" (Plested, *Macarian Legacy*, 31). Golitzen recognizes the reference to *Phaedrus,* but also notes that this is "Platonism with a difference," with Christ holding the reigns and guiding the soul by the Holy Spirit, rather than the intellect being in the driver's seat (Golitzen, "Christianity as Transfiguration," 140).

[14] The *Merkabah* is "God's throne-chariot" in the opening chapter of Ezekiel and was the subject of significant mystical speculation in Jewish antiquity (see Gershom Scholem, *Major Trends in Jewish Mysticism* [1946, repr.; New York: Schocken Books, 1995], 42).

[15] Joseph Stoffels, *Die Mystiche Theologie Makarius des Aegypters* (Bonn: Peter Hanstein, 1908), 79; cited in Gershom Scholem, *Major Trends*, 79.

[16] Pseudo-Macarius, *Homilies*, 37-38.

[17] Hannah K. Harrington, Review of *Holiness: Rabbinic Judaism and the Greco-Roman World*, by Alexander Golitzen, *St Vladamir's Theological Quarterly* 43 (January 2003): 462.

[18] Golitzen, "Christianity as Transfiguration," 133.

[19] Golitzen, "Christianity as Transfiguration," 150-51.

[20] Golitzen, "Christianity as Transfiguration," 138.

[21] This is in no way to imply that the Patristic writings were the sole or even primary influence on the development of the Wesleyan theology, including their distinctive understanding of sanctification. Apart from figures in the Patristic East such as Macarius-Symeon on whom I have focused here, there have been other Patristic figures from the West, such as Augustine, whose writings had an influence on Wesley.

[22] Richard P. Heinzenrater, "John Wesley's Reading of, and References to, the Early Church Fathers," in *Orthodox and Wesleyan Spirituality*, ed. by S. T. Kimbrough, Jr. (Crestwood, NY: St Vladamir's Seminary Press, 2002), 30-31.

[23] Albert C. Outler, *Introduction to John Wesley* (New York: Oxford University Press, 1964), 9-10.

[24] Outler, "Introduction," 9.

[25] Ted Campbell, "Back to the Future: Wesleyan Quest for Ancient Roots: the 1980's," *Wesleyan Theological Journal* 32, no. 1 (Spring 1997): 5-16.

[26] Ted A. Campbell, *John Wesley and Christian Antiquity* (Nashville: Kingswood Books, 1991), x.

[27] Campbell, "Back to the Future," 15. Of course, it has also been noted that Wesley edited virtually everything from *any* source; See Michael J. Christensen, "John Wesley: Christian Perfection as Faith Filled with the Energy of Love," in *Partakers of the Divine Nature: The History and Development of Deification in the Christian Traditions,* eds. Michael J. Christensen and Jeffrey A. Wittung (Grand Rapids, MI: Baker Academic, 2007), 221.

[28] Robert G. Tuttle, *Mysticism in the Wesleyan Tradition* (Grand Rapids, MI: Francis Asbury Press, 1989), 126.

[29] Randy L. Maddox, *Responsible Grace* (Nashville: Kingswood Books, 1994), 43.

[30] Howard Snyder, "John Wesley and Macarius the Egyptian," *Asbury Theological Journal* 45, no. 2 (Fall 1990), 59.

[31] Campbell, *John Wesley and Christian Antiquity*, x.

[32] "Macarius of Egypt," in *The Homilies of Macarius*. A Christian Library 1, ed. John Wesley. (London: T. Cordeux, 1819), XIX, accessed December 22, 2010, http://wesley.nnu.edu/john_wesley/christian_library/vol1/CL1Part2.htm, emphasis mine. Note that homily XIX in Wesley's revised Macarian corpus is the equivalent of Homily XLIV in the original Macarian corpus. See Hoo-Jung Lee, "The Doctrine of New Creation in the Theology of John Wesley" (PhD diss., Emory University, 1991), 235, for this particular homily, and numerous notes from 230-40.

[33] Maddox, *Responsible Grace*, 229.

[34] Maddox, *Responsible Grace*, 67.

[35] Maddox, *Responsible Grace*, 199.

[36] Pseudo-Macarius, *Homilies*, 173.

[37] Christensen, "Christian Perfection," 222.

[38] Christensen, "Christian Perfection," 226.

[39] John Fletcher, *The Works of the Rev. John Fletcher* (New York: T. Mason and G. Lane, 1836), 4.9.

[40] John Fletcher, *Works*, 4.9.

[41] Christensen, "Christian Perfection," 223.

[42] Christensen, "Christian Perfection," 227.

[43] John Wesley, *John Wesley's Sermons: An Anthology*, eds. Albert C. Outler and Richard P. Heinzenrater (Nashville: Abingdon Press, 1991), 21.

[44] Howard Snyder, "What's Unique about a Wesleyan Theology of Mission? A Wesleyan Perspective on Free Methodist Missions" (Presentation, FM Missions Consultation, Indianapolis, IN, October 11-13, 2002), 3.

[45] John Wesley, *The Bicentennial Edition of the Works of John Wesley: Sermons*, 4 vols., ed. Albert C. Outler (Nashville: Abingdon Press, 1985), 2.486.

[46] John Wesley, *WJW*, 2.487.

[47] John Wesley, *WJW*, 2.487-88.

[48] John Wesley, *WJW*, 2.496.

[49] John Wesley, *WJW*, 2.493-95.

[50] John Wesley, *WJW*, 2.495.

[51] John Wesley, *WJW*, 2.496-97.

[52] John Wesley, *WJW*, 2.498.

[53] Fletcher, *Works*, 4.227.

[54] Fletcher, *Works*, 4.44.

[55] Fletcher, *Works*, 4.45-46.

[56] Expressed in particular in Wesley's "On the Trinity," John Wesley, *WJW*, 2.377-86.

[57] John Wesley, *WJW*, 2.386.

[58] John Wesley, *A Plain Account of Christian Perfection* (New York: G. Lane and P. P. Sandford, 1844), 10.

Bibliography

Athanasius. *On the Incarnation of the Word of God*. Translated by Penelope Lawson. Crestwood, NY: St Vladamir's Seminary Press, 1993.

Bellini, Peter J. *Participation: Epistemology and Mission Theology*. Lexington, KY: Emeth Press, 2010.

Campbell, Ted A. *John Wesley and Christian Antiquity*. Nashville: Kingswood Books, 1991.

—————. "Back to the Future: Wesleyan Quest for Ancient Roots: the 1980's." *Wesleyan Theological Journal* 32, no.1 (Spring 1997): 5-16.

Christensen, Michael J. "John Wesley: Christian Perfection as Faith Filled with the Energy of Love." In *Partakers of the Divine Nature: The History and Development of Deification in the Christian Traditions.* Edited by Michael J. Christensen and Jeffrey A. Wittung, 219-29. Grand Rapids, MI: Baker Academic, 2007.

Clendenin, Daniel B. "Partakers of Divinity: The Orthodox Doctrine of *Theosis.*" *Journal of the Evangelical Theological Society* 37, no. 3 (September 1994): 365-79.

Fletcher, John. *The Works of the Rev. John Fletcher.* Translated by Miles Martindale. New York: T. Mason and G. Lane, 1836.

————. An Essay on the Doctrine of the New Birth. *The Asbury Theological Journal* 53, no. 1 (Spring 1998): 35-56.

Golitzin, Alexander. "A Testimony to Christianity as Transfiguration: The Macarian Homilies and Orthodox Spirituality." *Orthodox and Wesleyan Spirituality.* Edited by S. T. Kimbrough Jr., 129-156. Crestwood, NY: St Vladamir's Seminary Press, 2002.

Harrington, Hannah K. Review of *Holiness: Rabbinic Judaism and the Greco-Roman World.* By Alexander Golitzin. *St Vladamir's Theological Quarterly* 43 (January 2003): 461-68.

Greear, James D. "*Theosis* and Muslim Evangelism: How the Recovery of a Patristic Understanding of Salvation Can Aid Evangelical Missionaries in the Evangelization of Islamic Peoples." PhD diss., Southeastern Baptist Theological Seminary, 2003.

Heitzenrater, Richard P. "John Wesley's Reading of, and References to, the Early Church Fathers." *Orthodox and Wesleyan Spirituality.* Edited by S. T. Kimbrough, Jr., 25-32. Crestwood, NY: St Vladamir's Seminary Press, 2002.

Irenaeus. *Against Heresies.* In *The Apostolic Fathers, With Justin Martyr and Irenaeus.* The Ante-Nicene Fathers 1. Translated by Alexander Roberts and James Donaldson, 309-567. Buffalo: The Christian Literature Publishing Company, 1885.

Lee, Hoo-Jung. "The Doctrine of New Creation in the Theology of John Wesley." PhD diss., Emory University, 1991.

Lossky, Vladamir. *Mystical Theology of the Eastern Church.* London: James Clarke & Co., Ltd., 1957.

"Macarius." *The Homilies of Macarius*. A Christian Library 1. Edited by John Wesley. London: T. Cordeux, 1819. http://wesley.nnu.edu/john_wesley/christian_library/vol1/CL1Part2.htm. (December 22, 2010).

Maddox, Randy L. *Responsible Grace*. Nashville: Kingswood Books, 1994.

Outler, Albert C. *Introduction to John Wesley*. New York: Oxford University Press, 1964.

Plested, Marcus. *The Macarian Legacy: The Place of Macarius-Symeon in the Eastern Christian Tradition*. Oxford: Oxford University Press, 2004.

Pseudo-Macarius. *The Fifty Spiritual Homilies and the Great Letter*. Translated by George A. Maloney. Mahwah, NJ: Paulist Press, 1992.

Rakestraw, Robert V. "Becoming Like God: An Evangelical Doctrine of *Theosis*," *Journal of the Evangelical Theological Society* 40, no. 2 (June 1997): 257-69.

Snyder, Howard. Snyder, Howard. "John Wesley and Macarius the Egyptian." *Asbury Theological Journal* 45, no. 2 (Fall 1990): 55-60.

————. What's Unique about a Wesleyan Theology of Mission? A Wesleyan Perspective on Free Methodist Missions. Presentation, FM Missions Consultation, Indianapolis, IN, October 11-13, 2002.

Stoffels, Joseph. *Die Mystiche Theologie Makarius des Aegypters*. Bonn: Peter Hanstein, 1908.

Tuttle, Robert G. *Mysticism in the Wesleyan Tradition*. Grand Rapids, MI: Francis Asbury Press, 1989.

Wesley, John. *A Plain Account of Christian Perfection*. New York: G. Lane and P. P. Sandford, 1844.

————. *The Bicentennial Edition of the Works of John Wesley: Sermons*. Edited by Albert C. Outler. Nashville: Abingdon Press, 1985.

————. *John Wesley's Sermons: An Anthology*. Edited by Albert C. Outler and Richard P. Heinzenrater. Nashville: Abingdon Press, 1991.

Williams, Rowan. "Deification," In *The Westminster Dictionary of Christian Spirituality*. Edited by G. S. Wakefeld, 106-108. Philadelphia: Westminster, 1983.

4
Christian Witness as With-Ness in the Context of the 'Conversion' Controversy in India

Peniel Jesudason Rufus Rajkumar[1]

T he 'anti-conversion' rhetoric which has been voiced in India especially in justification of the Hindutva initiated communal violence against Christians is symptomatic of the gradual erosion of secular values in India. As the cultural critic Homi Bhabha has perceptively pointed out, the enemies of secularism are today waging a war *not simply in opposition to secularism* but *within secularism and in fact in and through secularism!*[2] This attack against secularism from within is blatant with regard to the issue of conversions, because here the Hindutva forces use the argument about the equality of all religions to protest against the attempts of Christians and Muslims to convert people from other religions, effectively threatening the fundamental right of these communities to propagate one's religion. In such a context this paper conceives of witness in the Indian context as 'with-ness' - as radical accompaniment and not abandonment - of those who have opted to convert, especially the subalterns, the term subaltern in this case implying those who have been rendered the 'Others' in the human story of exclusion, marginalization and oppression.

'With-ness' in this paper refers not to condescending forms of solidarity with the oppressed subalterns that has often been characteristic of certain forms of pro-'liberation' discourses. Rather the primary trajectory of 'witn-ness' that will be pursued in this paper is one which recognises the agency of the subaltern and offers resistance to all attempts to denounce or co-opt this agency of the subaltern. It also needs to be clarified that the concept of 'with-ness' that the paper proposes as a form of credible Christian witness cannot be confined exclusively to the question of practice. In fact the idea of 'with-ness' also functions as the methodological framework for this paper, as the primary epistemological premise which foregrounds the arguments for the pertinence of understanding Christian witness as 'with-ness.'

What I seek to do in this paper is:

a. Initially flesh out the methodological implications of 'with-ness' as a '(Re)-Turn to the Other.' The argument made in this section is that too often in contemporary academic discourses on power and emancipation there is a tacit inclination to reinforce structures of inequalities through the unconscious and uncritical acceptance of views of the privileged. Such elitism needs to be challenged.

b. Then move on to critically review the anti-conversion rhetoric of the Hindutva using as a lens the caste politics which seeks to thwart the mobility of the subalterns and thus seek to 'Re-cast(e) Conversions,' and

c. Briefly trace the contours of what 'with-nessing' as Christian witness might entail in the contemporary Indian context.

The Question of Methodology: With-ness as a (Re)-Turn to the Other

Despite a proliferation of discourses which have sought to address questions of power and inequality and take up the issues of the 'Other'/the subalterns, in several instances such discourses have been implicated in the politics of power as they have often denied the agency of the 'Other' and have remained elitist in their orientation. Such tacit inclination towards perspectives emerging from the 'elites' only function to reinforce the assymetrical status quo than change the status quo. This elitist orientation is true of Indian and Western discourses, both theological and secular. A few examples can be cited.

Analysing the discourses on economic poverty in the Indian context K. N. Panikkar critically exposes how even 'progressive thinking' in colonial India which employed rhetoric which critiqued inequality was clearly entrapped in a bourgeois perspective to such an extent that hierarchy and hegemony were reinforced and reproduced rather than being re-configured and re-dressed. Critiquing the thinking of people like Keshub Chander Sen, Bankim Chandra Chatterjee and Vivekananda, Panikkar says:

> That the intellectuals in colonial India were concerned with the problem of poverty is in itself not very significant; given the prevalent conditions, they would not have remained insensitive to it. What is important, however, is how they viewed this problem: whether their approach was from the standpoint of the poor or that of the privileged. Generally, it was the latter; therefore, while poverty was decried, the system and structure which decried it was not denounced.[3]

In a similar vein Edward W. Said for instance critically brings out how in the western circles even a philosopher like Foucault who is known for is discursive analysis of power did not really subvert the status quo by recognising adequately the agency of the subalterns at the level of discourses. According to Said, Foucault's 'interest in domination was critical but not finally as contestatory or as oppositional as on the surface it seems to be.'[4] This was primarily because of his reluctance to recognise the counter-discourses of the margins. Said goes on to flesh his arguments as follows:

> (t)o the extent that modern history in the West exemplifies for Foucault the confinement and elision of the marginal, oppositional, and eccentric groups, there is, I believe, a salutary virtue in testimonials by members of those groups asserting their right of self-representation within the total economy of discourse... What he (Foucault) seemed not as quite willing to grant is, in fact, the relative success of (these) counter-discursive attempts first to show the misrepresentations of discursive power, to show, in Fanon's words, the violence done to psychically and politically repressed inferiors in the name of an advanced culture, and then afterwards to begin the difficult, if not always tragically flawed project of formulating the discourse of liberation.[5]

This problem of not recognising the agency of the subaltern is what prompts a subversive methodology which seeks a *'(Re)-Turn to the Other'* - a way of analysing things from the perspective of the subalterns; and which, through according agency to the subalterns, contests any tacit inclination to accord normativity only to perspectives of the 'dominant.' We need to pay attention to a crucial question raised by the Tongan theologian Jione Havea who says, 'The crucial question is not just *Can the subaltern speak?*, which expects subaltern subjects to speak our dominant language, but *Can we understand, the subaltern-talk?*, in which we give ourselves to the language of the subaltern.'[6] This paper is an attempt to understand the 'language' of the subaltern through a methodological *metanoia* (repentance) which recognises the agency of the subaltern.

This paper seeks to explore what it might imply if we read the contemporary history of conversions against the grain – from the perspective of the agency of the marginalised. This paper is about privileging the voices of the subalterns and seeking to understand what epistemological irruption this would evoke, which would further justify our argument for 'with-ness' or radical accompaniment of the subalterns as a credible and appropriate form of Christian witness in the contemporary Indian context.

Such a '(Re)-Turning to the Other' has ethical implications because it helps us to reconfigure justice not in terms of the Rawlsian notion of fairness but as *preference* in an asymmetrical world. Recognising that 'to define justice as preference implies a stark contradiction in terms' and that justice as preference defies common sense logic and 'thus seems least fair', Joerg Reiger makes a cogent argument for justice as preference in the following manner:

> (t)his notion of justice, understood as "being in solidarity with those who experience injustice," and as "taking the sides of those who have been marginalized and excluded from relationship," is required to produce true opposition to the injustices of the status quo. This notion of justice is more radical than mere rejections of the status quo's notions of justice as fairness because it leads to unexpected reversals, implying not only attention to needs but closer attention to those pressured by injustice, and reminds us of alternative sorts of agency and energy that are often overlooked.[7]

It is this aspect of being reminded about 'alternative sorts of agency and energy' that is significant about understanding justice as preference. Very often these alternative sorts of agency are overlooked. Therefore a methodology of 'with-ness', which pays preferential attention to the subalterns has the potential to address this lacuna because it helps us to understand what can be called the 'productivity' of the subalterns. As Rieger puts it, 'Justice in touch with the lives of the marginalized leads to a new awareness and valuation of the productivity of the margins - and thus it might lead also to a new awareness of God's own mysterious productivity in places where we least expect it, even on a cross.'[8] With this perspective let us move on to analyse the issue of 'conversions' in a manner which affirms the agency of the subalterns, particularly Dalit and tribal Christians in the current context of aggressive and parochial nationalism propagated by the Hindutva.

Re-Cast(e)ing Subaltern Conversions

It is no secret that the rhetoric of 'religious conversion' has not only been pivotal in fomenting violence against the Christian Dalit communities in India and the violation of their basic human rights, but is also being widely used to justify atrocities against Christians in general and Christians from subaltern groups like Dalits and *Adivasis* in particular. A tirade has been launched against Christianity on the grounds of 'forcible conversions' and paradoxically this 'fight' against conversions has resulted in the forced re-conversion of many subaltern Christians to 'Hinduism'. The rhetoric of forcible-conversions obfuscates reality and thus needs to be viewed with suspicion.[9]

Delving into the issue of conversions it is important to locate the Hindutva's constant invocation of the rhetoric of debate on conversions at this juncture. We need to recognise that the question of conversions is the necessary foundation to sustain an anti-Christian campaign in India, because Hindu-Christian relations do not have other issues - like the memories of communal violence or partition or 'go-korbani' (cow slaughter) - which have affected Hindu-Muslim relationships. It needs to be mentioned that the issue of conversions has actually forged an unlikely marriage between Gandhi and the Hindu nationalists who, in spite of having played a role in the murder of Gandhi for his supposedly anti-national soft-corner to Muslims, have surprisingly 'heralded him as the voice of reason when he opposed Christian proselytisation.'[10]

The Hindu fundamentalists apprehension of conversions has a history which extends at least to the formation of post-Independent India having figured quite prominently in the discussions of the constituent assembly in the framing of the constitution. However, it was the report of the Niyogi commission, which was 'generated in a climate of chauvinism and ultra-nationalism' which introduced a new argument in the discussion on conversions and contributed to a distortion and demonising of conversions as, 'a form of exploitation threatening the integrity of the Indian state.'[11] The report introduced the argument that weakness, ignorance and poverty were reasons which made the poor lose control over free will. It hence rendered the deprived sections of the community as being 'vulnerable to the inducements of converting to another religion.'[12] It achieved this by essentialising India's economically weaker sections as 'essentially disabled, incapable of distinguishing motives and inexperienced in the exercise of their own judgement.'[13] The implications of this report for the current context are succinctly brought out by Gauri Viswanathan as follows:

> The Niyogi commission landmark report set the lines of an argument that have continued to the present day, blurring the boundaries between force and consent and giving very little credence both to the possibility that converts change over to another religion because they choose to. Interestingly in charging that Christian missionaries took advantage of the weakened will of the poor and disenfranchised, the report confirmed an elitist view of freewill and autonomy as the privileges of the economically advantaged classes.[14]

It is this argument floated by the Niyogi commission report that has become a tool in the hands of the Hindutva forces which refer to conversions as a diversionary tactic, to draw attention to a non-issue. The rhetoric of conversions functions as a double-edged political sword which can be used to both attack Christian mission agencies working among the downtrodden sections of the community as well as restrain subaltern groups to achieve upward social mobility through adopting a venue which is not sponsored by the Hindutva.

It needs to be mentioned that the conversion rhetoric has also been used by the Hindutva forces to attack the educational work of Christian missionaries at a wider all India level. The fact that Hindutva targets educational institutions by accusing them of forced conversions is actually an attempt to suppress the threat that literacy of the poor could pose to people with a vested interest in poverty.[15] Walter Fernandes points out as to how in UP for example dominant castes make it a point to send their own children to school while ensuring that no schools are built in the villages, 'lest their labourers gain access to it and then leave either the village or demand better wages and working conditions.'[16] Therefore, on the whole the Hindutva's rhetoric of 'forcible conversions' needs to be seen as a strategy to ensure the perpetuation of the caste-structure, which curtails the upward mobility of the subaltern communities like the Dalits and also ensures that they are obligated to the caste hierarchy. It is true then that Hindutva politics aims to 'strait-jacket and to chain the potential assertion of the subalterns.'[17]

From the perspective of 'with-ness' which recognises the agency of the subaltern, it would be naive to buy into this rhetoric of inducement perpetuated by the Hindutva forces, which renders the subalterns as placid and inarticulate in the whole process of conversions. We need to recognise that 'the whole emphasis placed on such popular discourse on conversions falls into the Orientalist's pitfall, which accentuates the agency of the western agents, whether colonial or missionary, and devalues the instrumentality of the native subjects themselves in such historical events.'[18] In such a context arguments such as those made by the Hindutva merely seek self-perpetuation of their self-identity through the tacit invocation of binaries which constructs the other as a placid, weak and inarticulate object and reduces the other to a controllable, unthinking self, perpetuating new patterns of sustaining the asymmetries in the relations between them. These arguments obfuscate the real framework of meaning in which conversions have to be understood. An alternative framework for understanding subaltern conversions is brought out perceptively by Sathianathan Clarke as follows:

> Religious conversion (thus) can be interpreted to be one strategy whereby Dalits seek to pursue and secure release from the cosmically engendered, and, more importantly, comprehensively and concretely actualized world vision of caste communities. Religious conversion to another symbolic world vision, in this case Christianity, was an effort at community-initiated bailing out from the constructs of the Brahminic symbolic world vision and contracting of newer pictures of the world. In a sense this cumulative and comprehensive discriminatory treatment at the hand of the Brahminic caste communities that surrounded them for many centuries must have been responsible for the stirring in Dalit communities to seek another symbolic world vision.[19]

In this context one needs to understand conversions as the articulation of self-assertion by the Dalits. It functions as a mode of upward mobility for the Dalits in their search for equality and dignity.

Conversion as a strategy of self-assertion and symbolic emancipation of the subalterns is also counter-intuitive to the

Hindutva's agenda of cultural nationalism which thrives on the perpetuation of binaristic notions of identity as the 'Hindu' and the 'non-Hindu.' Conversion contests nationalism's recourse to water tight conceptualisations of identity by demonstrating how porous these reifications of identity are. Conversions also demonstrate that identity can be formulated and reformulated at will, which makes it particularly threatening to cultural nationalism which resorts to positivist ways of conceptualising difference through such essentialising markers as race, religion, colour, ethnicity and nationality. As Viswanathan states:

> When identity is destabilised by boundaries that are so porous, that movement from one world view to another take place with the regularity of actual border-crossings, a challenge is posed to the fixed categories that act as an empirical grid for interpreting human behaviour and action.[20]

In this context conversion contests the essentialising of identity to serve interests in a way in which it is more dynamic than either the concept of hybridity or syncretism. Conversion conveys a dynamism of movement of identity-crossings which is different from hybridity. Unlike hybridity, conversion conveys the *remaking of the very categories that constitute identity* and does not view border-crossings as exchange or fusion. It is more concrete than syncretism which is more *a blurring of differences* than a negotiation of differences.[21] As such it contests the very agenda of Hindu nationalism which seeks to reify the subalterns as passive beings not capable of autonomous agency.

The Shape of Christian With-ness in India

Taking into consideration the above mentioned reasons, Christian witness in the contemporary Indian context needs to be re-imagined in terms of 'with-ness' in the context of the conversion controversy. Such 'with-ness' would carry with it the moral imperative for us to recognise conversions as a means of furthering human flourishing. The shape of such with-ness should take the form of accompanying the subalterns in their quest for freedom from systems of human un-flourishing. Usually subaltern conversions are considered to be merely 'social' and as lacking a religious or spiritual dimension. Many of us are only too familiar with the derogatory epithet 'rice-christianity' which is used synonymously with Dalit conversions. However, dividing conversions in terms of binaristic notions of social and the spiritual hardly does any justice. One can affirm that it is precisely the political nature of subaltern conversions which makes them religious, given the 'polity' of Jesus who came so that life can be lived in abundance and affirmed that the key to salvation is in responding to human predicament (Matthew 25:31-46).

In line with this thinking, the contours of 'with-ness' in the Indian context can be imagined in relation to three different areas.

Firstly, Christian witness as 'with-ness' in the Indian context today would entail recognising subaltern conversions to Christianity as signposts which point to ways in which alternative version of nationalisms can be affirmed or articulated because these conversions are attempts to create a caste-free nation with justice and equality. They are to be seen as prophetic attempts towards exposing how Hindutva politics has distorted the face of Indian nationalism in the third millennium by being overtly or covertly involved in a barbaric and aggressive effort to facilitate a shift from the 'secular-territorial' version of nationalism of the 1950's. Subaltern conversions in a way affirm and strengthen the 'secular-territorial' version of nationalism which refused to make the nation co-terminus with a particular religion.[22] This secular-territorial version of nationalism of the 1950's recognised 'the dangers inherent in the religious and fascist varieties of aggressive nationalism' and did not accord general approbation to 'nationalism not tempered with morality.'[23] Such nationalism 'was a humane nationalism, comprehending within it political freedom, economic justice, and social solidarity' and today 'given the resurgence of a communal politics that conflates religion and culture,' such a version of nationalism is under threat.[24]

Subaltern conversions should be seen today as attempts to recover a humane nationalism. They should be seen as a continuum of the liberative project of 'oppressor conversion,' whereby oppressors are challenged to give up religion validated forms of control which stifle freedom, autonomy and social mobility. These conversions are challenges to the oppressor to recover explicitly humane versions of nationalism in which the defining category is not adherence to a particular 'religious world view' but concern for our neighbours. Subaltern conversions take up the challenge of enabling the oppressors to rethink the notion of loyalty to the nation. Catholic theologian Ambrose Pinto's in his critique of the misguided notion of loyalty to the nation that is expected by the Hindutva Vadis and the rightists says, 'If burning of SCs/STs, discrimination on the basis of caste against BC's, and hatred towards minorities is considered as a sign of loyalty to national culture and heritage, one needs to redefine loyalty in terms of a concern for the poor, compassion for the suffering and integrity and rectitude. None of these social qualities is highlighted by the Hindutva right as loyalty.[25] Subaltern conversions need to be understood in these circumstances

Secondly, Christian witness as 'with-ness' also needs to prompt a re-definition of the notion of interfaith dialogue.

With regard to the issue of inter-faith dialogue, it needs to be stressed that a critical approach to interfaith relations is needed in a context where there is a growing recognition of the nexus between dominance, power and religion. In such a context it is the task of Christian theologising and social thinking to bring a socio-political lens to the various attempts at interfaith dialogue. Shantha Premawardhana brings such a corrective lens appropriate for the Indian context when he points out that in a context where caste is legitimated by dominant religion, it is right 'to question whether we should be in dialogue with them.'[26] Out of such 'political consciousness' emerges the affirmation that '(T)oday our partners in dialogue are not necessarily those religious leaders who are a part of the exploitative structures, but those who suffer from exploitation.' Such a view subverts the traditional and popular views of interfaith dialogue.[27] Recognizing that those affected by exploitative structures are 'overwhelmingly the poor,' Shanthawardhana identifies these people as the 'partners in dialogue, to build alliances and to challenge the power structures of government, corporations and indeed religions that exploit and destroy our communities.'[28] It is this counterintuitive mode of dialogue which we need to embark upon in a context of rising religious fundamentalism so that inter-religious dialogue becomes a viable means of furthering the flourishing of relationships.

Thirdly, the other area where Christian 'with-ness' can be practiced in the context of subaltern conversions relates to the predicament of subaltern re-conversions. Very often such re-conversions are viewed as instances of 'un-faith.' Perhaps this issue can also be linked in a much broader manner to the issue of 'dual-identity' which is maintained by several Dalit-Christians, who do not want to have their identity registered in Churches as Christians but choose to retain their Dalit identity. It has not been unusual for the Church to criticise their actions as 'unfaith' and as not having a liberative dimension. In both these circumstances of seeming 'apostasy,' subalterns are accused of fickle faith which does not actively and openly resist oppression and domination. In these contexts our Christian with-ness should take the form of pastoral-sensitivity which does not view these actions as the rescinding of faith, but rather recognises that at certain times these actions can also be manifestations of alternative subaltern agency. It however needs to be said that these forms of alternative-agency should neither be romanticised or idealized. In making this argument - that acts which seem to be compromising may actually be manifestations of the alternative agency of the 'ordinary people' the so-called dominated, who may actually be enacting their own agenda of liberation through these outward acts of 'compromising their faith' - I am following the line of thought proposed by James C. Scott. In his work *Domination and the Arts of Resistance: Hidden Transcripts*[29] C. Scott speaks of 'arts of resistance' which in the words of Gerald West involve:

> first, the establishment of a safe sequestered site offstage, behind the backs of the dominant forces in society, where they are able to articulate and act out a hidden transcript of defiance and affirm their dignity; and second, an insertion of resisting forms of discourse into the public realm which assert their presence.[30]

With regard to the second strategy the argument that is made is 'that subordinate groups have typically learned to clothe their resistance and defiance in ritualisms of subordination that serve both to disguise their purposes and to provide them with a ready route of retreat that may soften the consequences of a possible failure.'[31] In such a context we need to accept an 'alternative analysis that the poor and marginalized are already engaged in forms of resistance.'[32] In such a case even what looks like the culture of silence and culture of accommodation may actually be disguised forms of defiance, 'an elaborate act, a show' which oppressed people 'practice and perform in order to survive, while they wait for an opportunity to transform their reality.'[33] Between the two moments – 'of hidden transcript offstage' and 'of public irruption at center-stage', there is 'a zone of constant contestation.'[34] Inhabiting this zone are 'disguised forms of resistance' which 'are a constant reminder that all is not as controlled as it appears.'[35]

In such a context we need a conversion 'from below' when we look at the reservations issue and at the issue of re-conversions and not easily judge them as being apolitical, benign and passive acts of accommodating to the status quo. We need to tread cautiously never forgetting that 'what is hidden is hidden for good reason, so any attempt to penetrate the disguise ... is potentially dangerous.'[36] Despite whatever activist unrest that such seeming accommodation to domination may evoke within us we need to recognise that, 'Rituals of subordination have their place. And when dignity and autonomy demand an irruption or an articulation, this must be done in ways determined by the dominated.'[37] Christian witness as 'with-ness' in this context would imply that we follow the agenda set by the dominated themselves and not our own agendas which may more often than not seek to bolster our own egoistic images of ourselves as 'self-styled activists.'

Conclusion

Talking of the productivity of the margins, Rieger says 'Below the surface, at the level of what has been repressed, lie tremendous energies that push toward transformation and justice, not primarily in its punitive or redistributive forms but as creating the space for alternative productivity.'[38] In line with this observation, in conclusion it can be stated that subaltern conversions can be understood not only as 'speaking truth to power' – the power of religious fanaticism, but also as the carving out of visions of equality and the creation of alternative or surrogate spaces where justice and freedom thrive. Subaltern conversions are the active and concrete pursuit of the dreams of visionaries who envision modes of living which are radically and subversively life-affirming and transformative not only for them but also for those who actively suppress them. It is important that at this point of history the wider Indian Church partners the dreaming visionaries – the subaltern converts - in dreaming the un-dreamable. In this pursuit of dreams lies the hope of life in all its fullness because it is not only an act of carving out a life-affirming 'tomorrow' in the dreams of 'today' but also an act of making sure that a life-denying 'yesterday', with its gruesome murdering of the motivations of the most marginalised, is actively prevented from repeating itself!

Endnotes

[1] Peniel Jesudason Rufus Rajkumar teaches in the Department of Theology and Ethics at the United Theological College, Bangalore. He is the author of *Challenges of Transition: Religion and Ethics in Changing Contexts* (New Delhi: ISPCK, 2007); *Dalit Theology and Dalit Liberation: Problems, Paradigms and Possibilities* (Farnham: Ashgate 2010); editor of *Asian Theology on the Way: Christianity, Culture and Context* (London: SPCK, 2012); and co-edited with Emma Wild-Wood, *Foundations for Mission* (Oxford: Regnum, 2013).

[2] Interview with Homi Bhabha, *The Book Review,* December 1995, 19:12 cited in Brenda Crossman and Ratna Kapur, eds., *Secularism's Last Sigh: Hindutva and the (Mis)Rule of Law* (New Delhi: Oxford University Press, 1999), 1.

³ K. N. Panikkar, *Colonialism, Culture, and Resistance* (New Delhi: Oxford University Press, 2007), 67&68.

⁴ Edward W. Said, *Reflections on Exile and Other Literary and Cultural Essays* (New Delhi: Penguin, 2001), 242.

⁵ Said, *Reflections on Exile,* 243-44.

⁶ Jione Havea, "*Unu'unu Ki he loloto,* Shuffle over to the Deep, into Island Spaced Reading," in *Still at the Margins: Biblical Scholarship Fifteen Years after the Voices from the Margin,*" R. S. Sugirtharajah (London: T&T Clark, 2008), 91.

⁷ Joerg Rieger, "'That's Not Fair': Upside-Down Justice in the Midst of the Empire," in *Interpreting the Postmodern: Responses to "Radical Orthodoxy,"* eds., Rosemary Radford Ruether and Marion Grau (New York/London: T&T Clark, 2006), 100. Emphasis is mine.

⁸ Rieger, "That's Not Fair," 101.

⁹ Using the Right to Information Act 2005, which makes it mandatory for the government to disclose to any citizen information relating to public issues the leader of the AICC (All India Christian Council) Samson Christian discovered that even in the state of Gujarat where 'forcible conversions' have been cited as an issue only three complaints of forcible conversions were filed over the last few years, of these only two concerned Christian conversions and were filed in 1997 and 2007 respectively. See *Compass Direct News.*

¹⁰ Gauri Viswanathan, "Literacy and Conversion in the Discourse of Hindu Nationalism," *Race and Class* 42, no. 1 (July 2000): 1.

¹¹ Viswanathan, "Literacy and Conversion," 4.

¹² Viswanathan, "Literacy and Conversion," 4.

¹³ Viswanathan, "Literacy and Conversion," 4.

¹⁴ Viswanathan, "Literacy and Conversion," 4 & 5. Emphasis is mine.

¹⁵ Walter Fernandes, "Attacks on Minorities and a National Debate on Conversions," in *Economic and Political Weekly* 34, no. 3/4 (January 16-23, 1999): 82.

¹⁶ Fernandes, "Attacks on Minorities," 82.

¹⁷ P. R. Ram, "Left Ideology, Ends and Means and Hindutva," *Economic and Political Weekly* 31, no. 34 (1997): 1428.

¹⁸ Sathianathan Clarke, "Conversion to Christianity in Tamil Nadu: Conscious and Constitutive Community Mobilization Towards a

different Symbolic World Vision," in *Religious Conversion in India: Modes, Motivations, and Meanings*, eds. Sathianathan Clarke and Roweena Robinson (New Delhi: Oxford University Press, 2003), 336.

[19] Clarke, "Conversion to Christianity in Tamil Nadu," 336.

[20] Viswanathan, "Literacy and Conversion," 6.

[21] Viswanathan, "Literacy and Conversion," 6.

[22] Panikkar, *Colonialism, Culture and Resistance*, 87.

[23] Panikkar, *Colonialism, Culture and Resistance*, 87.

[23] Panikkar, *Colonialism, Culture and Resistance*, 87.

[25] Ambrose Pinto, "Hindutva," *Economic and Political Weekly* 35, no. 41 (October 7-13, 2000): 3633.

[26] Shantha Premawardhana, "The Strange Exorcist," *Masihi Sevak: Journal of Christian Ministry* XXXIV, no. 2, (August 2009): 63.

[27] Premawardhana, "The Strange Exorcist," 63.

[28] Premawardhana, "The Strange Exorcist," 64.

[29] James C. Scott, *Domination and the Arts of Resistance: Hidden Transcripts* (New Haven & London: Yale University Press, 1990.

[30] Gerald West, "Disguising Defiance in Ritualisms of Subordination: Literary and Community-based Resources for Recovering Resistance Discourse within the Dominant Discourses of the Bible," in *Reading Communities Reading Scripture*, eds., Gary A. Philips and Nicole Wilkinson Duran (Harrisburg, Pennsylvania: Trinity Press International, 2002), 197.

[31] West, "Disguising Defiance in Ritualisms of Subordination," 197.

[32] West, "Disguising Defiance in Ritualisms of Subordination," 198.

[33] West, "Disguising Defiance in Ritualisms of Subordination," 198.

[34] West, "Disguising Defiance in Ritualisms of Subordination," 199.

[35] West, "Disguising Defiance in Ritualisms of Subordination," 199.

[36] West, "Disguising Defiance in Ritualisms of Subordination," 199.

[37] West, "Disguising Defiance in Ritualisms of Subordination," 199.

[38] Rieger, "That's Not Fair," 102.

Bibliography

Rajkumar, Peniel Jesudason Rufus. *Challenges of Transition: Religion and Ethics in Changing Contexts*. New Delhi: ISPCK, 2007.

──────. *Dalit Theology and Dalit Liberation: Problems, Paradigms and Possibilities*. Farnham: Ashgate 2010.

————————, ed. *Asian Theology on the Way: Christianity, Culture and Context*. London: SPCK, 2012.

————————, and Emma Wild-Wood, eds. *Foundations for Mission*. Oxford: Regnum, 2013.

Crossman, Brenda and Ratna Kapur, eds. *Secularism's Last Sigh: Hindutva and the (Mis)Rule of Law*. New Delhi: Oxford University Press, 1999.

Panikkar, K. N. *Colonialism, Culture, and* Resistance. New Delhi: Oxford University Press, 2007.

Said, Edward W. *Reflections on Exile and Other Literary and Cultural Essays*. New Delhi: Penguin, 2001.

Havea, Jione. "*Unu'unu Ki he loloto*, Shuffle over to the Deep, into Island Spaced Reading." In *Still at the Margins: Biblical Scholarship Fifteen Years after the Voices from the Margin*." Edited by R.S. Sugirtharajah, 88-97. London: T&T Clark, 2008.

Rieger, Joerg. "'That's Not Fair': Upside-Down Justice in the Midst of the Empire," in *Interpreting the Postmodern: Responses to "Radical Orthodoxy*." Edited by Rosemary Radford Ruether and Marion Grau, 91-106. New York/London: T&T Clark, 2006.

Viswanathan, Gauri. "Literacy and Conversion in the Discourse of Hindu Nationalism." *Race and Class* 42, no. 1 (July 2000): 1-20.

Fernandes, Walter. "Attacks on Minorities and a National Debate on Conversions." *Economic and Political Weekly* 34, no. 3/4 (January 16-23, 1999): 81-84.

Ram, P. R. "Left Ideology, Ends and Means and Hindutva." *Economic and Political Weekly* 31, no. 34 (1996): 1426-428.

Clarke, Sathianathan. "Conversion to Christianity in Tamil Nadu: Conscious and Constitutive Community Mobilization Towards a different Symbolic World Vision." In *Religious Conversion in India: Modes, Motivations, and Meanings*. Edited by Sathianathan Clarke and Roweena Robinson, 323-50. New Delhi: Oxford University Press, 2003.

Premawardhana, Shantha. "The Strange Exorcist." *Masihi Sevak: Journal of Christian Ministry* XXXIV, no. 2 (August 2009): 61-70.

Pinto, Ambrose. "Hindutva." *Economic and Political Weekly* 35 no. 41 (October 7-13, 2000): 3633-36.

Scott, James C. *Domination and the Arts of Resistance: Hidden Transcripts*. New Haven & London: Yale University Press, 1990.

West, Gerald. "Disguising Defiance in Ritualisms of Subordination: Literary and Community-based Resources for Recovering Resistance Discourse within the Dominant Discourses of the Bible." In *Reading Communities Reading Scripture.* Edited by Gary A. Philips and Nicole Wilkinson Duran, 194-217. Harrisburg, Pennsylvania: Trinity Press International, 2002.

5
Witnessing Christ to a Community in Chaos

A. Selvaraj

Introduction

Chaos is never an isolated reality. It is usually linked with violence and violation of rules and justice. Often such chaos in turn results in poverty. Social inequalities and casteism bring division in the society. Terrorism and militant attacks shatter the peace of a nation. This paper provides a socio politico religious context in which Christian mission can apply justifiable means to communicate Christ for holistic transformation. Independent India is struggling to satisfy the aspiration of the needy. But there are social inequalities, fanaticism, corrupt cultism and political extremism disturbing the common citizen. The mission must be aware of this chaotic situation to answer the question of the people.

Sharing good news to chaos hit people and to help them in their needs is not an option for the church and Christian organizations. It is a compelling necessity. Chaos hit people are extra ordinary in their cases and uniquely created in the image of God. These people are vulnerable to physical pain, emotional stress, and spiritual depression. There are people who are oppressed by chaos situations or victims of such incidents socially, economically, politically, culturally and spiritually. There are certain incidents which hamper the common people and break their peace. The measure of inadequacy on the part of the Christian church is that the needy cry out for help, but there are few who respond to their needs. We feel the values of democracy today are fraudulent, and not real. Corruption has reached its peak. Our leaders at the top are found to be guilty.[1] Many chaos situations do not arise by themselves but when law protectors became law breakers they provoke the grass root people groups to develop into militants.

We have enough Biblical foundations that we need to share the good news and rescue these people in their needs. The very nature of the Nazareth manifesto of our Lord Jesus identified with this very fact. To sustain a ministry like this we need a Christ- centered motivation. As He went beyond the boundaries and barriers so we should do the same. Unless we are motivated by God himself we cannot perform well. As with all missionary work we need to have a strong sense of God's call to this most difficult of all tasks.

The Stirring Problem/The Cruel Face of Chaos

Persecution is on the increase. After the Graham Staines' martyrdom there has been widespread persecution in Orissa particularly visible in the Kandamal incident and it has spread to the South as well as to the North. In Karnattaka after the BJP rule a resurgent form of persecution against churches, nuns and priests is visible. It would appear that the BJP government agenda is only to attack and destroy Christians and their mission.

Cult movements are much active in India and their followers range from farmers and house wives to politicians and rock stars. Cults play a role to confuse the needy and marginalized in the name of god men and god women: Sathya Sai Baba, Bhagavan Nityananda, Bhagwan Shree Rajneesh, Swami Premananda of Tiruchirapalli, and Matha Amritanandamayi Devi. These human forms have become much like pan shops and every part of the nation has hundreds of god men who have thousands of followers. When one of them is harmed, their followers are in panic.[2] It has clearly become a lucrative business, the business of making you see God. These god men have fleets of luxury cars, fly in choppers and live in palatial houses. They survive on huge donations from their followers and are extremely well connected. Money and cult power are trade marks of modern day ascetics. It is spiritual chaos making business out of sacred things. So there is need to witness to cult members who are deceived by these false ideas of human gods and goddesses.

Political extremism in the name of Maoism, Naxalism and so forth is a cause for concern. The extreme poverty and Government inaction to develop the poor has resulted in violence. The recent Maoist attack on the Mumbai-bound Express killed at least 98 people in West Bengal's Midnapore district. There are at least 15,000 'child soldiers, between the age of 6 to 16 who are fighting for the Maoist cause across the country. The police operation Green Hunt led to the Dantewada massacre, in which a CRPF platoon was ambushed. The States anti Naxal team claimed to have flushed the Naxals out of AP a few years ago. As a result the armed movement spread along the red corridor to neighboring states. Here is a field for missions to exercise the model of being light of the world and salt of the earth. The paper will highlight how to promote

Jesus mission in the midst of such chaos contexts. For instance in Simultala, in Bihar there is a congregation which provides hostel facilities to the children of the Maoists and there are 47 poor children there. This is surely a model for mission in the midst of Maoist extremism.

Terrorism has spread throughout the nation. For instance there was the recent incident in Kerala where a lecturer's palm was cut off for blasphemy. The terrorist attack in Mumbai is not exceptional. How can Christian mission give response to this sort of fanaticism? This paper will provide the cause of terrorism and how church can exist as an agent of peace in the midst of terror situations. By doing this we are fulfilling the purpose of Jesus' mission in word and deed.

India today is infested with a large number of socio-economic problems such as the population explosion, poverty, illiteracy, ill-health, unemployment, corruption, crime, prostitution, alcohol, and suicide and drug addiction. Social disorganization and social problems are the worst of the ill-effects. Disorganization has brought about disruption of social institutions and personal life. Political parties twist corruptions like the "*Adharsh*"[3] issues in Maharashtra and the land scam by the son of the chief minister of the Karnataka government and the Spectrum scam case created by minister Raja at the centre. These have widespread repercussions and we have many symptoms of a sick society in India today. The rate of beggary, prostitution, rape, suicide and violence is steadily increasing, reaching chaos proportions. The church has to get ready to face this pathological condition of the society in India.

Inequality is a serious issue. At least in principle, the members of the communities are considered equal: one man is the other man's brother, irrespective of his origin, social rank, or nationality, but in reality things are highly different.

In our country one third of the population are illiterate while paradoxically India is an Information Technology superpower. Chatting online, tickets online, banking online, books online, mail online, dating online, travel online, jobs online, shopping online, cinema online, gaming online and everything in this world seems to be going online. In spite of this our 78 million rural homes have never seen electricity while we are an economic superpower. While India's educated elite are reveling in their new found status on the global stage, inequitable distribution of wealth and opportunities are shaking the very foundation of India's new economy. In the last 12 years India's economy has grown at an average annual rate of about 7 percent, reducing poverty by 10 percent. However, 40 percent of the world's poor still live in India. Kay Marshall Storm says, "India is undergoing a dramatic transformation, but that transformation has not reached the majority of Indians."[4]

Hyderabad is the capital city of Andhra Pradesh. In the last decade, Hyderabad has established itself as a worthy successor to Bangalore. Companies like Microsoft, Wipro, Infosys, GE, HSBC have all made their presence felt in the city. Bill Gates, Bill Clinton, Jack Welch and a host of other global biggies have visited the city and proclaimed their confidence in its role in the global world. Yet, a continuing drought and a lack of government support has led to 4500 farmer suicides in the last 7 years in the state of Andhra Pradesh. Kerala and other states of India are not an exception in regard to this.

And the scenario is not too different in smaller cities. For example, Nagpur is a bustling metropolis in the heart of India, in a region known as Vidarbha. There are signs of economic boom every where in the city- shopping arcades, multiplexes, pubs, and luxury clubs. Yet, right out side the city; farmers are committing suicide due to their inability to repay debts as small as is Rs 5000. In the last five years, almost two thousand farmers in the region have killed themselves.

The poor and the poverty struck require our attention because they are suffering people. According to Tom Houston, "The poor to whom Jesus and the early church brought good news included the naked, the hungry, the disabled, the oppressed, the imprisoned, the sick, the bereaved, widows and orphans."[5] Today all these categories are sufficiently out there for help.

The caste system even after independence is a troublesome organization in India. It has created untouchability, discrimination, feelings of low and high and gaps between man and man that are becoming wider day by day. Such a caste system is not only detrimental to society but is also harmful to national integrity. So the social revolution is still incomplete in India.[6]

We can see the caste inequality and poverty in India within the context of caste based discrimination. It does so by creating differences between (caste) Hindu and Scheduled Caste (SC)[7] and Scheduled Tribe (ST)[8] households in: their average household incomes; their probabilities of being in different income percentiles; their probabilities of being at different levels of poverty and turning these into a "discrimination effect," which stems from the fact that a household's income level, into which its (income- generating) profile translates, depends on whether it is SC/ST; on "attributes (or residual) effect," which stems from the fact that there are systematic differences between SC/ST and Hindu households in their (income- generating) profiles. The results, based on unit record data for 28, 922 households, showed that at least one- third of the average income/ probability differences between Hindu and SC/ST households was due to the "unequal treatment" of the latter.

Such discrimination brings social inequality, poverty and disunity. They feel not only helpless, desperate and angry but they are also ashamed of this kind of division. They feel inferior and deprived of their human dignity. The sense of shame and indignity is subjective but it depends to a great extent upon the attitude of others toward them. The lower caste is disliked and deserted by the upper caste. So they become more poor. Believing Christians are, both for the sake of justice and of love, obligated to stand on the side of the suffering innocent and try to change the structures.

The Biblical Views on Chaos

The heart of God does not desire anyone to perish (John 3:16) but gives ample opportunities to turn back from sinful lifestyles. In Isaiah 24:10 we see the term chaos emphatically used which says the result of God's judgment will be a world that is empty, laid waste, and distorted, and whose inhabitants will be scattered. Similar things are happening in India too, where the judgment of God can be seen to be happening. This judgment is not an end but acts as a starter to get them to the Kingdom of God. People who are proud of their wealth and position will find themselves poor and without power. Why does God punish the inhabitants of the world, is a matter to be clarified. Probably the Bible will say that they have defiled the world by their sins.

The Biblical account of creation in Genesis chapter one does bear similarities to ancient near eastern creation myths, but the description of the divine purpose in creation omits any reference to a cosmic struggle between God and the forces of chaos.[9] John Watts sees the seriousness of cosmic union in destruction of the land. The sun, moon, and stars join the battle to make the land desolate.[10] When we study the book of Isaiah chapter 24, it is clear that human beings caused the world to become a desert.

The secular meaning for the word chaos is a state of total confusion and lack of order.[11] According to George Gorden Noel Byron, "Out of chaos God made a world, and out of high passions comes a people."[12] According to Georg Büchner, "The world is chaos. Nothingness is the yet-to-be-born god of the world."[13]

When we look around the people have a great capacity to create chaos by sinning. Our biblical concept of chaos theory does not care what religion you belong to. You could be a Christian and fail to recognize that you are partaking in sinful chaotic behavior. This rebellious liberalism first produces an irritated grumbling in others, but it can soon build into general disorder and confusion. In due course, a whole culture's energies are expended merely to survive, effectively destroying the development of spiritual, creative, and intellectual qualities essential to an individual's and society's well being. The mind set of people who are involved in any type of chaotic act have a hard time in cooperating because their minds are filled with insecurities, they feel they are being taken advantage of, or they feel driven to compete in everything. As time goes on, they feel put upon, and thus become quite defensive.

The need for money, position and a comfortable life style leads to the polluting of land, water and atmosphere as well as to the exploiting of the earth of its God given treasures. For such reasons God punished the earth with the flood.[14] John A. Martin says, "The cause of world wide pollution is that men have broken the everlasting covenant which people implicitly had with God to obey His Word.[15] Let us study some chaotic situations of the recent past to understand violence and in particular religion and violence.

Recent Violence Between Hindus and Muslims

The recent Hindu-Muslim violence in a small Gujarati town called Godhra[16] is a case in point. Conflict with Pakistan over Kashmir and communal violence has dominated human rights developments in India during the year. To the Muslim mind, the loss of power over Hindu India represents an aberration to be circumvented through a radical spiritual re-orientation.[17] Islam is a minority faith in India and is perceived by the Hindus as actively engaging in a pan-Islamic ideology in order to recover the past-something that contributes to the heightening of the Hindu sense of insecurity.

Even though there was an appreciable Verdict recently made on the Ayodhya issue[18] for both, still the internal agitation between them is very clear in many areas. For example the Muslims demand for a separate Jammu and Kashmir and the resultant violence by VHP.[19] In 1992, extremist Hindus encouraged by the cultural organizations such as the Rashtriya Swayam Sevak Sangh (RSS) and the VHP and their political division, BJP[20] tore down the 16th century babri masjid (Babri Mosque). This mosque, it was claimed, was built by a Mughal conqueror on an original temple commemorating the birth of lord Rama.[21] During the riots which followed throughout India, over 1100 Muslims were murdered and countless injured or mutilated. After this the Godhra Train incident took place which caused the loss of many lives. Based on these two issues later on in India many, chaotic incidents took place namely bombs being placed in temples and so on....

Violence afflicts cultures from within and without, even those that are not necessarily global in their vision, such as Hinduism. Hindu extremism has been on the Indian soil for well over a century. What is unprecedented is the speed with which it has expanded its cultural and political power through the RSS, the VHP and the BJP. These organizations are generally known to be led and inspired by the elite Hindus, the Brahmins and the Khshatriyas.[22] Hindutva stands for Hindu nationalism by treating the minorities like Muslims and Christians as second class citizens. The Christians have set up remarkable institutions in the area of health and education, especially in backward tribal areas and promoted love and peace. In spite of this Hindu nationalists seek to tarnish Christians by calling them anti-national.

Fanaticism: Violence Against Christianity

Another area of chaos is fresh violence against the Christian minority by other fanatic religious groups. Clearly, there is enough to suggest a cover-up and a reluctance to even examine the possibility of a nascent Hindu terror network.[23] But the endeavor in India is always threatened by anti-Christian groups. Christians are caught between two identifications: nationalism on the one hand and commitment to the cause of the marginalized on the other. At the same time there is a strong awakening of the Tribals and Dalits. In this context, the question comes to our mind: how do Christians in India serve both so called nationalist groups and marginalized groups when both of them are opposing each other?

The word religion comes from the Latin word *religio*, which means the sense of binding together, but also provides them with a system of beliefs, rituals, institutions, traditions and a sense of the sacred. It also gives meaning to their life and the way of relating themselves to the universe and its creator.[24] The Hinduism of the nineteenth century tried to recover the glory of the ancient past ignoring the rich contribution of cultural varieties and religious manifestations. To achieve this they used the notion of Hindu religion and Hindu community. They started Purification rituals to bring the people back to their home. Thus re-conversion became a 'force method' used by the fundamentalist Hindus.[25] Pannikar writes, "Hinduism cannot be described as a historically evolved religion. The historicity of Hinduism is relatively recent as a part of the reformist-revivalist movements."[26]

The anti- Christian violence that began in Orissa a year ago has still not died down: Instead, it has spread to other parts of India. The situation also remains tense in Karnataka, and the Christian citadel state of Kerala. Probably the best example was the chopping of the hand of a Christian professor by the Muslims. The church also expressed callousness in dealing with the issue.

The wave of anti- Christian violence is spreading to other parts of India. The Catholic Jaya Mata School was attacked by unknown persons on the night of September 14. This took place in the district of Kasargode (Kerala, southeast India). The school building was being used as a chapel on a temporary basis, since the parish church was being restored. The police have opened an investigation and have reinforced security around the churches, fearing attacks like in Orissa and Karnataka. There was also tension in Mangalore on September

14, 2010. 20 churches were ransacked by radical Hindus of the Sangh Parivar.

Among possibly several others, two examples of sacrifice without any other ulterior motive than to further reconciliation and peace come from the Henry Martyn Institute (HMI) in Hyderabad, India and St. Mary's Dominican Hospital in Ahmedabad. Post-6 December 1992 saw a string of violent clashes between extremist Muslims and Hindus in several towns of North India and Hyderabad in South India. Often the victims were innocent men, women and children lacking protection in contexts where police neutrality was a rare commodity. The HMI, true to its commitments to reconciliation, put together a peace corps called the '*aman-shanti* forum.' The forum obtained special permits and roamed the old city, the epicenter of violence, and assisted and rescued those wounded and affected by the riots which were sweeping through the heart of the city. Since then the HMI has not only expanded its proactive peace effort through actually establishing itself in centers[27] associated with violence in the old city, but has also incorporated conflict resolution as a proactive in-house and external training program.[28]

Another example comes from the Spanish Dominicans who run St. Mary's Hospital in Ahmedabad. Sister Lusia Carabias and her colleagues gave refuge to over 6,000 Muslims fleeing angry Hindu mobs in the city. The St. Mary's compound which includes a hospital and a *Mahila Shikshan Kendra*[29] is surrounded by Muslim homes. After pleading with the local police for several days to provide security for the frightened Muslims seeking refuge in their compound, the nuns finally convinced the police to come and patrol the gates, protecting the Muslims inside from mobs of angry Hindus. People responded to this act of courage, mercy and sacrifice by sending money to St. Mary's to help feed the refugees. Several others sent money to help rebuild the homes of Muslims, which were totally razed to the ground by the mobs.[30]

These fanatic groups work with political protection. They use the law when convenient to and abuse the same to frustrate minorities from getting justice. Hindutva targets Christians and Missionaries because they empower the poor. Missionary work lets the poor get out of the clutches and control of upper caste Hindus.

Terrorism: The New Face of Chaos

It would appear that the recent terrorist attacks and the involvements of human gods and goddesses is a short cut to make a Hindu Rashtra. For the last ten years there have been several minor and major bomb blasts in various parts of our nation. The involvement of Hindu right-wing members was alleged but there has never been concrete proof.[31]

Indian intelligence agencies say a new terror channel has emerged that begins in Pakistan, passes through Male in Maldives and then goes on to the southern Indian cities that have direct flights to Male. The recent attack in Mumbai shows, how easily people can intrude in to Indian soil. Often people from India help international terrorists to stay home and plan terrorist activities. Often terrorism uses religion as a curtain. It is evident that Headley had been under the FBI scanner for a while. His original name was Dawood Gilani, which he changed when he converted to Christianity in 2006.[32] He says that Lashkar-e-Toiba trained him to spy on India.[33] India and Christian organizations should try to mobilize international opinion to contain the threat of violence and terrorism emanating from any country of the world, not only from Pakistan. The terrorist attacks leave the families and individuals in a horrific chaos.

Militants: Maoists

Another source of chaos is Naxalism. Marxist Leninst and Maoist ideology has been responsible for Nexalism which has now a spatial spread from Nepal to Andhra Pradesh. They fight for the poor. Maoists target Hindutva but generally not the Christian missionaries. It is simply because they have seen the missionaries empower the poor with their education, health and development programmes. Official sources have confirmed Maoist presence in 182 districts in 16 states. But other sources say there are many more states with confirmed Maoist activity.[34]

The recent brutal killing of policemen, blowing up railway tracks and burning of vehicles by the Naxalites and the Maoists alike can be equated to terrorism! Maoists blew up a bus and killed 36 people. It was the second attack.[35] What is the reason for this uprising of the disgruntled elements of society? While unemployment can be assigned the first and the foremost reason, the main reason can be attributed to the ever rising divide amongst the rich and the poor without any hope for equality. The government should pay prime attention to this problem and take effective steps to develop all the states of the country equally.

The states in the North East remain totally ignored and underdeveloped. There are no proper roads or infrastructure leave alone industries in the North East which form an integral part of the country! During the elections or inauguration of some festivals or games you can see the central politicians dancing with the locals otherwise there is absolute neglect of these states despite 60 years of independence! Unemployment and backwardness force the young and the unemployed to take up arms and term themselves as Naxals and Maoists states!

Unemployment and poverty force young men and women to become numbers of militant group. In turn they work against the state and the central government. Power and money are the two most important reasons that have attracted these young men and women.[36] And also many young Hindu men in Kashmir are lured by easy money and gun-power and they are generally in the age group of 16 to 25. We can learn one thing and that is that Christians are on the right track as long as we empower the poor through what we are best known for: education and health. However the killing of Swami Lakshimananda by Maoist rebels was not justifiable.[37] That caused a lot of loss for Christianity.

Rape Victims and Armed Forces

Rape was common on both sides in the Vietnam War. Between a quarter and a half million Tutsi women were raped in Rwanda in 1994 as per the Human Rights Watch 1996.[38] Irom Sharmila's 'fast unto death' is 10 years old. Sharmila was 28 years old when she started the fast in November 2000, after an Assam Rifles contingent killed 10 innocent people at Mallom. As they were returning to their camp militants detonated a battery operated improvised explosive device at Mallom, Manipur. There was no casualty, but the troops went berserk. All the victims were waiting for their buses when they were shot randomly by the Jawans.[39]

In the North East of India with the apparent sanction of the Government, hundreds of women have been raped and murdered. The culprits are never brought to book as they are members of the armed forces and have been granted complete immunity. In Manipur the AFSPA has been in force for the past 24 years. As a result of this the Manipuris feel that they have been deprived of civil and human rights. The extent of military deployment in Manipur is such that at the height of anti-insurgent operations in the 1990s there were at least four divisions and 270 paramilitary companies stationed in the small state. Today the military forces harm the common life.

On 27th December, 1994 following an exchange of fire between militants and army personnel in Manipur a major of the army was killed. Members of the Task Force of the 16 Maratha Light Infantry took out their anger on the innocent people of Mokokchung town. During this incident several women were raped and sexually assaulted. Their clothes were then dipped into petrol to burn their homes. Dr. Yangerla Ao, a doctor and President of the United Women's Forum, examined and treated at least 15-16 cases of rape and molestation.[40]

During "Operation Birdie" in 1997-98 in Meghalaya, many Khasi tribal women were raped. Soldiers of the Assam Rifles regiment also used women as human shields, placing the muzzle of their guns on the women's shoulders as they battled with the rebels. This is a complete violation of the laws of war.[41] While the violence in Meghalaya has largely died down, widespread allegations of arbitrary detention, rape, and torture have never been properly investigated.[42]

The famous case of Thangjam Manorama (Manipur) clearly reveals the brutality and lawlessness prevalent. Sometime in the night of 10-11 July 2004, Assam Rifles took Manorama from her house, issuing an arrest memo to her family. Later her dead body was found covered with scratch marks, a deep gashing wound, in all probability caused by a knife, and seven fatal bullet wounds to her back, one of which passed through her vagina.[43] The next day, July 12, the home department of the government of Manipur appointed a commission of inquiry presided over by a retired district and session judge, C Upendra Singh, as per section 3 of the Commission of Inquiry Act 1952. However, the Assam Rifles challenged the authority of the commission asserting that a commission established by the State Government had no authority over the Indian Armed Forces, as per section of the AFSPA. The Guwahati High Court endorsed section 6 of the AFSPA on 23 June 2005, and thereby removed any possibility that Manorama's killers would be brought to justice.[44]

These are just a few instances. Many more women have been raped and killed, but their stories lie hidden, especially as people are reluctant to file complaints against the security forces, since investigations launched in the past have not succeeded in bringing the perpetrators of these heinous crimes to justice. Sister Anju Kshetrimayum says, it is very difficult to bring these people who are socially exploited to the ways of Christ unless we bring some changes to their lives.[45]

Christian Mission

I have indicated some of the emerging concerns for chaos hit people. The question is, is there a significant shift in methodology to witness Christ to them? In one sense the fundamental commitment to the poor remains unchanged, but newer dimensions of the struggles of the chaos in relation to the capitalist resurgence, solidarity of the subaltern and their unsolved struggles, the social and political crisis require newer emphasis. Christian witness to chaos hit people is best done by cooperating with local Christian communities of faith.

Thus the Christian development agency can happily restrict its activity to that part of holistic mission which complements the evangelistic work of the local church. Here are a few methods to be adopted by the church for the work among chaos hit people.

After having seen the tragedies that people face we may ask a question what Jesus would do here, or what is the role of the gospel of Christ? The answer is: to all who come to Him in repentance and faith He offers new life. He is the only hope of a broken and suffering India. His good news is about building relationships. God created in his own image, male and female, for a plurality of in-depth relationships unknown in the rest of creation. Therefore, sharing good news through Christ with the chaos affected people becomes a reality only when interpersonal relationships of mutual respect are established.

While the good news begins with personal salvation it does not end there. It is about new and transformed communities of people, living in peace and hope with God. Thus rescuing these people or witnessing Christ to these people the primary goal should be to create households of faith in which Christ reigns. When they see the kingdom of God inaugurated among them and chaos hit people see other victims transformed and their lifestyle changed they respond to the message of Christ, thus the church is born. Here evangelism and servant services of the church are much needed for further spreading of the gospel.

We have seen the importance of building relationships by which we could introduce Christ the Savior to them. Next we can help them to overcome the crisis. We can ask the victimized community to unite which would bring strength. This approach reflects the credo of the International Institute for Rural Reconstruction: Go to the people; live among them;

learn from them; serve them, plan with them; start with what they know; build on what they have; learn by doing; teach by showing; not a piecemeal but an integrated approach; not a showcase but a pattern; not relief but release. This is not the time to preach alone but act upon the needs. Help them to stand alone. Several things clearly undermine the credibility of Christians witnessing the gospel among the chaos hit people: immoral or insensitive behavior; paternalism; ignoring the culture and environment of the people.

Empowerment through organizing enables the chaos hit victims to achieve the power which unity brings. It helps them to have a common understanding of the problems of their exploitation, and therefore to develop ways of improving their situation. Improving health becomes another factor to consider. In order to raise the health and sanitation levels of the people Para- church should work hard because health cannot be an after thought in Christianity. They can assist the NGOs and government public health center workers in immunization, vitamin distribution, and other public health programs.

Nurturing faith is another concern. In the relationship building process we have seen that the gospels are not just to be preached but to be lived. Local churches around the incident places should take up the responsibilities of Christian nurture: service and witness to the chaos hit people. When we do so, we help them to rearrange things on earth and set them in line with things in Heaven. The role of the local church is important to direct proclamation but it would also have to be sensitive.

From the social aspects churches and para- churches did indeed engage in providing relief to the victims in Gujarat, but it was largely reactive. Christians did not have any significant part in actually doing something for the people as they were being murdered. This is different from the pathological elements in the martyrdom sought by those who die killing the 'enemies of God' or invite death foolishly by choosing to abuse the cultural, ethnic and religious feelings of the people of other faiths.

Even though the government brought certain projects to save people from this crisis they did not work out timely. Like the rehabilitation of the destitute and the protection for victims of the flesh trades. The provisions of the government failed due to corruption and mismanagement. For instance, is the Destitute Rehabilitation Center in Bangalore where the filthy living conditions caused 27 inmates to die.[46] Irrespective of violence against Christianity, Christians continue to serve and sacrifice for the good of the nation. Our inspiration is taken from Scripture that nothing can separate us from the love of God.

Jesus too came to redeem those who were captives. There exist many historical proofs of church and para-church organizations becoming part of nation building. We of the church today should help the government bring about a social transformation that would drastically change the living conditions of people living in chaos. David was sure in Psalm 72:4, He will bring justice to the poor. He will save the children of the needy and will break in pieces the oppressor. Down through the centuries the poor and needy have been oppressed, underpaid, persecuted and even killed. In the Millennium, the King Himself will be their Advocate. He will emancipate them once for all and punish those who took advantage of them.

And in 82:4, he is seeking God's intervention to deliver the needy, and free them from the hands of the exploiters. The church is called to order and do. The Judge has taken His place at the bench. It is God Himself. Let the church not be rebuked for malfeasance and ignorance towards the socially exploited society. Christ's Kingdom expects equity and justice from all the courts in the land-from the Supreme Court all the way down to the local magistrate. But the secular rulers have been guilty of graft and corruption. Under their administration the rich have been favored while the poor and needy have been oppressed. Criminals have escaped unpunished and the innocent have had to suffer loss without recourse. The scales of justice have become scales of oppression. Then the Judge of all the earth reminds them once more of their responsibilities in the area of social justice. The church is to champion the rights of the afflicted and needy. Church should be the helpers of all who are dispossessed and downtrodden through a chaos. Whereby she will be able to witness Christ effectively and bring meaning for the message of Cross.

In her "Last Word" Mallika Sarabahai in *The Week* dated Oct 24th, 2010 gives a story which explains the failure of the church. Wilson's father was a manual scavenger in the Kolar gold mines but managed to become a gardener. By the time Wilson was born, he belonged to a church. Wilson started attending the seminary, and was confronted by dry latrines and manual scavengers. He fought with the priests to banish it but they wouldn't listen. He tried to join the brotherhood to abolish this disgrace but the priests threw him out because they thought he was bringing shame to them by talking of such things. He then started working in a factory. The Church till today remains so immune to this inhumanity around us. In spite of an official ban on manual scavenging since 1993, panchayats and even city municipalities heap this indignity on our brothers and sisters.[47] Christianity is supposed to be the representative of Jesus who taught love, forgiveness, sacrifice, unity, and humility. Though that may be true to a large extent, Christianity has demonstrated an ability to overlook many of its professed virtues.

Participating in God's work calls for involvement in the struggles of the people and we should be encouraged to continue the work irrespective of the political and social interference. The Bible says in Ecc 4:1, the oppressed were crying and no one would help them because on the side of the oppressors there was power. God intervened everywhere for the rescue of the people. The church has to play a liberative role to work for equality and justice to free people from the bondages of chaos, discrimination, poverty, and exploitation. That way we can offer through Christ a new life and meaning to them. Now that we have been taught we should not be fearful and idle in the chaos situations. Let us arise and shine, be salt to the earth and light to the world. In the words of Sir Wintson Churchill as quoted by Oswald J. Smith, in the *Challenge of Mission* "Give us the tools and we will finish the job."[48] We have the tools i.e. the teaching of the scriptures and therefore let us finish the job.

The churches in India should know that the tools are in our hands we just need to be available to the hands of Jesus Christ. In general there are millions of chaos hit people in need and seeking the help of Christians. They are all still waiting to receive the whole salvation of Christ. To reach these people with the gospel which changes the whole person is the responsibility of the church. Christians can keep on doing that over and over again, because of the very mission of Christ's gospel. Because of good news, we know God loves the victims and the oppressors. All are important; the help should go out from the church right now, and we cannot remain silent. We believe in the resurrection and we know for sure that the Kingdom of God is coming soon.

Christians should seek active solutions facing our contemporary world today. Rehabilitation of terror hit people due to riots or bomb attacks should be implemented on an emergency basis. Every Christian should be prepared mentally and spiritually to offer first aid in terms of sheltering, providing food and counseling grief stuck families. At the next level every Christian should be aware of the government rehabilitation programs and help the destitute to reach these sources. Earthquakes and other related disasters are also on the increase. Every Christian should learn some elements of disaster management. Due to the caste conflict when the oppressed castes are discriminated against, every Christian should be able to speak for the underdog. The Christians of the rich churches are generally content to give financial aid and material aid and then sit back complacently. But we live in a world where complacency cannot be enjoyed. Any thing can happen in our own backyard. When disaster strikes our country it is the NGOs who reach first. This is because these people are highly motivated and have been prepared almost to drill perfection and know exactly what to do. When we attempt to rescue people from their chaos situations then we have a receptive audience for the preaching of the gospel. Jesus' miracles are a case in point. He healed the sick, the maimed and the blind and thus had a good context to teach concerning the Kingdom of God.

Christians can learn from fine individuals who have initiated and sustained social transformation models. In this respect, the magazine *The Week* gives space in its pages to focus on individuals who have brought changes in society in the perimeters in which they live. A Christian can always go further. He can point to God, to Jesus who has inspired him/her. And in this way they can enable people to look up instead of just around. It is a sad statement today that the Christian church is silent on many basic problems of the country. National integration is a crying need. How should we show this in our own churches? The churches are rift with divisions on the basis of region, language and caste. How does one fight prejudice within the Christian church? It is a known fact that in the Muslim world brotherhood is an achieved ideal. There are no overt caste distinctions. But this is absent in the Christian church. How do we overcome this?

Endnotes

[1] Solomon P. Benjamin, "The Other Side of Indian Independence - People Yet Set Free," In *Mashi Sevak: Journal of Christian Ministry* (July 2004): 21.

[2] Ramu Patil, "Allegations are More Shocking," *The Week*, June 13, 2010, 16.

[3] The Adarsh Housing Society has been in the eye of a storm for violating norms and misusing the land granted to it.

[4] Kay Marshall Storm, *The Presence of the Poor Challenging the Face of India* (Hyderabad: Authentic, 2008), 7.

[5] Tom Huston, "Good News for the Poor," *Transformation* 7, no. 1 (1990): 4-5.

[6] Saeed Naqvi, "Toppling the Caste Pyramid," *The Week Anniversary Special*, December 2009, 92.

[7] Scheduled Caste.

[8] Scheduled Tribe.

[9] Allen C. Myers, ed., *The Eerdmans Bible Dictionary* (Grand Rapids: William B. Eerdmans Publishing Company, 1987), 201.

[10] John D. W. Watts, ed., *Isaiah,* vol. 24 of *Word Biblical Commentaries* (Texas: Word Books, 1985), 322.

[11] Paul Procter, *Cambridge International Dictionary of English* (Cambridge University Press, 1995), 216.

[12] Lesslie A. Marchand, ed., *Lord Byron: Selected Letters and Journals* (Harvard University Press, 1982).

[13] Georg Büchner, *Georg Büchner: The Complete Collected Works* (Avon Books, 1977).

[14] Warren W. Wiersbe, *The Wiersbe Bible Commentary* (Colorado: David C. Cook Publishing Company, 2008).

[15] John A. Martin, "Isaiah," in *The Bible Knowledge Commentary: Old Testament*, eds., John F. Walvoord and Roy B. Zuck (Colorado: David C. Cook, 1983), 1072.

[16] Godhra train burning is a 2002 incident in which a Sleeper class coach numbered S-6 of the train "Sabarmati Express" which was coming from Darbhanga (Bihar) and was destined to Ahmedabad (Gujarat) was burned, killing 58 people, mostly Hindu pilgrims, in Godhra, Gujarat. The event triggered widespread violence in Gujarat, resulting in the deaths of about between 790 and 2,000 Muslims and 254 Hindus.

[17] Myra MacDonald, "Hindu Campaigners Combat Christian Conversions," *Yahoo News*, March 11, 2003.

[18] *Mosque of Babur* was a mosque in Ayodhya, a city in the Faizabad district of Uttar Pradesh, on Ramkot Hill ("Rama's Fort"). It was destroyed in 1992 when a political rally developed into a riot involving 150,000 people. despite a commitment to the Indian Supreme Court by the rally organisers that the mosque would not be harmed. More than 2,000 people, mostly Muslims, were killed in ensuing riots in many major Indian cities including Mumbai and Delhi. The mosque was constructed in 1527 by order of Babur, the first Mughal emperor of India. Mir Baki, after seizing the Hindu structure from priests, named it Babri Masjid.

[19] Vishva Hindu Paricad.

[20] Bhratiya Janata Party.

[21] A virtuous god from the popular Hindu Epic, Ramayana.

[22] The two chief castes of the priests and the warriors respectively.

[23] Smita Gupta, "A Call to Arms," *Outlook*, September 15, 2008, 12.

[24] Asgar Ali Engineer, "Religious Fanaticism and Communalism," *Economic and Political Weekly* 32, no. 15 (April 5-11, 1997): 701.

[25] C. V. Mathew, *Neo- Hinduism: A Missionary Religion* (Madras: Church Growth Research Centre, 1987), 31-32.

[26] K. N. Pannikar, *Communalism in India: History, Politics and Culture* (New Delhi: Manohar Publications, 1991), 2.

[27] Wedged between Hindu and Muslim communities.

[28] Robert Marquand, "In India, a Pattern of Attacks on Christians," *Christian Science Monitor*, June 29, 2000, 89.

[29] Training centre for women learning handcrafts.

[30] Manohar Murukesh, *The Past Two Decades of Christian Mission in India* (New Delhi: Christian Discoveries, 2005), 79.

[31] Anupama Katakam, "Terrorist Face," *Frontline*, August 13, 2010, 8.

[32] Payal Saxena, "Web or Terror" *The Week*, November 2009, 50.

[33] Payal Saxena, "Headley in; Pak Out New Mystery about Headley's Parsi Girl," *The Week*, April 4, 2010, 42.

[34] Payal Saxena, "Late Vigil," *The Week*, April 25, 2010, 32.

[35] Vijaya Pushkama, "Half-hearted Battle," *The Week*, May 30, 2010, 44.

[36] Tariq Bhat, "The Hindu Face of Jihad," *The Week*, November 2009, 20.

[37] Anto Akkara, *Shining Faith in Kandhamal* (Bangalore: ATC Publications, 2009), 109.

[38] Roland Littlewood, "Military Rape," *Anthropology Today* 13, no. 2, (April 1997): 7.

[39] Iboyaima Laithangbam, "Batting On," *Frontline*, November 19, 2010, 41.

[40] North East Network (NEN) and International Women's Rights Action Watch Asia Pacific, Baseline Report: Women in Armed Conflict Situations in India.

[41] Mandy Turner, "Armed Violence and Poverty in Northeast India: A Mini Case Study for the Armed Violence and Poverty Initiative," accessed December 1, 2010, https://bradscholars.brad.ac.uk/bitstream/handle/10454/995/AVPI_India.pdf?sequence=1&isAllowed=y

[42] Human Rights Watch, "Getting Away with Murder: 50 years of Armed Forces (Special Powers) Act," accessed August 13, 2008, http://www.hrw.org/backgrounder/2008/indiao8o8/

[43] Ramanujan, interview by author, November 22, 2010.

[44] Human Rights Watch, "'These Fellows Must Be Eliminated': Relentless Violence and Impunity in Manipur," accessed September 29, 2008, https://www.hrw.org/report/2008/09/29/these-fellows-must-be-eliminated/relentless-violence-and-impunity-manipur.

[45] Interview with Anju, a Hindu convert from Meitei community of Manipur on 23/11/10.

[46] Ramu Patil, "Bangalore's Hellhole," *The Week*, September 12, 2010, 26.

[47] Mallika Sarabhai, "Last Word," *The Week*, October 24, 2010.

[48] Oswald J. Smith, *The Challenge of Missions* (1959; repr., Hyderabad: Authentic Publication, 2010), 84.

Bibliography

Akkara, Anto. *Shining Faith in Kandhamal*. Bangalore: ATC Publications, 2009.

Ali Engineer, Asgar. "Religious Fanaticism and Communalism." *Economic and Political Weekly* 32 (April 5-11, 1997): 701-4.

Benjamin, P. Solomon, "The Other side of India 57th Indian Independence - People Yet Set Free." *Mashi Sevak: Journal of Christian Ministry*. July 2004.

Bhat, Tariq. "The Hindu Face of Jihad." *The Week*. November 2009.

Christian Discoveries, 2005.

Cumont, Franz. *Oriental Religions in Roman Paganism*. New York: Dover Publications Ltd., 1956.

Das, Prafulla. "Project Orissa." *Frontline*. September 26, 2008.

Gupta, Smita. "A Call to Arms." *Outlook*. September 15, 2008.

Human Rights Watch. "'These Fellows Must Be Eliminated': Relentless Violence and Impunity in Manipur." Accessed September 29, 2008. https://www.hrw.org/report/2008/09/29/these-fellows-must-be-eliminated/relentless-violence-and-impunity-manipur.

Human Rights Watch. "'These Fellows Must Be Eliminated': Relentless Violence and Impunity in Manipur." Accessed September 29, 2008. https://www.hrw.org/report/2008/09/29/these-fellows-must-be-eliminated/relentless-violence-and-impunity-manipur.

Huston, Tom. "Good News for the Poor." *Transformation* 7, no. 1 (1990): 3-8.

Katakam, Anupama. "Terrorist Face." *Frontline*. August 13, 2010.

Laithangbam, Iboyaima. "Batting On." *Frontline*. November 19, 2010.

Littlewood, Roland. "Military Rape." *Anthropology Today* 13, no. 2 (April 1997): 7-16.

MacDonald, Myra. "Hindu campaigners combat Christian conversions." *Yahoo News*. March 11, 2003.

Marchand, Lesslie A. ed. *Lord Byron: Selected Letters and Journals.* Harvard University Press, 1982.

Marquand, Robert. "In India, a Pattern of Attacks on Christians." *Christian Science Monitor* (June 29, 2000).

Martin, John A. "Isaiah." *The Bible Knowledge Commentary: Old Testament.* Edited by John F. Walvoord and Roy B. Zuck, 1029-1122. Colorado: David C. Cook, 1983.

Mathew, C. V. *Neo-Hinduism: A Missionary Religion.* Madras: Church Growth Research Centre, 1987.

Murukesh, Manohar. *The Past Two Decades of Christian Mission in India.* New Delhi:

Myers, Allen C. ed. *The Eerdmans Bible Dictionary.* Grand Rapids: William B. Eerdmans Publishing Company, 1987.

Nandy, Ashis, Shikha Trivedy, Ashail Mayaram, and Achyut Yagnik. *Creating a Nationality: The Ramjanmabhumi Movement and Fear of the Self.* Delhi: Oxford University Press, 1997.

Naqvi, Saeed. "Toppling the Caste Pyramid." *The Week Anniversary Special.* December 2009.

Panikkar, K. N. *Communalism in India: History, Politics and Culture.* New Delhi: Manohar Publications, 1991.

Patil, Ramu. "Allegations are More Shocking." *The Week.* June 13, 2010.

———. "Banglore's Hellhole." *The Week.* September 12, 2010.

Pushkarna, Vijaya. "Half-hearted Battle." *The Week.* May 30, 2010.

Ramanujan. Interview by author. November 22, 2010.

Samuel, Jayakumar. *Mission Reader: Historical Models for Holistic Mission in the Indian Context.* Delhi/Oxford: ISPCK, 2002.

Sarabhai, Mallika. "Last Word." *The Week.* October 24, 2010.

Saxena, Payal, "Headley in Pak. Out New Mystery about Headley's Parsi Girl." *The Week.* April 4, 2010.

———. "Late Vigil." *The Week.* April 25, 2010.

———. "Web or Terror." *The Week.* November 2009.

Smith, Oswald J. *The Challenge of Missions.* 1959. Reprint. Hyderabad: Authentic Publication, 2010.

Storm, Kay Marshall. *In the Presence of the Poor Challenging the Face of India.* Hyderabad: Authentic, 2008.

Turner, Mandy. "Armed Violence and Poverty in Northeast India: A Mini Case Study for the Armed Violence and Poverty Initiative." Accessed December 1, 2010. https://bradscholars.brad.ac.uk/bitstream/handle/10454/995/AVPI_India.pdf?sequence=1&isAllowed=y

Watts, W. John D., ed. *Isaiah*. Vol. 24 of the *Word Biblical Commentaries*. Texas: Word Books, 1985.

Wiersbe, Warren W. *The Wiersbe Bible Commentary*. Colorado: David C. Cook, 2007.

Wingate, Andrew. *The Church and Conversion: A Study of the Recent Conversions to and from Christianity in the Tamil Area of South India*. New Delhi: ISPCK, 1999.

6
Witnessing to Christ in a Pluralist Context:
Five Models from the
Madras Christian College[1]

Joshua Kalapati

Madras Christian College[2] is on the threshold of celebrating its 175th year of great service to the Nation. Founded as a school by the Scottish missionaries in 1837, the institution was served by a host of distinguished educationists, many of whom were outstanding theologians as well, who adopted different ways of relating Christ to the predominantly Hindu people in a rigidly stratified social context. I have taken up for discussion FIVE different, but by no means exclusivist, models of Mission gleaned from the life and thought of five former Principals of our college.

Rev. John Anderson: Uncompromising Evangelical

Theologically trained in Edinburgh, Rev. John Anderson (1805-1855) arrived in Madras in 1837, and developed the General Assembly School until he died in 1855. He was an uncompromising evangelical in his convictions, who had to face several challenges from the Hindu orthodoxy of the day. Nonetheless, the converts he won, such as Rev. Rajagopaul, Rev. Venkataramiah, Rev Ettirajulu, and many other women, made a huge impact to the Scottish educational mission in Madras.[3]

Alexander Duff (1806-78), the first prominent Scottish missionary, who laboured in Calcutta since 1830, profoundly impacted the missionaries in Madras. Duff's missionary strategy was two-fold: To use English as a medium of instruction, and through the westernization of education, he believed, Christianization of the Indian masses could be realized; and two, to target especially the high classes (castes) of the society, because, as he reasoned, if the higher classes were converted to Christian faith through English education, they would in turn do the same for those below them in social hierarchy, a theory which came to be known as 'downward filtration theory.'[4] Anderson pursued both these strategies successfully, which were aimed at winning souls for Christ.

Training in Christian Apologetics

In the Prospectus widely circulated in the local newspapers, Anderson made the character and objective of the school clear:

> The object is simply to convey through the channel of a good education as great an amount of truth as possible to the Native mind, especially of Bible truth. Every branch of knowledge communicated is to be made subservient to this desirable end... Each department of science and knowledge important for the students to know, will be taught to them as soon as they can with advantage to receive...[5]

Anderson trained his young men in Christian apologetics, equipping them in the art of discussion and rhetoric. He prepared his students to debate with the Hindu intellectuals of the day. The first issue of the *Native Herald* would reveal its character and scope. Its contents included-- An exposure of the idolatry of the Hindus; Remarks on the Christian school books; A defense of the conduct of the three converts by A.Venkataramiah; The Mysticism of Polycarp etc., The expected reaction came from the newspaper edited by a European Christian, who sought to defend Hinduism. When the first issue of his magazine Native Herald, received rejoinders to his critique of certain Hindu practices, Anderson remarked, Nothing could work better for advancing our great object. To examine, defend, discuss, is the way to pull down error and to establish God's truth in India. Anderson believed that spiritual transformation should be holistic i.e. when a person accepted Christ, he or she would be radically changed, and they in turn would transform people around them without compromising one any of the core values. The articles of his converts in the Native Herald also reflect their training in apologetics.

Evangelism through Education

Anderson and his colleagues never believed for a moment that education and evangelism stand separated; they in fact believed that education process is incomplete without spiritual formation and spiritual training. With this conviction the missionaries endeavoured to make their students, both boys and girls, to follow the Christian ideals. Therefore the spiritual and pedagogical training went hand in hand in the Central Institution as well as in the branch schools. Anderson always began and ended his classes with prayer. The students were required to study portions of the Bible, Catechisms, Christian classics and literature related to the Church history. Anderson firmly believed that a Christian institution should be different from a Government one.[6]

Besides, Anderson held uncompromising views on conversion, baptism, and fighting the social evils such as untouchability (his admitting three untouchable students was a milestone in Christian missions[7]), and suppression of women. As a result, he and his colleagues paid a heavy price while pursuing these goals. When three untouchables were admitted into the school, and whenever he boldly baptized his students, Anderson had to face the wrath of the high castes in Madras Presidency. Anderson as a radical reformer, was hailed as the 'Luther of South India.'[8]

Is Gospel Antagonism to Indian Culture?

Although Anderson encouraged Christian faith to be expressed in prominent local languages such as Tamil and Telugu, he was critical of the native culture. He targeted not only the major Hindu beliefs and practices but also Indian culture. The native names, not all of them, were changed into anglicised, Christian ones. For example, the five Hindu girls, who were converted, received baptism with new names: Unnum became Joanna, Mooniatta became Ruth, Venkatalutchoomoo was christened as Lydia, Yaygah was named Rachel, and Mungah became Elizabeth.[9] However the first three converts of the mission were allowed to retain their names, although Rajagopal became Rajagopaul.

Likewise Anderson was against the native rituals. S.P. Ramanujooloo's wife, when she became a Christian after her husband did, was asked to lay aside her Taulee (the sacred thread around the neck, which a woman wears at the time of marriage), as he perceived it to be part of 'heathenish ceremonies.'[10] Yet another harsh act was asking the Brahman to remove his poita (Brahman's string) and Coodomy (tuft of hair), when he was preparing for his baptism.[11] Although these were isolated incidents, these nevertheless reveal certain negative attitudes of the missionaries of Anderson times towards Indian culture. It however swung to the opposite when William Miller took over.

This 'old fashioned evangelical model' of Anderson certainly has both positive and negative sides: Anderson's uncompromising ways of presenting Christ to the Hindu community, the way he went about training and transforming the lives of scores of young Hindus, who became great leaders, and the determination with which he fought casteism---were all truly inspiring. But Anderson, in his times, did not know the distinction between Indian culture and the Hindu culture, which is a problematic even today.

Rev. William Miller: Christ the Fulfiller of Hinduism

Having arrived in Madras in 1862, Miller (1838-1923) took the College to great heights as its Principal for 45 long years until 1907. In contrast to Anderson, Miller was liberal and broadminded in thought and temperament, and demonstrated through his life and writings a very positive understanding of Hinduism and its traditions. Miller looked at Christ from a trans-historical perspective, and as One who enlightens every civilization on earth.

Education as *Praeparatio Evangelica*

Unlike his predecessor John Anderson, Miller believed that conversion and baptism, though important, were not primary to the educational mission, but only subsidiary. Christian institutions were not places for conversion, but for preparation. In the Missionary Conference held in Allahabad in 1872, Miller gave reasons why Christian Colleges were not meant for conversion, but for diffusion of Christian values. In his paper titled, "The Place of Education as a Missionary Agency,"[12]

Miller argued that the additions made to the visible Church by means of these Institutions were far fewer than they once were. Miller asked provocatively whether the colleges were in fact brought into existence as a means of increasing the number of Christians in India. The object of the Christian Church investing "so much money, so much thought, so many lives" in India was "to bring India to Christ." But if the Churches insist that the sole object of the Colleges was to add numbers, then "I at least join the enemies of Indian missions and should denounce them as an immoral waste of strength."[13] The true purpose of the educational missions should be the establishment of the kingdom of Christ and his Church in India rather than that of adding as many numbers as possible to the rolls of the disciples of Christ.[14]

Thus Miller was totally opposed to the "bait theory" viz. using the educational institutions as a bait to gather souls. Christian Colleges must believe that their job was mainly to prepare the students in a Christian direction. Therefore these cannot be centres for direct evangelism, but for the spread of Christian ideals. The task of Christian colleges was to diffuse the Christian ideas in concentric circles from the focus of the College. Miller used the metaphor of 'sowing and reaping.' The main task of a Christian college according to him was sowing, and reaping was for others, and at other times. The province of Christian education, Miller maintained, "was not directly to save souls, but to make the work of saving them more speedy and more certain than it would be without them."[15] Christian higher education, thus for Miller, was *praeparatio evangelica*, preparing the minds to be receptive to Christian principles. In a lecture he delivered on a furlough in 1878, Miller reasoned: "Now the main result of the work I have been describing is a change of thought and feeling, a modification of character and formation of principles tending in a Christian direction, which has begun to leaven the whole lump of Hinduism."[16]

Eric Sharpe summarised Miller's contribution to say, "Miller provided the Christian Colleges of India with a new and controversial raison d'etre--not to convert, but to spread Christian thought and Christian influence throughout non-Christian India."[17]

Hindu-Christian Relations: 'Christ the Fulfiller of Hinduism'

Miller had a broad, catholic understanding of Christ and Christianity. As his biographer O. Kandaswamy Chetty puts it, Miller believed that Christ was the friend of all that was good and true not only in Christianity, but also in Hinduism and an enemy of all that was evil and erroneous wherever found.[18] Therefore Miller argued that Christ was present in all religions including Hinduism, fulfilling all noble longings and aspirations.

Although J. N. Farquhar lucidly articulated 'Fulfilment theology' through his scholarly work, *The Crown of Hinduism* (1913), he was certainly not the first in that direction. 'Fulfilment theology' had already gained solid ground in Madras, as Eric Sharpe observes that Farquhar's work should be seen as one built upon the foundations originally laid in Madras, especially in the ideas of educationists such as Miller, T. E. Slater and F. W. Kellet.[19] Incidentally all these three were intimately connected with the Madras Christian College,[20] with Miller leading the way.

While Alexander Duff devoted all his attention and energy trying to utterly undermine Hindu religion and its social system, Miller believed that such a critical and negative attitude

was a sure way of alienating the Hindu masses, especially
those students in his College. Miller was the first educational
missionary in India who spoke boldly that Hinduism could
not be excluded from the plans and providence of God.[21] He
continued, "Hinduism has a place, real, though for the present
undefinable, in the mysterious whole of the divine purposes
and plan."[22] Also, "India has her own contribution to make,
and that a valuable one, for the working out of the story of
the world."[23]

While writing *Madras Christian College: A Short Account of
its History and Influence*, in 1905, Miller threw more light on his
understanding of Hinduism. Hinduism he admitted contained
much that was harmful and corrupt. To dwell upon that side
of it was however very cheap and easy. But one could see that
in a non-Christian land, just as in the Christian, the tares grow
mingled with the wheat. This is a uniform principle of all God's
dealings with mankind.[24] The purpose of Christianity coming
into contact with Hinduism was not to result in the overthrow
of the latter, but to accomplish "complete contact between East
and West," the religious ideas of both are to be laid aside each
other for the purpose of mutual enlightenment.[25]

'Christ the fulfiller' is the idea implicit in many of the
writings of Miller. For instance, he writes, "Christ's religion
was one which sought to fulfil the aspirations in other religions
and which itself sought its own fulfilment or completion
by being furnished with the peculiar contributions of other
religions."[26] Miller emphasized the fact that Christ alone is
the judge of everything, and not churches or missionaries.[27]
As O. Kandaswamy Che tty points out, "If the idea of Christ
as the Fulfiller had become more familiar and more agreeable

to the minds of South Indian Christians, it was largely due to the teachings and influence of Miller."[28]

Today, this Miller model raises these questions: Is Christ at work in the lives of non-Christians as much as He is in that of believers? Is Christ the source of all that is good and moral, true and beautiful in every one's life, irrespective of their religious affiliation? If so, is there any room for evangelism? How can we make them realize this truth, and lead them to a more fuller realization of the presence of Christ in their lives? Besides, the other disturbing question is: What is Christianity vis-à-vis Casteism in India today? Should we like Anderson take it head on, or simply condone and accept it as an unsolvable social reality, as Miller did?

Rev. Alfred George Hogg: Mission as Challenging Relevancy

Hogg (1874-1954),[29] who was the Principal of MCC during the years 1930-1938, used to tell his students that he was a *world-citizen*—born in Scotland, brought up in Egypt, educated in Germany and now serving in India. He studied Philosophy under Andrew Seth Pringle-Pattison between 1893 and 1897. His studies at Halle University under the Ritschlian, Arthur Titius, profoundly influenced his theological perspective. Ritschlian theology ingrained in him the idea that the centre of revelation is not the doctrinal formulations but the historical person of Jesus Christ. Hogg thus understood that Christian faith was in contrast with the dogmatic, doctrinal formulations. It is this broadminded worldview that endeared him to many a Hindu student, including S. Radhakrishnan and C. T. Krishnamachari.

It was the year 1903 that Hogg joined the faculty of MCC, a year before the college's most illustrious student, Sarvepalli Radhakrishnan entered its portals, and who was initiated into Hindu-Christian apologetics.[30] For Hogg, teaching of philosophy was 'a matter of life and death.'[31] A prolific writer, Hogg contributed number of penetrating and insightful articles in the college Magazine on areas like comparative religion, Hindu-Christian relations, Christian theology and practice etc., His philosophically penetrating books, though small in size, include *Karma and Redemption* (1905); *Redemption from this World* (1922); *Christian Message to the Hindu* (1947).[32]

Mission as Challenging Relevancy

Hogg was known for his philosophical rigor and unusual religious sensitivity towards Hinduism and his Hindu students. One of his unique contributions was the distinction he made between faith and belief, the distinction, which was made use of by several noted theologians including Wilfred Cantwell Smith. For Hogg, 'faith' was an existential commitment to a higher reality, while 'belief' is an intellectual, doctrinal formulation. Among the different religions, argued Hogg, chief obstacles crop up in the realm of belief more than that of faith. Left to himself, a Hindu was like a man in stupor, who might cross the chasm with narrowest of the doctrinal planks, but shake him a little, he would fall into the abyss. Hogg, in his later years became a more explicit Christian apologist when argued in his *Christian Message to the Hindu* (1947) that even a Hindu should take seriously the invitation of Christ--*Come and follow Me*.

Method of Selective Contrasts

Hogg suggested a method, which could be very effective in comparative religion, which came to be known, as the *Method of selective contrast.*[33] Hogg argued that the comparisons between religions could at best be facile and superficial, but if any one fundamental contrast is chosen, and subjected to rigorous intellectual analysis, it could lead us close to Truth. It is with this conviction that Hogg took up *Karma and Redemption* for analysis,[34] and showed how Redemption through Christ could provide a solution to the problem of Karma. Hogg also argued that Christianity might be offering solutions, which Hinduism is not looking for. But under certain conditions, a Hindu could be made to feel for ideas and solutions available only in Christianity. This process Hogg called as *Challenging Relevancy*, which inspired a number of Indian thinkers such as P. D. Devanandan and M. M. Thomas.

Extending Hogg's 'Method of Contrasts,' a Christian believer could raise the fundamental question: How is Christ different from the 'gods' of other religions? Many have endeavoured to trace similarities between Christ's life and teachings and those of others. But Hogg's method enables us to think how Christ's uniqueness lies in His being a contrast—in holiness, service, love, forgiveness etc.,– to the every other personal god.

Rev. Alexander John Boyd: People-to-People Relationship

Alexander Boyd (1896-1980) was the Principal of the college for 18 long years (1938-1956) in Tambaram. As a Professor of English, Boyd was known for his erudite teaching and personal care. He had a legendary memory of remembering all the 800 odd names of his students in the college, even with their surnames. It is this personal touch that endeared Dr. Boyd to hundreds of his Hindu students.

The best of his scholarly writings came only after his retirement in the form of the *Warrock Lectures* he delivered in Edinburgh and St Andrews, which were developed into a book titled, *Christian Encounter* (1961), which is a reflection of Boyd's grasp of Indian philosophy and religions. After delineating the philosophies of Sankara and Ramanuja, Boyd attempts to show that the ancient Hinduism underwent much reform in the modern times. Describing Dr. S. Radhakrishnan as one of the most distinguished scholars of our times in east or west,[35] and his books as the outstanding exposition of modern liberal Hinduism, Boyd discusses the various problems that crop up in the context of Hindu-Christian dialogue. There are theological and doctrinal differences between the two religions, but the best way he advocates was that of the 'people-to-people contact. We as people must be genuinely open to them as people…not simply as material on which we should like to get to work.'[36] Boyd gives an example of how, in his own college, a group of Christian students went to live among the people of criminal tribes. A Christian College, Boyd argued, should not be a college for Christians alone, but a College inspired by a Christian motive, seeking to make the best that we know available to all who desire to receive it.[37]

One of the most effective ways of witnessing to Christ in a pluralist context is through our love and service, our personal touch--a fact demonstrated by countless believers like Mother Teresa. During the height of Quit India movement in 1942, MCC under the leadership of Boyd, was the only city college which admitted students who were sent out of other colleges, without insisting on a Transfer Certificate. That Boyd touched the lives of thousands of his students was amply demonstrated by the fact that when he visited India in 1964-65, ten years after he retired, there was a groundswell of support by the hundreds of alumni all over. *What ye do to the least of these brethren, ye are doing it to Me*, is perhaps the most effective way of witnessing to Christ in a pluralist context.

Dr. Chandran D. S. Devanesen: Gandhian Christianity

Educated at Cambridge, and with a doctorate from Harvard, Chandran Devanesen (1917-1982) was the first Indian Principal of the college during the years 1962-1973. Greatly influenced by his famous uncles, the Kumarappa brothers, Devanesen chose to follow Gandhian path towards fulfilment of life. His interest in Gandhian thought led him to the Harvard University, where he did a Doctorate on the topic-- *The First Forty Years of Mahatma Gandhi* (1958-61), which was published as *The Making of the Mahatma* in 1969. This seminal work is broadly a lucid historical survey of the formative influences on the life and thought of Gandhi. In his foreword, Devanesen explains that the book seeks to explore how Gandhi, though rooted in Indian tradition, was subjected to the 'very profound forces of acculturation,' and how Gandhi had experienced the intellectual and spiritual impact of more than one great civilization. One particularly challenging task for Devanesen in this book was to deconstruct Gandhi's attitude to Christianity, and the latter's impact on him. In a crucial passage, he writes, the solution for many sensitive Hindus like Gandhi was to accept Christ, while rejecting organized Christianity and its packaging of Western culture.[38]

Devanesen vigorously used the Gandhian model to expand the horizons of the College life. He strengthened the Rural Service League programme founded by Dr. Malcolm Adiseshiah, started the Family Life Institute in Mappedu, near Tambaram, and a huge Farm well inside the College. Hundreds of students found near meaning and scope to their educational training in the nearby villages.

In the recent decades, a distinct development was the emergence of Gandhian Christianity. *Gandhi's Satyagraha is Christianity in action*, writes S. K. George.[39] For Gandhi, Christ appeared to be *Supreme Satyagrahi*, argued M. M. Thomas.[40] Gandhi, writes Martin Luther King Jr. "was probably the first person in history to lift the love ethic of Jesus above mere interaction between individuals to a powerful and effective social force on a large scale."[41] BUT the problems remain in Gandhian approach to Christianity: He denied the uniqueness of Christ, and frowned upon direct evangelism. He advised missionaries to carry out their charitable works such as running schools, hospitals, and other charitable institutions without indulging in conversions. Gandhi therefore looked at Bishop V. S. Azariah as *the enemy number one*, because of the latter's crusading zeal to lead the untouchable masses into the fold of Christianity.[42]

Can Gandhi's ideals further the cause of Mission in India? Surely yes! It is Gandhi's combat of communalism, his ideals of ahimsa (non-violence) and satyagraha (righteous anger), his plea for tolerance and respect for all religions---that had all inspired, and continue to inspire countless Christian leaders including Chandran Devanesen. Gandhi's challenge to Christianity is an invitation to practice, what John R. Mott calls, "larger evangelism."[43] At the same time, believers need to respond intellectually and critically to those views of Gandhi which run counter to the message of Christianity, especially the uniqueness of Jesus Christ.

Conclusion

All these five models of mission discussed are being used today in the larger Indian context. The mission field of India is so vast and complex that mission needs to be defined and redefined, and mission strategies to be constantly evolved. Perhaps, there can be no ONE way of presenting Christ and His message in the Indian context. We need to employ culture-specific, context-specific, people-specific models of Christian witness. In this endeavour, the leaders of Madras Christian College cited above provide some strategies!

Endnotes

[1] This paper has grown out of the one presented by the author at the Edinburgh Centenary Conference held in Edinburgh, June 2-6, 2010, titled, "Mission Spirituality in the Indian Context: Some Opportunities, Challenges and Strategies."

[2] This author and Ambrose Jeyasekaran have recently brought out a publication with a title, *Life and Legacy of Madras Christian College, 1837-1978* (Madras: Zha Communications, 2010). It chronicles the five historic phases of the Institution (I:1837-1862; II: 1862-1907; III: 1907-1937; IV: 1937-1962; and V: 1962 and henceforth), besides the contribution of more than fifty most illustrious alumni of the College.

[3] For details see, Jeyasekaran, *Life and Legacy of Madras Christian College, 1817-1978*, 24-43.

[4] D. F. Wright, ed., *Dictionary of Scottish Church History and Theology* (Edinburgh: T&T Clarke, 1993), 259.

[5] John Braidwood, *True Yoke Fellows in the Mission Field: The Life and Labours of the Rev. John Anderson and the Rev. Robert Johnston* (London: John Nisbet and Co., 1862), 61.

[6] He once observed in Braidwood, *True Yoke Fellows in the Mission Field*, 118-19; quoted as; "A Government normal school for mere intellectual drill, would merely turn out a few heartless machines in the shape of trained teachers with a keen eye for their salaries, but without one spark of feeling for their wretched fellow countrymen. A (Bible) normal school is wanted for the heart as well as the head, thoroughly informed and leavened with Bible truth."

[7] For more details see, Jeyasekaran, *Life and Legacy*, 20-22.

[8] For Colonel Rowlandson on Anderson's death, see *True Yoke Fellows in the Mission Field*, 559.

[9] Braidwood, *True Yoke Fellows in the Mission Field*, 352.

[10] Braidwood, *True Yoke Fellows in the Mission Field*, 261.

[11] Braidwood, *True Yoke Fellows in the Mission Field*, 249.

[12] W. Miller, "The Place of Education as a Mission Agency," *Reports of the Allahabad Missionary Conference, 1872-73*, ed., John Barton (London: Seeley, Jackson, and Halliday, 1873), 105-114.

[13] Miller, "The Place of Education as a Mission Agency," 106.

[14] Miller, "The Place of Education as a Mission Agency," 106

[15] Miller, "The Place of Education as a Mission Agency," 110.

[16] W. Miller, *Indian Missions and How to View Them* (Edinburgh, 1878), 29.

[17] Eric Sharpe, *Not to Destroy, But to Fulfill: The Contribution of J. N. Farquhar to the Protestant Missionary Thought in India Before 1914* (Uppsala: 1962), 82.

[18] O. Kandaswami Chetty, *Dr William Miller* (Madras: CLS, 1924), 43. This booklet grew out of the two articles O. K. C. wrote for the *Madras Christian College Magazine* in 1923, soon after William Miller died.

[19] Sharpe, *Not to Destroy, But to Fulfill*, 83.

[20] F. W. Keller, representing the Wesleyan Methodist Society taught History in the college for a long time, while T. E. Slater of the LMS was a close associate of Miller in Social Reform meetings, besides published many articles on Hindu-Christian relations, in the College Magazine.

[21] William Miller, *Madras Christian College: A Short Account of its History and Influence* (Edinburgh: Macniven and Wallace, 1905), 8; quoted as, "Future generations will see as clearly as we see this, that Hinduism and the Hindus are embraced within the limits of God's plan. The time will come when it will be deemed simply foolish to deny that Hindu thought, as truly as Greek philosophy, or Roman law, is a factor in the building of the historic fabric of which the foundation was laid when Abraham was called and of which the cornerstone is Christ."

[22] Miller, *Madras Christian College*.

[23] William Miller, "The Place of Hinduism in the Story of the World," *Madras Christian College Magazine*, April 1896, 583.

[24] Miller, *Madras Christian College*, 7.

[25] Miller, *Madras Christian College*, 13.

[26] Chetty, *Dr William Miller*, 49.

[27] Once while addressing his students, who were predominantly Hindus, Miller observed that in "The Place of Hinduism in the Story of the

World," 583; quoted as, "You have not to do with churches or with missionaries. The very plan of the world shows, as we have seen, that in them there is evil and mistake. They are not to be your standard. They have no authority as your guides. It is of Christ you have to judge. He stands apart, seeking to found no sect and to upset none, seeking only to make men know that each one of them has a place in the Father's heart."

[28] Chetty, *Dr William Miller*, 44.

[29] The chief sources on Hogg include; Eric Sharpe, *The Theology of A. G. Hogg*, (Madras: CLS, 1971); Eric Sharpe, *Alfred Hogg*, (Madras: CLS, 1999); and James L. Cox, "The Development of A. G. Hogg's Theology in Relation to Non-Christian Faith: Its Significance for the Tambaram Meeting of the International Missionary Council, 1938" (PhD diss., Aberdeen University, 1977).

[30] For details see Joshua Kalapati, *Dr. S. Radhakrishnan and Christianity: An Introduction to Hindu-Christian Apologetics* (Delhi: ISPCK, 2002), 1-36.

[31] While tracing the formative influences of Radhakrishnan, his biographer-son, Sarvepalli Gopal writes in, *Radhakrishnan: A Biography* (Oxford University Press, 1989), 15; quotes as, "Hogg was so meticulous a thinker that in his lectures and writings, and even in informal conversations, there was throughout a restrained hesitation of thought, a qualified moderation, a scrupulous regard for all sides of a case and an anxiety to ensure all the qualifications for any statement. A dedicated missionary with an unshakeable belief in the person of Christ and in the indispensability of belonging to the visible Church, Hogg was yet flexible in matters of doctrine and regarded himself as more a philosopher than a theologian; and Radhakrishnan always acknowledged the permanent mark on his own mind of Hogg's influence, in both response and reaction."

[32] For an excellent introduction to Hogg's ideas, see Eric Sharpe, *The Theology of Hogg*.

[33] Cf. Cox, "The Development of A.G. Hogg's Theology in Relation to Non-Christian Faith."

[34] A. G. Hogg, "Karma and Redemption," *Madras Christian College Magazine*, January 1904, 357-369.

[35] Alexander Boyd, *Christian Encounter* (Edinburgh: St Andrew's Press, 1961), 29.

[36] Boyd, *Christian Encounter*, 86.

[37] "The Principal's Report," *Madras Christian College Magazine*, March 1947, 69-70.

[38] Chandran D. S. Devanesen, *The Making of the Mahatm*a (Delhi, 1969), 59.

[39] S. K. George, *Gandhi's Challenge to Christianity* (Ahmedabad: Navjivan Trust, 1947), xv.

[40] M. M. Thomas, *Acknowledge Christ of Indian Renaissance* (Madras: CLS, 1970); see chapter VIII

[41] Cited in Susan Billington Harper, *In the Shadow of the Mahatma: Bishop V.S. Azariah and the Travails of Christianity in British India* (Grand Rapid, Michigan: William B. Eerdmans Publishing Company, 2000), 7.

[42] Paul D. Devanandan uses this phrase of John Mott while articulating Gandhi's challenge to Christianity. See his article, "Gandhi's Challenge to Christianity," *Christianity and Crisis* 8 (1948): 75-78; cited in Joachim Wietzke, ed., *Paul D. Devanandan*, vol.1 (Madras: CLS, 1983), 238.

Bibliography

"The Principal's Report." *Madras Christian College Magazine*, March 1947.

Boyd, Alexander. *Christian Encounter*. Edinburgh: St Andrew's Press, 1961.

Braidwood, John. *True Yoke Fellows in the Mission Field: The Life and Labours of the Rev. John Anderson and the Rev. Robert Johnston*. London: John Nisbet & Co., 1862.

Chetty, O. Kandaswami. *Dr William Miller*. Madras: CLS, 1924.

Cox, James L. "The Development of A. G. Hogg's Theology in Relation to Non-Christian Faith: Its Significance for the Tambaram Meeting of the International Missionary Council, 1938." PhD diss., Aberdeen University, 1977.

Devanesen, Chandran D. S. *The Making of the Mahatm*a. Delhi, 1969.

Devanandan, Paul D. "Gandhi's Challenge to Christianity," *Christianity and Crisis* 8 (1948): 75-78.

George, S. K. *Gandhi's Challenge to Christianity*. Ahmedabad: Navjivan Trust, 1947.

Harper, Susan Billington. *In the Shadow of the Mahatma: Bishop V.S. Azariah and the Travails of Christianity in British India*. Grand Rapid, Michigan: William B. Eerdmans Publishing Company.

Hogg, A. G. "Karma and Redemption." *Madras Christian College Magazine*, January 1904.

Kalapati, Joshua and Ambrose Jeyasekaran. Life *and Legacy of Madras Christian College (1837-1978)*. Madras: Zha Communications, 2010.

Kalapati, Joshua. *Dr S Radhakrishnan and Christianity: An Introduction to Hindu-Christian Apologetics*. Delhi: ISPCK, 2002.

Miller, William. *Madras Christian College: A Short Account of its History and Influence*. Edinburgh: MacNiven & Wallace, 1905.

Miller, W. "The Place of Education as a Mission Agency." *Reports of the Allahabad Missionary Conference, 1872-1873*. Edited by John Barton. London: Seeley, Jackson, and Halliday, 1873.

—————. *Indian Missions and How to View Them*. Edinburgh, 1878.

Gopal, Sarvepalli. *Radhakrishnan: A Biography*. Oxford University Press, 1989.

Sharpe, Eric. *Alfred Hogg*. Madras: CLS, 1999.

—————. *Not to Destroy, But to Fulfill: The Contribution of J. N. Farquhar to the Protestant Missionary Thought in India before 1914*. Uppsala: 1962

—————. *The Theology of A.G. Hogg*. Madras: CLS, 1971.

Thomas, M.M. *Acknowledge Christ of Indian Renaissance*. Madras: CLS, 1970.

Wright, D. F. ed. *Dictionary of Scottish Church History and Theology*. Edinburgh: T&T Clarke, 1983.

Wietzke, Joachim. ed., *Paul D. Devanandan*. Vol. 1. Madras: CLS, 1983.

7
Witnessing to Christ
Among Postmodern Intellectuals

Joshua Iyadurai

Introduction

The British journal *New Scientist*, February 2005, portrayed India as the next Knowledge Super Power. Kabil Sibal spoke about India becoming Knowledge Super Power by 2020. Dr. Mashelkar, Director General of CSIR predicted, "Even if India does not do anything it is inevitable that we will emerge as the knowledge power in the next 5-10 years."[1] Hence the focus of Mission in 21st century needs to be shifted towards intellectuals in campuses and corporate world. There is no separate gospel for intellectuals than the one Jesus offered to everyone. So, what is so special about witnessing to intellectuals? We are not here to define a new gospel for intellectuals; the message is the same. But the question is, in what plate we serve the gospel which will be appealing to them? This paper is an attempt to understand philosophical trend of postmodernism among intellectuals and draw some implications for presenting the gospel to them. I would like to draw some inspiration from the different approaches Jesus adopted to reach individuals in his time. Then discuss the features of postmodernism, the religiosity of intellectuals and the implications for witnessing.

Jesus Style of Approaches

Jesus used different approaches to touch different individuals.

- Nicodemus: A Jewish official and Teacher

  Jesus reasoned with him on spiritual truths. (Jn 3:1-21)

- Nathaniel: A religious person

  Jesus appreciated him for his sincerity. (Jn 1:45-51)

- Young Official: A rich man, Jewish Official and a self-righteous man

  Jesus brought out the positive elements in him and pointed out what was lacking in him. (Lk. 18:18-27; Mk 10:17-27)

- Pharisees: Considered to be the most holy people in the Jewish society

  Jesus rebuked them for their hypocrisy. (Matt. 23)

- Samaritan Woman: A sinful woman

  Jesus dealt with her sinful life without using the word sin. He offered living water which aroused a thirst in her. (Jn 4:1-42)

- Blind Man: Considered to be cursed

  Jesus offered him vision; his blindness brought God's glory. (Jn 9)

- Leper: Socially outcast

  Jesus offered social acceptance by touching him and offered physical healing too. (Mk. 1:40-45)

We need to adopt different approaches in presenting the gospel to reach the intellectuals. Our knowledge on the philosophical trends among the intellectuals will be helpful to address their worldviews while presenting the gospels. In the next section we will be dealing with the features of postmodernism briefly.

Postmodernism

We need to understand the current philosophical trend of postmodernism in order to witness to intellectuals. Postmodernism is a term being used today in all fields and it is very difficult to define. It is an intellectual trend of the present day emerged from the later part of 20th century as a reaction to modernism.

Modernism established supremacy of reason and considered science as the vehicle to make life better for humanity. However, the two world-wars, Nazi holocaust etc. awakened philosophers to question the claims of modernism. Postmodernism emerged by rejecting *reason* as the sole arbiter of knowledge and truth. The tall claims of science being objective and providing solutions to all problems of humanity are set aside by postmodernism.

Postmodernism does not have a set of philosophies and theories; in fact it is against such grand philosophical frame work. However, postmodernism has a say in every sphere of life, and the essence of postmodernism is pluralism. Joe Mannath identifies seven traits of postmodernism.

1. World is evolutionary: Changing and it is not a machine but expands.

2. Everything is Relational: Everything exists in relation to other.

3. Reality is Mysterious: Reality cannot be fully comprehended.

4. Knowledge is a process and cultural artefact: Knowing is a process and it is culturally conditioned.

5. Science and technology not necessarily always good: Science cannot save humanity and progress is not always good. Loss of lives due to wars and ecological destruction due to advanced technology are some indicators.

6. New World order: There is no one centre: The West.

7. Rejection of grand narratives: Grand theories with universal claims are rejected and particularities found space.[2] Here we will be discussing some of the main features of postmodernism: Plurality of Truth, Experience, Absence of Metanarrative (absolute truth), and Community.

Plurality of Truth

In postmodernism, truth is subjective as one perceives it. Truth varies person to person, community to community and culture to culture. Truth is understood from a community's perspective. "[T]ruth is what fits within a specific community; truth consists in the ground-rules that facilitate the well-being of the community in which one operates."[3] In other words truth is what works or what is good for a person/community. Postmodernism rejects any claim for absolute truth; hence truth is plural.

The rejection of the absolute truth by postmodernism is a great challenge to Christianity. Though, postmodernism rejects absolute truth, it accepts what works as truth. We need a shift in the starting point of declaring the absolute truth. Instead, show what works in one's life and invite people to experience the truth. We are not presenting an abstract idea as the truth but Christian witness is presenting the truth: the person Jesus Christ. We can set aside all theological jargons about Christology and introduce Jesus as a person who brings transformation. So the challenge is to show people that Jesus works in our lives. The ongoing transformation in individual lives and in the church is the evidence that the truth—Jesus—works today. When a person experiences the 'truth that works' then he/she may be in a position to understand the absolute claims.

People are not inclined to believe what we say but would like to try something that worked in our lives. My study on conversion finds that converts do not accept the gospel as it is presented. However, they test it's workability in their lives. Nathan, a Charted Accountant, experienced conversion at the age of 18. He reported his prayer to a generic God, addressing God without using any names:

> I couldn't accept Christ was the true God. The struggle in my heart was that I was good outside and bad inside, that was troubling me. One day, as I was alone, I felt, I need to pray, but I didn't want to pray to Jesus, as I was not sure of who was the real God. So I prayed "I don't know who you are, I have committed many wrongs, I am ready to accept the penalty for the wrongs I have done. I wanted to be good but I couldn't. Help me."
> Immediately after I said this, there was a great joy in my heart: it was bubbling. Since then I began to seek sincerely to learn what is in it.[4]

We need to understand how the Pentecostal movement thrive forward all over the world because they demonstrate that the truth—Jesus— works in the lives of the people. Rationalized gospel does not appeal to people, even to the intellectuals. Postmodernism attributes great significance to experience, so people are interested in experiencing or knowing the truth. Modernism talks about possessing knowledge objectively, but postmodernism gives room to experience the truth and gain knowledge through subjective experience.

Experience

Modernism enthroned reason as the arbiter of knowledge. Unfortunately, theologians bent backward to prove the rationality of Christian claims. According to Lesslie Newbigin "The defense is in fact, a tactical retreat. But as later history has shown, these tactical retreats can—if repeated often enough—begin to look more like a rout."[5] Modern mission was also highly influenced by enlightenment thinking. Postmodernism limits the role of reason by rejecting the notion of objective knowledge. The knower and the knowable cannot be separated because the reality is not 'out there.' It opens the doors of experience, intuition, and aesthetics to gain knowledge. We can take postmodernism as an ally in this aspect as it creates space for us to talk about revelation, spiritual experiences which result in knowledge.

The biblical understanding of 'knowing' is experiential and knowing God is encountering God. When we present the gospel, we expect the person to encounter Jesus; it is not merely a rational understanding of what Jesus taught and did. In the conversation with Nicodemus, Jesus was talking about the spiritual experience of being born again, while Nicodemus missed the whole point by rationalizing it. Though rational aspect of the gospel is important but if a person has not experienced Jesus, the rational knowledge is meaningless.

My study has highlighted that religious experience in conversion is central. Mala, a medical doctor narrated her religious experience:

> One day, as I was reading the Bible, I was stuck while reading the verse: "I am your God.... do not follow other gods." I felt I should read it again. I read it again. Then I realized that I haven't yet removed the statues from my room, immediately, I disposed of the idols which I possessed. Again I came and read, the same verse was repeated then I found one guru's photo and I removed that also. Again, I started reading the Bible and the same verse was repeated to me, then I found my drawings of gods and I disposed them also. That was how first I got the conviction. Till then, I knew Jesus was God but only at that moment I realized, "Jesus is the only God." God didn't appear before me, but revealed in my mind.[6]

Nithya, a medical student, expressed her inability to explain how the realization came to her, "One day, suddenly a change came into my mind, 'Christ is the only God.' I can't tell you exactly (she laughs). You won't know when one would fall in love. I fell in love; it was like my love towards my Lord. I don't know when it really happened. What I can say is that I love Jesus."[7] Similarly others also pointed out that it was not a rational understating but a sudden realization, an inner experience.

Modernistic paradigm of witnessing would appeal to the intellect by offering convincing proofs for the gospel, whereas, postmodern paradigm of witnessing would invite a person to encounter Jesus. "Experiential knowledge is valid in postmodernity and one can openly talk about one's experience without being branded as irrational."[8] Therefore, our focus in witnessing is to invite people to experience Jesus. Knowledge of God through religious experience is valid for intellectuals in a postmodern world.

Absence of Metanarrative (No Absolute Truth)

Metanarrative means universal claim or overarching theory which claim universal implications. Postmodernism rejects any universal claims, whether it is scientific, socialistic, religious or philosophical etc. Craig Van Gelder points out Lyotard's view on this:

> He [Lyotard] believed that Enlightenment thinkers made a great mistake when they set one particular kind of knowledge—scientific knowledge—above all others and insisted that all experience be interpreted in terms of it. He challenged the premise that it was possible or desirable to construct a grand narrative, especially one that focussed all reality through the narrow lens of instrumental reason.[9]

There cannot be one single theory or universal claim on reality, truth or knowledge. Reality is looked at from the perspective of the individual which varies from community to community and culture to culture. Postmodernism claims no one has the right to impose any metanarrative as the absolute truth for all. It questions the traditional logic of 'excluded middle' by enforcing 'either' 'or'. Postmodernism considers all universal claims or metanarratives as the constructs of societies or communities in order to have control over others.

Plurality in understanding of reality in diversity and in particularity is real. Postmodernism attaches significance to local narratives and particularities. Christianity can walk with postmodernism in terms of rejecting metanarratives produced by the Enlightenment project such as reason as the sole arbiter of knowledge. However, universal claim/metanarrative of Christianity, Jesus is the only saviour, is challenged by postmodernism. This limits us in presenting Jesus as the saviour of the world and to present God's commandments as the moral laws for every human being. Here, we have to defend the universal implications.

The Biblical claims are metanarratives encompassing the entire human race. However, Chris Wright points out that these metanarratives are basically emerged out of particularities of local narratives:

> [T]he Bible... glories in *diversity*, and celebrates multiple human *cultures*, the Bible which builds its most elevated theological claims on utterly *particular* and sometimes very *local* events, the Bible which sees everything in *relational*, not abstract, terms, and the Bible which does the bulk of its work through the medium of *stories*.[10] [emphasis as in original]

In a postmodern world, witnessing to Christ is not offering a metanarrative (a grand theory of salvation) but presenting the truth—Jesus Christ—who appeared *locally* in Nazareth. The biblical grand narrative is not a universal theory but an invitation to experience the truth—Jesus Christ who has universal appeal. The focus in witnessing need not be on the universal claims of Christianity but the person of Jesus who is rooted in history and in particularity.

Community

Community is another term widely used these days. Modernism exalted the self to great extend that self is supreme. Postmodernism views self in the context of community. Self is a product of community. Self cannot exist in isolation, but only in a social context. Community plays a vital role in many dimensions of human life.

In Indian context, families are closely knitted together and the head of the family wields power. Caste is another factor which binds people together. People hesitate to accept Jesus because Christianity is considered as a religion of low caste.

On the other hand, Dalits hesitate to embrace Christianity because of the caste discrimination within the church. Others consider the church as an institutional form of Christianity which requires change of social identity by breaking away from their communities.

While witnessing to Christ in a postmodern world, we need to take the community factor into consideration. When a person accepts Jesus generally we expect the convert to break away the old ties. Discontinuity is emphasized in conversion in order to demonstrate the loyalty of the converts to Jesus. Inadvertently our witnessing is influenced by modernism which elevates the individual above the community. It would be strategically and theologically congruent to let the convert be part of his/her community. In my research on conversion, many of the converts preferred to be the secret followers of Jesus till an opportune time came.[11] Jeyaraj Dasan studied about non-church movement in Chennai[12] and claims that it is widespread; this trend seems to be widely present worldwide especially in Islamic countries.[13]

On the other hand, the impact of globalization leads to breaking away of community bonds among younger generation. They do not have a sense of belonging and they are looking for a group where they can find acceptance and love. They do not get it in a real life situation; they try it in the virtual world. We know how social sites in the web are growing in magnitude and how people spend their time for online chatting. In virtual communities one can be anonymous but still gets a feeling that he/she is accepted. A comparative study of college students in Chennai and Maastricht, Netherlands finds, "virtual interaction taking place in these sites is just a supplement to real life interaction.[14]

Christian spirituality is all about relationships: Love God and love your neighbour. We are called to create a genuine community where people will find genuine love and acceptance. Our fellowship cannot be merely an activity; it should be an active community where each one feels accepted and wanted. One of the reasons converts find attractive in Pentecostal churches is the personal touch and follow-up.

Religious Intellectuals

In our Indian society, great number of intellectuals are religious. They follow their traditional religions (Hinduism, Islam, Sikhism, Jainism, and Buddhism) without any inconvenience to the position they hold in the intellectual arena. Religious beliefs and practices can coexist with scientific views, even if they are contradictory. ISRO chairman along with 10 scientists offering prayer for the launch of GSLV last month was one such illustration. Meera Nanda in an article in Frontline brought out this paradox vividly:

I learnt of *yagnas* being done in the laboratories of a major university to ward off ghosts; I learnt of *jagrans* being held on university campuses, presided over by the members of the science faculty. My friends saw nothing particularly objectionable to such compartmentalisation between the work you do as a scientist and what you do in the rest of your life outside the laboratory. But what happens when what you do outside directly contradicts and negates all that you know as a scientist, I asked. How do you live with the contradictions of praying to supernatural forces for the safety of a rocket that you have fashioned out of your own hands without invoking anything but natural forces? Where, in modern physics and astronomy, is there room for a supernatural power that listens to our prayers? Or for that matter, where in modern biology is there any evidence whatsoever for immaterial spiritual energy, *prana*, that is routinely treated as an actual force of nature in the discourses of our yogis and gurus?[15]

Intellectuals in our country generally are religious and for them spiritual practices and experiences need not be ratified by reason. They are legitimate in holding such a view because it was modernism which made reason as the arbiter of all forms of knowledge. For an Indian mind reason is not supreme and one's experience of divine is greatly valued. Because of this atmosphere, we have mushrooming of gurus offering various kinds of techniques for healing, prosperity and to arouse the energy within. The followers of these gurus are not merely the poor and the illiterates but educated as well. Unlike the West, where the intellectuals are generally secularists, in other words atheists, here in India, intellectuals are religious. This is a positive factor which can be a starting point for us to talk about Jesus. While witnessing, we need to keep our focus on the person of Jesus, his life and what he could offer instead of presenting Christianity; because Christianity is associated with the institutionalized form of religion. One of the factors that attracts people to Jesus is the personal relationship with God in Jesus. This was highlighted by the participants of my study that having such relationship is unique in Jesus.[16] We can present Jesus as a companion for life who is committed to the welfare of the person who receives him.

Conclusion

While witnessing for Christ to intellectuals, we need to be aware of different world-views and religious beliefs. We should be ready to appreciate the positive factors in their views and practices. We can be genuinely interested in understanding their positions and the values they attach to their beliefs and practices so that we can be sensitive to them. We can try to discuss the limitations of their beliefs and practices as a matter of fact, without getting into any arguments.

It is important to identify their felt needs and express our sincere concern for their welfare. Make use of such situations to show how Jesus helped us to get over the crisis. We can always assure them of our prayers; generally people are happy to accept when we say we will pray for them. We can invite them to try Jesus and pass on New Testament and the rest God will take care. We can dialogue through lives by developing genuine friendship with them. Thus we expose our lives to them and they can read our lives to see what Jesus can do.

Once, Dr. Martin Lloyd Jones delivered a sermon in Oxford, a law student and the head of the Debating Society rose and said that the sermon was well prepared and presented, but it was suitable to any farm laborers or any one; sounding that it was not an intellectual stuff that was suitable to the intellectual community. Lloyd Jones replied that whether intellectuals or farm laborers the condition of human beings is same with sin. We need to keep in mind that our intellectual presentation is not going to win a person to Christ; but it can clear the philosophical barriers in understanding the gospel intellectually. Our responsibility is to present the gospel in an effective manner; the Holy Spirit does the conversion.

Endnotes

[1] Raghunath A. Mashelkar, "India to Emerge as Knowledge Power: Dr Mashelkar," accessed January 06, 2010, http://www.rediff.com/money/2003/sep/25 india.htm.

[2] Joe Mannath, "A Fad, a Cult of Jargon, or a Significant Intellectual Trend?" *Indian Philosophical Annual* 22 (1999): 122-34.

[3] Stanly J. Grenz, "Postmodernism and the Future of Evangelical Theology: Star Trek and the Next Generation," *Crux* XXX, no. 1 (1994): 24-32.

[4] Joshua Iyadurai, "Self-transformative Religious Experiences: A Phenomenological Inquiry" (PhD diss., University of Madras, Chennai, 2008).

[5] Lesslie Newbigin, *The Gospel in a Pluralist Society* (Grand Rapids: Eerdmans, 1989), 3.

[6] Iyadurai, "Self-transformative Religious Experiences."

[7] Iyadurai, "Self-transformative Religious Experiences."

[8] Joshua Iyadurai, "Mission in Postmodernity: An Asian Perspective," *Theme 3 Mission and Postmodernities - Papers*, accessed December 12, 2011, http://www.edinburgh2010.org/en/study-themes/main-study-themes/3-mission-and-postmodernities/theme-3-papers.html

[9] Craig Van Gelder, "Mission in the Emerging Postmodern Condition," in *The Church between Gospel and Culture*, eds. George R. Hunsberger and Craig Van Gelder (Grand Rapids: Eerdmans, 1996), 128.

[10] Christopher Wright, *The Mission of God: Unlocking the Bible's Grand Narrative* (Downers Grove: IVP, 2006), 47.

[11] Iyadurai, "Mission in Postmodernity."

[12] Dasan Jeyaraj, *Followers of Christ Outside the Church in Chennai, India* (Zoetermeer: Boekencentrum Academic, 2010).

[13] See for detailed discussion on movements within Islamic countries: Rebecca Lewis, "Promoting Movement to Christ within Natural Communities," *IJFM* 24, no. 2 (Summer 2007): 75.

[14] Rajalakshmi Kanagavel and Chandrasekharan Velayutham, "Impact of Social Networking on College Students: A Comparative Study in India and the Netherlands," *International Journal of Virtual Communities and Social Networking* 2, no. 3 (2010), accessed January 5, 2011, http://www.igi-global.com/Bookstore/Article.aspx?TitleId=49704, DOI: 10.4018/jvcsn.2010070105.

[15] Meer Nanda, "Is India a Science Super Power?" *Frontline*, September 10-23, 2005, accessed December 9, 2011, http://www.hinduonnet.com/fline/fl2219/stories/20050923002109200.htm.

[16] Iyadurai, "Mission in Postmodernity."

Bibliography

Gelder, Craig Van. "Mission in the Emerging Postmodern Condition." *The Church between Gospel and Culture*. Edited by George R. Hunsberger and Craig Van Gelder, 113-38. Grand Rapids: Eerdmans, 1996.

Grenz, Stanly J. "Postmodernism and the Future of Evangelical Theology: Star Trek and the Next Generation." *Crux* XXX, no. 1 (March 1994): 24-32.

Iyadurai, Joshua. "Mission in Postmodernity: An Asian Perspective." *Theme 3 Mission and Postmodernities – Papers*. Accessed December 12, 2011. http://www.edinburgh2010.org/en/study-themes/main-study-themes/3-mission-and-postmodernities/theme-3-papers.html.

—————. "Self-transformative Religious Experiences: A Phenomenological Inquiry." PhD diss., University of Madras, Chennai, 2008.

Jeyaraj, Dasan. *Followers of Christ Outside the Church in Chennai, India*. Zoetermeer: Boekencentrum Academic, 2010.

Kanagavel, Rajalakshmi and Chandrasekharan Velayutham. "Impact of Social Networking on College Students: A Comparative Study in India and the Netherlands." *International Journal of Virtual Communities and Social Networking* 2, no. 3 (2010): 55-67. Accessed January 5, 2011. http://www.igi-lobal.com/Bookstore/Article.aspx?TitleId=49704, DOI:10.4018/ jvcsn.2010070105.

Lewis, Rebecca. "Promoting Movement to Christ within Natural Communities." *IJFM* 24, no. 2 (Summer 2007): 75-76.

Mannath, Joe. "A Fad, A Cult of Jargon, or a Significant Intellectual Trend?" *Indian Philosophical Annual* 22 (1999): 122-34.

Mashelkar, Raghunath A. "India to Emerge as Knowledge Power: Dr Mashelkar." Accessed January 06, 2010. http://www.rediff.com/money/ 2003/sep/25 india.htm.

Nanda, Meera "Is India a Science Super Power?" *Frontline*. September 10-23, 2005. Accessed December 9, 2011. http://www.hinduonnet.com/fline/fl2219/stories/20050923002109200.htm.

Newbigin, Lesslie. *The Gospel in a Pluralist Society*. Grand Rapids: Eerdmans, 1989.

Wright, Christopher. *The Mission of God: Unlocking the Bible's Grand Narrative*. Downers Grove: IVP, 2006.

8

The Early Mizo Mission School Teachers' Role in Witnessing to Christ

Marina Ngursangzeli Behera

Introduction

It is a historical fact that foreign missionaries had brought about spectacular changes among the Mizos and in Mizo society at large. Christianity transformed the worldview and standard of values held by the Mizos of the time. Undoubtedly, education was an important by-product of Christianity. Saiaithanga clearly asserted that the desire to be able to read the Good News and the hymns promoted in the Mizos the desire for education – the ability to be able to read and write.[1] In 1937 Edwards commented in his reports of the Lushai Hills 1936-37, "Education has become one of the accepted 'values' of Lushai life."[2]

There has been considerable research dealing with and emphasizing the contributions of the missionaries towards education as well as on the education system which they had introduced in Mizoram.[3] However in the past few years there has been born an interest in and a recognition of the need among the Mizos to give emphasis on the Mizos' contributions and their role in terms of the transformation they and their society had undergone during the past hundred odd years with the advent of the British and along with that of Christianity. There have been efforts to reclaim the story of the early Mizo Christians as active historical agents participating in the journey towards the Christianization of the region and the transformation they underwent. The life and witness of the early Mizo pastors, the evangelists, the Church elders and the "Bible Women" have been given much prominence nowadays in writings and researches dealing with the history of Christianity and the Church in Mizoram. There have also been some passing comments about the contribution and role played by the mission school teachers, but these have never really been the focus of the latest researches or the writings. Almost all the writings emphasize the ministry of the ordained pastors and to a certain extent the evangelists and the itinerant preachers.[4]

In a time when Christian mission or witnessing is understood to be 'by everyone from everywhere to everywhere' this paper attempts to highlight the role and contributions of the mission school teachers, specifically the village primary school teachers during the early period of the history of Christianity in Mizoram. The paper begins with the premise that the village school teachers were the foundations of the churches in Mizoram before there were any ordained Mizo pastors and elders among the early Mizo faith community. And even after 1913 when the first Mizo pastor was ordained, they continued to witness to the Gospel message and God's redeeming love through their life and selfless work in partnership with the ordained pastors and church elders. The paper will specifically deal with the period from 1894 (the year the foreign missionaries started work in

Mizoram) to 1934. This is because though by this time there were ordained ministers, they were still few in number and so the school teachers continued to pay an important role through their multifarious activities in consolidating the place of Christianity in Mizo society. They were subsequently able to build on the foundations of their earlier work of proclaiming the Gospel until the Church in Mizoram was in a better position to look after these churches with more people getting ordained.

The understanding of witnessing in partnership is embodied in the understanding of mission as *Missio Dei*, which by definition is a collaborative action by Father, Son and Holy Spirit (John 14:26) and also a divine action which invites human participation, if not collaboration: "As the Father sent me so I send you" (John 20:21). It shows the necessity of engaging humanity as agents of God's mission. This point is further underlined by Jesus' own calling of the disciples as co-workers to whom He eventually entrusts the task of global mission (Matt 28:18-20). We can also point to many biblical images of the missional ecclesia which are of a networking nature, such as the Body (Rom. 12:I Cor. 12; Eph. 4:12; etc) and the Vine (John 15). We live in a well networked world, our God exists in Trinitarian partnership, and God's mission into which we are drawn is characterized by collaboration and partnership, as Christ 'reconciles to Himself all things, whether on earth or in heaven' (Col. 1:20).[5] Thus this paper will attempt to bring to light an understanding and a perspective that witnessing to Christ and God's redeeming love does not rest only on those who are ordained ministers or on those who are trained specifically for Christian ministry. All of us have the responsibility and ability to witness to Christ wherever we are located and situated.

Authentic witnessing to Christ demands of us the acknowledgement that each of us- irrespective of our differences and geographical location needs the other in our task of proclaiming the good news of Jesus Christ. We cannot deny the fact that there is still a sense of competition, even of superiority amongst us, which raises serious concerns about our commitment as individuals as well as a Church towards partnership and by implication towards unity.

Mission Schools (Primary and Middle Schools)

J. Herbert Lorrain and F.W. Savidge opened a small school in Aizawl and devised a script for the Mizo language in 1894. The school had to close for sometime but was reopened on 15th February 1898 by D.E. Jones. Prior to this a small school had been opened in Aizawl and another one by the Government where the Bengali script was being used and taught which the Mizos found very difficult.[6] Jones and Rowlands could provide food and lodging for about thirty pupils whereas the others had to find their own way of coping with the problems of schooling. Many Mizo boys started working in the Assam Rifles' camp as unskilled labourer in the kitchen and the canteens. They scrubbed and cleaned the cooking pots, and did a lot of other work, to support themselves in school. The subjects taught in the Aizawl School were the basic ones needed up to Primary, and, later up to Middle School standards. Lloyd rightly remarks that, "The interest in education was usually two fold. It was not merely a desire to learn, but also a spontaneous desire to share with others what had been acquired."[7] It is from the school that the early leaders of the Mizo Church received their education and emerged as leaders of their community.

The Mizos' passion for education was clearly evident from their eagerness to learn how to read and write right from the earliest years. Jones giving a report of their first year's work states:

> We gathered a few children and young men together, teaching them to read and write.... It is from four or five villages that most of them come, but occasionally some come from villages several days' distance. They carry enough rice to last for some time, and when they have had a head start they return again to their villages, and teach their fellows. In this way the number of readers increases even among those that have never been to school.[8]

Soon other schools were started by both the government and the missionaries. In 1901 schools were set up in three villages-Khawrihnim, Phulpui and Chhingchhip on an experimental basis. These schools were combined and set up permanently in Changzawl village with Hranga as the teacher.[9] By 1902 apart from the Mission school at Aizawl there were two other schools —one in Aizawl for the children of non- Mizos mainly the Nagas, and the other in Dokhama's village about two miles from Aizawl for Mizo children. These two schools were conducted and kept by unpaid Mizo students of the Mission school. Another school was also kept and conducted at Lalhrima's village (Sesawng), about twenty miles from Aizawl by Rowlands and two Mizo boys.[10] In 1903 three more schools were set up at Hriangmual, Thakthing and Chaprasis which were for the girls and three women who were studying in the Mission School taught in these schools.[11] It was only in 1903 that nine regular schools were started in the villages- the first one was opened at Khandaih in July and the other eight in the month of October.[12] An examination of the first report of the schools in Mizoram in *Mizo leh Vai Chanchin Bu*, a monthly magazine officially published by the Superintendent of Lushai Hills will show that 15 schools were listed in this report.[13]

In 1904 the Chief Commissioner of Assam visited Mizoram and was very impressed with the Mission schools in Aizawl and Lunglei. He therefore put the entire educational work in North Mizoram under the Presbyterian Mission and the education of the whole of South Mizoram under the Baptist Mission. Government schools at both stations were closed and incorporated with the Missions schools.[14] Since then for the next fifty years, until the Indian Government took over the schools in 1952, all education was in the hands of the Mizo Church.

Several primary schools were started as a result of the growing desire among the Mizos to have their own schools in their villages. The school buildings were always built by the Mizos themselves. Schools were set up even in villages where there were no or few Christians. Very soon there were about more than 200 primary schools just in Mizoram.[15] The first English Middle School Examination took place in 1909 and here six students - Saitawna, Khianga, Ngaihthangvunga, Saptea, Kawlkhuma and Lianhmingthanga passed the examination.[16] By 1973 Nair could state, 'No other part of the country can boast so many primary schools, middle schools, and high schools in relation to the size of its population.[17]

Hminga discussing the growth of Christianity during the first decade of the 18th century (1904-1914) states:

> The growth during the first half (1904-1909) then was mainly through the mission school at Aizawl and Serkawn. About half of the Christian community was likely to be in and around the two mission compounds and the rest were perhaps, one by one conversion here and there in the villages through the work of the itinerant evangelists and those converted in the mission schools, and [who] had gone back to their villages.[18]

Thus it is clear that we cannot underestimate the value and contributions of the Mission schools and the Mizos themselves in the evangelization of the Mizos. We would not be wrong in saying that many people became Christians because of the education they received in these schools. Examining the studies and research done by Hminga on the period 1915-1924 it is evident that the Church in South Mizoram was comparatively smaller than that of North Mizoram. Hminga attributed the difference in growth to the number of schools: "The outstanding difference, I noticed, was the number of schools in the North.... Since these early missions school teachers were all preachers, church planters and church leaders, North Mizoram had a much larger number of workers to gather the harvest."[19]

Saiaithanga had listed out eight major impacts and influences of the schools among the Mizos which cannot really be considered or separated from the impact and influence of Christianity namely- change in the manner of socializing as well as in the venue where such socializing would take place; giving up of bad habits; promoting solidarity among the Mizos; rendering help to neighbours during festivities and in times of bereavement; end to superstitions; encouraging acts of love among the people, promoting selflessness and humility and the overall development of the people.[20] It is quite obvious then, that education and the spread of the Gospel went together. They were like two streams flowing together in harmony.

The Mizo Teachers

According to J. Herbert Kane, Education has always been an integral part of the missionary movement.... Teaching held an important place in the public ministry of Christ... and played a large role in the development of the early church.[21] This was especially true in Mizoram. The whole system of school education during the early period which was under the missionaries had a great impact in the Christianization of the state.

Commenting on the growth of education in Mizoram Mendus, acknowledging the role played by the Mizo schools teachers stated:

> ...it surprises one that such progress in education has been achieved within so short a time. Such progress would not have been possible apart from the sacrificial devotion and effort of my predecessors, Rev. D.E. Jones and Rev. Edwin Rowlands who founded this schools, also Rev. and Mrs. Sandy, who, with the help of their Lushai assistants, were responsible from bringing this school, together with village school education in general, to the present standard.[22]

Saiaithanga while commenting on how the missionaries would as soon as possible open schools, send out evangelists and start some medical work, also pointed out how the missionaries took care of several poor young men, mostly victims of the famine of 1911.[23] They were provided food and lodging and also given education. The homes that were set up for them were known as "*Chawm In*" (Sponsored Homes). These homes produced some important early Mizo Christian leaders: pastors such as Hranga; itinerant preachers such as Thangupaa and Vanzika and school teachers like Vaikhawla and Dohleia. Saaithanga however added that these homes were more important and significant in terms of taking care of the poor rather than as centres for the spread of the Gospel.[24]

Lalnghinglova has grouped the native teachers into three groups:

1. Travelling teachers who were sent by the missionaries to tour the villages and teach the villagers how to read and write. They were not paid by the mission and had to accept and

live on the hospitality of the villagers they visited during their stay in those particular villages. Even non- Christians were involved in this kind of teaching.

2. Permanent teachers who are employed by the Mission. The Mission began appointing permanent mission teachers to villages by 1903.

3. Those teachers who underwent the teachers' training course. The Mission began training their teachers from 1927 onwards.[25]

It has already been pointed out that right from the beginning the Mizos who learnt to read and write would go and teach the others as soon as they themselves had mastered it. They therefore played a very important role in the spread of education and thereby creating a new awareness among the people. Apart from this they also shared their new knowledge of the Gospel. As early as 1900, Jones was able to write in his report, "By this time some of the Lushais help us in our work, both in teaching and preaching."[26]

Education in Mizoram did not begin in a formal western manner, but began initially in a small groups sitting on the floor following the tribal style of informal learning. As Lorrain stated:

> Should a boy be doing simple words only, one who can read better than himself has to help him along, so as a rule they are allotted off two and two, and they do not learn in silence, but the hum of their voices the whole of the time is a strange feature of their mode of grasping knowledge: it greatly increases their ability to receive instruction, and so such a thing as silence in the school is unknown.[27]

Jones probably referring to the three schools that were opened in three villages in 1901[28] describes in his report of 1901-1902 how for the first time Mizo teachers were sent out to conduct schools in other parts of the country for a short period. He states:

> Thanga, Chonga, and Toka were the first teachers to start elementary schools in the villages. They, with five others, are supported by us personally, so that they went without salaries, on trial. While they are out in the villages they get their food by public subscriptions of so many tinful of rice, & c. schools have been built at those villages by the villagers some months ago.[29]

These teachers were the first group of teachers as grouped by Lalnghinglova. These were the young men and women who had taught in the temporary schools which have been mentioned earlier in this paper. Rowlands expresses how their Mizo students especially those in the higher classes have proved very useful, both in preaching and teaching saying, "The school could not be carried on without paid teachers were it not for their aid- they make excellent teachers."[30]

The second group of teachers- those employed by the Mission and appointed to certain villages in 1903, were Dorikhuma, Chhunruma and Hrangsaipuia. After them Viakhawla, Lianhnuna, Chalkunga, Tumbila and Dohnuna were appointed. These first mission teachers were one of the most important foundations of the Church in Mizoram as well of the society. Their work, apart from teaching, consisted of preaching the Gospel, planting churches as well as looking after these churches.[31] Often they would be travelling, preaching the Gospel in far off places.

By 1927 mission teachers received training at the Mission station in Aizawl.[32] The training was a one year course. The first Mizo teacher was Pasena.[33] Williams gives us a clear picture on how the Mission teachers were trained in his report, which reads:

Besides studying the Theory and Method of teaching they had an opportunity of doing practical teaching in a vacant school near here which can be visited day by day.... They received some theological training in the Theological School here, so that they might be able to lead with the Sunday School and other meetings.[34]

Evangelization

As already mentioned the Mizo Mission school teachers played an important role in the evangelization of the Mizo people. They were more concerned about evangelization and the preaching of the Gospel than the everyday regular school work, and consider preaching and sharing the Gospel as the most important and foremost responsibility and duty of a school teacher.[35] One of the subjects taught in the Schools was the Scriptures.[36]

Only two or three missionary families were in each half of the state at any one time. The missionaries simply followed Paul's exhortation to Timothy: 'And the things which you have heard from me in the presence of many witnesses, these entrust to faithful men, who will be able to teach others also' (2 Tim. 2:2). Jones and Rowlands first took teenage boys with them on evangelistic tours. When village schools were started, Mizo Christian teacher-evangelists were left in charge of these.[37] Apart from these foreign missionaries and the few itinerant evangelists, the school teachers were the ones who preached the Gospel and brought many to Christ. Through education they managed to rouse the interest of the people to become Christians. Teachers at the end of the school term would go off on their own, travelling to distant places to preach the Good News to others. As early as 1901 we have a report of Toka, one of the first three Mizo teachers sending to the missionaries the *kelmei*[38] of a man, which signified that the owner had discontinued his belief in the protection of the spirits, and that he wished to become a Christian.[39]

Zairema writing in 1978 clearly asserted that "It is not possible to talk about the work in the Lushai hills without considering the contribution made by primary school teachers."[40] Mendus, describing his visit to villages on the Mizoram- Chin Hills border in 1939, believed that pagan superstitions still existed in the region because of the lack of sufficient schools and Christian teachers. He later found out to his joy and surprise that there were many who were willing to become Christians but were still not because they did not have teachers and the mission stations were nine or ten days journey away from these villages and the pastor of the district could only pay them occasional visits. He had also expressed his hope that the very next year a teacher would be placed there.[41]

Church Planting and Administration

During the early days of Christianity in Mizoram, the churches in Aizawl were taken care of by the missionaries. In villages there were self made leaders, and wherever there was a school it was the school teachers who were the Church leaders. Right from the start, the leadership in the churches was taken over by those involved and responsible for the schools. Many of those who later became ordained pastors were earlier school teachers.

The school teachers had the responsibility of planting a church in the villages where they had their school. Wherever a Christian congregation came into existence, they were the natural leaders. The teachers were given the status of Church elders by the foreign missionaries and were given membership to the presbytery.[42] They served as Chairman, Secretary, Preacher and Sunday School teacher of the churches. After the ordination of Elders was introduced in 1910, most of the Mission teachers were ordained. Though there were still a considerable number of teachers who were not ordained, they were usually looked up to as leaders. Lalhmuaka comments, "We would not be wrong in saying that the Pastors and the Evangelists ministered the Churches which the teachers have planted"[43] thus makes clear the position of the Mission teachers.

The schools under the care of by the Mission encouraged the spread of the Gospel because the teachers were like pastors though they were not ordained. Even in villages where there were no Christians, there were soon believers because of the the schools and subsequently a congregation soon grew. For a long time these schools were the main agents for the growth of the Church and the Christians in Mizo society. The teachers did not confine their teaching to basic education but were also religious teachers. They played the multiple roles of school teacher, preacher as well as evangelist.[44]

Even after the emergence of ordained pastors from 1913, such pastors were still very few in number and their pastorates were very large. The pastors had to spend most of their time travelling from one village pastorate to another. They would be responsible for a district of roughly 30 to 50 square miles, and often had to undertake a day's journey through the jungle between each village.[45] Therefore they do not have enough time to even look after the church in the area where they were residing. It fell on the Mission teachers to look after these churches. Their position was somewhat like the position of modern days Probationary Pastors or Assistant Pastors.[46] Mendus writing about new village school teachers being sent by the Mission commented on their usefulness saying, "This is a great help for the Church. If the mission can put a teacher in every village, it will be very good for the Church."[47]

Even after the Presbyterian system of Church administration was introduced in North Mizoram the schools teachers continued to play an important role and position in the Church administration. According to the Minute of the first presbytery held in North Mizoram in April 22 1910 at Aizawl, one of the decisions taken (listed as decision no. 10), was the inclusion of the teachers as members in the Presbytery meetings.[48]

Village Leaders

The school teachers were considered leaders of the villages and the community.[49] They emerged as the key-figures in village life. Their schools were there with the consent of the village chiefs and the villagers. They were recognized by the Government and supported by the missionaries. Their position therefore was a strong one.[50]

According to Lalchhinga as told to him by his father who was one of the advisers to a chief, the chief would often seek the advice of the teachers in the administration of his village.[51] The chiefs would even want to have school teachers as their elders to help rule the villages. Some of the Mission teachers accepted this position, but most did not. They are often invited to attend the village meetings called by the chiefs. If the teachers accepted the invitation, they were treated almost like the chief's prime minister.[52] Lalnghinglova has given us a description of one such meeting- The village elders of five villages- Phulpui, Sateek, Sumsuih, Hmuifang and Tachhip, which was under one chief, Kamliana met together. A Mission teacher Dorikhuma led the meeting. The issues he raised were:

1. No one should drink liquor, including the chief and his elders, in such meetings.

2. The meeting should begin with a Bible reading.

3. The chief should be like the British Queen

4. The chief should favour his elders.

5. The chief should have a good relationship with the Church leaders.[53]

Thus it is clear that teachers had great influence in village life. Lloyd rightly comments that they "usually raised the moral tone of a village, guided people away from superstition and provided for many an access to the wider world."[54]

The teachers were expected to do what no one else could do. They represented the development and changes that were taking place in Mizoram. In them the sacred and secular activities were inextricably linked. They were the leaders in both the religious and the social spheres of the villages. They took part and were involved in all religious and social activities. They were members of different committees such as the Church, the Young Lushai Association, the Sunday School, etc. They educated the villagers in how to lead more hygienic lifestyles. Jones has given us insights of the teachers' activities from the diary[55] of one village-teacher named Kunga.

> This is how Kunga describes his own work day by day- "A teacher has to do a lot of unpaid work…. Some of the odd jobs he has to do are to dig a grave…. Make a hoe,,, help the chief to make a chest… and stay with the mourners. At one time those who stayed to comfort the mourners spent their time telling funny stories, but now the teacher talks about salvation through Christ…. The teacher may suggest a way of improving the village and may point out some of the bad habits in the village (bad for either health or morals)[56]

According to Mendus, "A good teacher is more than a teacher. He is a leader. If he is a strong spiritual personality he may transform a whole village."[57]

A course in First-Aid was also given to the teachers[58] and so they played an important role in the health care of the community. They would visit the sick-praying and giving medical advice as best as they could.

Conclusion

This brief study of the role of the Mission school teachers in the spread of the Gospel in Mizoram in the early days of Christianity has attempted to put into perspective the vital and largely unsung role that they had played. In doing so, the paper clearly points out the important connection between education and the transformation it brings about in society.

We need to remind ourselves in a gathering such as this that witnessing to Christ will always be closely linked with humanitarian services that will promote beneficial change in society. "Witnessing" to Christ has, over a period of time conjured up a rather romantic image of either "speaking out" bravely in adverse conditions about the message of the Gospel, often at the risk of one's life or, on the other extreme, confining oneself to writing scholarly pieces of work, without being involved in the daily struggles of the common person on the street or even, of those of the Christian of today.

We need to sort out for ourselves what it is that witnessing to Christ today means. Indeed, does any church, denomination, culture or even scholar have the right to define what the ideal manner of witnessing is? Is witnessing only about "proclamation"? Is it only through the establishment of schools, colleges and hospitals? When a certain church or denomination boasts of being "missionary minded," what gives that church or denomination the right to boast? Additionally, what is the effect of such a boast on those around?

Our brief study has shown us the impact of education not just for social change but also for spiritual change. This is relevant for the times that we live in where we are caught between the two extremes of exclusive schools charging expensive fees and schools with overcrowded classrooms but charging lesser fees. In such a situation, what roles do Christian teachers and schools play?

The Church in India today boasts of some of the finest educational institutions under its care: from the Presbyterian and Baptist schools in the North-East to schools and colleges belonging to the Church of North India; from the educational institutions of the South Indian churches to the reputed schools and colleges run by the Roman Catholic Church that are spread over almost all parts of the country.[59] Parents aspire to get their children admitted into 'missionary schools' and those who have had a 'convent education' are much in demand when it comes to employment or even at the time of matrimony.[60]

Consequently the Church in India today faces the enormous responsibility of making education relevant so that those who learn will find employment and make themselves useful members of society. At the same time Church-run institutions must proclaim the good news of Christ and His relevance in today's world. It must balance the need to proclaim the Gospel, with its responsibility towards social issues and clearly show the connection between the two.

We can thus observe the struggle the Church must go through as it seeks to use education as a tool for empowerment, both socially as well as spiritually. A relevant and dynamic curriculum must be developed which will address the needs not only of society but also of the total person studying it. There are bound to be struggles and questions, not just within the Church but also between the Church and secular society. One of the lively issues within the Christian schools "… is the serious conflict being experienced theologically or politically, concerning the contemporary meaning of the Gospel and the church's responsibility towards social issues."[61]

In examining the unsung role that the mission school teacher in Mizoram played, we too must be challenged to reexamine our understanding of mission. We need to be reminded that school education is also Christian mission and that we are in danger of sacrificing this important aspect of witnessing for the sake of more income from our schools in the form of higher fees, "donations," and other subtle forms of corruption in our educational system as well as in the administration of many Church-run schools.

In recognizing the vital role of education in witnessing to Christ, we are then reminded of the Teacher whose sacrificial love forms the basis and core of our mission here on earth.

Endnotes

[1] Saiaithanga, *Mizo Kohhran Chanchin* (History of the Mizo Church), 1969, 1973, 3rd ed. (Aizawl: Mizo Theological Literature Committee, 1993), 19.

[2] David Edwards, "Reports of the North Lushai Hills 1936-37," in *Reports of the Foreign Mission of the Presbyterian Church of Wales on Mizoram 1894-1957*, comp., K. Thanzauva (Aizawl: The Synod Literature and Publication Boards, 1997), 137. Mizoram was known as the Lushai Hills District till September 1954 when it was changed to 'Mizo Districts'. In 1972 it was made a Union Territory and in 1987 it was granted full statehood. Therefore, the term Lushai and Mizo will be interchangeably used.

[3] The first missionary to visit Mizoram was Rev. William Williams a young Presbyterian missionary who arrived at Aizawl on 20th March1891 and remained there till 17th April. On January 1894 J.H. Lorraine and F.W. Savidge came under the Arthington Aborigine Mission and worked for almost four years. Then on 30th August 1897 Rev D.E. Jones of the

Welsh Presbyterian Mission (then known as The Calvinistic Methodist Foreign Mission arrived in Aizawl and on 1898 was joined by Rev. Edwin Rowlands. These two missionaries had the whole of Mizoram as their field of service till the coming of the Baptist Missionary Society which took over the South Mizo Hills and started work in 1903. Within a few years the whole of Mizoram was Christianized and today all but for a few who claim to be Jews are Christians.

[4] For example, in R. Lalsawmliana, *Rawngbawltu Ropui Rev Saiaithanga* (Aizawal: Lalthanliani Tuikhuah Tlang, 1993), written in Mizo and considered to be a very important resource book about the history of the Church in Mizoram, a very clear distinction appears to have been made between pastors and evangelists and Church elders on one hand and the Mission School teachers on the other hand. The first group are referred to as '*Kohhran Rawngbawltute*' (Church workers or those serving the Church or in service of the Church). There are also several writings and lists made of ordained pastors, evangelists and Bible women, and church elders in order that their contributions to the life of the Church in Mizoram would be remembered and their stories not forgotten. One example would be Rev. Lalnghinglova, *Zoram Nghahchhan* (Zoram Foundation) (1993), where the author had given space to the mission school teachers and their contributions. At the end of the book he lists out the names of the early evangelists, the pastors and the Bible women beginning from the year 1903 to 1994 (up to 1968 with references to the evangelists and up to 1939 with references to the Bible women). Both the books were written to commemorate the Gospel Centenary in Mizoram (1894-1994), emphasizing and given importance to the life and witness of the early pastors- in other words specifically to ordained ministry.

[5] The concept of mission/witness as partnership and networking is emphasized under Study Theme V: Forms of Missionary Engagement. For more details see Daryl Balia and Kirsteen Kim, eds., *Edinburgh 2010: Witnessing to Christ Today* (Oxford: Regnum Books International, 2010), 128-32.

[6] John Hughes Morris, *The Story of our Foreign Mission* (Presbyterian Church of Wales) (Aizawl: Synod Publication Board,1990), First published by Hugh Evans & Sons Ltd., in 1930, 81; Mention must be made here of the contributions and the important roles played by Rai Bahadur, an evangelist from Meghalaya and his wife who taught in the school; Lalhmuaka stated that the first school in the whole of Mizoram was a Government primary school in a certain village called Khawngbawk,

which was later shifted to Lunglei around 1902. See Lalhmuaka, *Zoram Zirna Lam Chhinchiahna* (The Records of Zoram Education) (Aizawl: Tribal Research Institute, 1981), 1.

⁷ L. Merion Llyod, *History of the Church in Mizoram* (Aizawl: Synod Publication Board, 1991), 63.

⁸ D. E. Jones, "The Report of the Lushai Hills 1898-99," in *Reports of the Foreign Mission Missions of the Presbyterian Church of Wales on Mizoram 1894-1957*, 3. It is significant to note that by the time the Mizos got formal education from the missionaries, other parts of North East India had already established their educational institutions and the respective governments had also established their own institutions and made grants to mission schools. For instance, the first English school in Assam was established at Guwahati in July 1835 with 58 students. The Serampore Baptist Missionaries started their first educational work among the Khasis in 1833. The first school in the Naga hills was opened in 1871. Missionaries started working in the Garo hills in 1868 and by 1891-92 there were 40 aided schools there. During 1891-92, in the Naga Hills there were 9 schools, and in the Khasi-Jaintia hills there were 141 schools. During the same period, in Mizoram there was neither a script for the language nor formal education in the modern sense. See J. V. Hluna, *Education and Missionaries in Mizoram* (Guwahati, Delhi: Spectrum Publications, 1992), 21-22. However, it is to be noted that as early as 1931 till date Mizoram ranks second in India about the literacy percentage.

⁹ The reason why the schools were not continued in the three villages is not known. Lalhmuaka is of the opinion that the revival of 1907 which had spread to Mizoram from Meghalaya was also felt in Changzawl village (the only known village in Mizoram where the revival was felt) because of the impact of the Mission school. During the revival 120 persons accepted the Christian faith. See Lalhmuaka, *Zoram Zirna Lam Chhinchiahna*, 17.

¹⁰ D. E. Jones & Edwin Rowlands, "The Report of the Lushai Hills 1902-1903," in *Reports of the Foreign Mission of the Presbyterian Church of Wales on Mizoram 1894-1957*, 16-18.

¹¹ Jones & Rowlands, "The Reports of the Lushai Hills 1903-04," in *Reports of the Foreign Mission of the Presbyterian Church of Wales on Mizoram 1894-1957*, 19-20. In the beginning education for girls was not much given importance as this was regarded as being of little or no value compared to the work which the girls could do at home in helping their parents. But the missionaries recognized its importance and believed that the Church could not develop soundly until women were treated as equals

and given their rightful place in it. Conditions began to change gradually and soon a number of girls' schools were opened. Out of these schools emerged many leading church workers like the Bible Women, and also school teachers. For details on female education in Mizoram see Hluna, *Education and Missionaries in Mizoram*, 148-81.

[12] The eight schools were opened in Khawrihnim, Phulpui, Zukbual, Lungtan, Biate, Khawreng, Hmunpui and, Maite. Hluna, *Education and Missionaries in Mizoram*, 20.

[13] Lalhmuaka, *Zoram Zirna Lam Chhinchiahna*, 17-19; and J. V. Hluna, *Education and Missionaries in Mizoram*, 56.

[14] Saiaithanga, *Mizo Kohhran Chanchin*, 41-42.

[15] Saiaithanga, *Mizo Kohhran Chanchin*, 42-43.

[16] Lalhmuaka, *Zoram Zirna Lam Chhinchiahna*, 21; and Saiaithanga, *Mizo Kohhran Chanchin*, 42.

[17] C. N. S. Nair, "Mizoram," in *The Illustrated Weekly of India Annual*, ed. Khuswant Singh (Bombay: Times of India Press, 1973), 184, quoted in Donna Strom, *Wind through the Bamboo: The Story of Transformed Mizos* (Madras: Evangelical Literature Service, 1983), 66.

[18] C. L. Hminga, *The Life and Witness of the Churches in Mizoram* (Lunglei, Mizoram: The Literature Committee, Baptist Church of Mizoram, 1987), 93.

[19] Hminga, *The Life and Witness of the Churches in Mizoram*, 111-121.

[20] Lalhmuaka, *Zoram Zirna Lam Chhinchiahn*, 66-67, quoting from Saiaithanga, *Mizo Kohhran Chanchin*, 131-144.

[21] J. Herbert Kane, *Understanding Christian Missions* (Grand Rapids, Michigan: Baker Book House, 1974), 318 as quoted in Donna Strom, *Wind through the Bamboo*, 49.

[22] Enoch Lewis Mendus, *The Diary of a Jungle Missionary* (1956; repr., Aizawl: The Synod Publication Board, 1984), 25.

[23] The famine was caused by the flowering of a certain type of bamboo, which flowers regularly every fifty years. They produce seeds, the main stems die off and new plants grow from the seeds. Insects, birds and rats feed on these seeds. With this unlimited natural food supply and perhaps due to some special vitamins or chemical contents, rats increased in astronomical proportion. When this food supply is exhausted they attack standing crops. They are known to destroy as much as twenty acres of rice field in a single night. Zairema, *God's Miracle in Mizoram: A Glimpse of Christian Work among Head-Hunters* (Aizawl: Synod Press, 1978), 7.

[24] Saiaithanga, *Mizo Kohhran Chanchin*, 23.

[25] Lalnghinglova Ralte, *Zoram Nghahchan*, 2nd ed. (Aizawl, Mizoram: The PresCom Production, 2000), 18-20.

[26] D. E. Jones, "The Report of The Lushai Hills 1900-1901," in *Reports of the Foreign Mission of the Presbyterian Church of Wales on Mizoram 1894-1957*, 9.

[27] Reginald A. Lorrain, *Five Years in Unknown Jungle* (London: Lakher Pioneer Mission, 1912), 232-233, quoted in Donna Strom, *Wind through the Bamboo*, 65.

[28] Schools in the villages of Khawrihnim, Phulpui and, Chhingchhip.

[29] Jones, "The Report of the Lushai Hills 1901-1902," 13.

[30] Edwin Rowlands, "The Report of the Lushai Hills 1902-1903" in *Reports of the Foreign Mission of the Presbyterian Church of Wales on Mizoram 1894-1957*, 18.

[31] Ralte, *Zoram Nghahchan*; Jones, "The Report of the Lushai Hills 1901-1902," 20.

[32] Jones, "The Report of the Lushai Hills, 1901-1902."

[33] Pasena had the privilege of visiting the mother church in 1895 when he was taken to Britain to do his training at Gold Smith College. He returned in the early part of 1926. See Banrilang Ryngnga, *The Life and Work of Revd. William Williams* (Aizawl: Synod Publication Board, 1994), 77; *Assembly of the Presbyterian Church in North East India, Golden Jubilee Souvenir* (1926-76), 6; and Lalhmuaka, *Zoram Zirna Lam Chhinchiahna*, 49.

[34] John Williams, "Report of the North Lushai Hills 1923-1929," and Jones, "The Report of the Lushai Hills 1901-1902," 89; both in in *Reports of the Foreign Mission of the Presbyterian Church of Wales on Mizoram 1894-1957*.

[35] Lalchhinga, *Mizo Kristian Kohhran: A Chanchin Hmasa Lam Leh Presbytery Neih Hnulamte* (1894-1939) (Aizawl: L. M. Press, 1996), 14.

[36] Lalhmuaka, *Zoram Zirna Lam Chhinchiahna*, 30.

[37] Strom, *Wind through the Bamboo*, 55-56.

[38] *Kelme*i is a tuft of goat's hair hanging from a string around the neck.

[39] Jones, "The Report of the Lushai Hills 1901-1902," 13.

[40] Zairema, *God's Miracle in Mizoram*, 29.

[41] E. L. Mendus, *Diary of a Jungle Missionary*, 118.

[42] P. C. Lalhmuaka, *Zoram- Thim Ata Engah* (Aizawl: Synod Publication Board, 1998), 112; and Lalchhinga, *Mizo Kristian Kohhran*, 14.

[43] Lalhmuaka, *Zoram- Thim Ata Engah*, 159.

[44] Saiaithanga, *Kohhran Chanchin*, 43&44; Lalchhinga, *Mizo Kristian Kohhran*, 14.

[45] E. L. Mendus, *The Diary of a Jungle Missionary*, 55.

[46] See Lalnghinglova Ralte, *Zoram Nghahchan*, 82.

[47] E. L. Mendus, "Report of the North Lushai Hills 1926-1927," in *Reports of the Foreign Mission of the Presbyterian Church of Wales on Mizoram 1894-1957*, 82.

[48] Lalchhinga, *Mizo Kristian Kohhran*, Appendix 1-2.

[49] Lalchhinga, *Mizo Kristian* Kohhran, 14.

[50] Llyod, *History of the Church in Mizoram*, 109 & 146.

[51] Lalchhinga, *Mizo Kristian Kohhran*, 14.

[52] Ralte, *Zoram Nghahchan*, 21-22.

[53] Ralte, *Zoram Nghahchan*, 21.

[54] Llyod, *History of the Church in Mizoram*, 146.

[55] Careful reports of the progress of their schools and activities were maintained by the village school teachers. These were assessed and scrutinized at regular intervals by the missionaries.

[56] D. E. Jones letter written on 18th May 1911 as cited by Llyod, *History of the Church in Mizoram*, 147.

[57] Mendus, *The Diary of a Jungle Missionary*, 118.

[58] F. J. Sandy, "The Report of the Lushai Hills 1916-1917," in *Reports of the Foreign Mission of the Presbyterian Church of Wales on Mizoram 1894-1957*, 61.

[59] A survey of the top engineering, medical and business schools in the country has thrown up the following results with reference to Christian institutions: in medicine CMC Vellore ranks 2nd with 54.7% and St John's Bangalore 8th with 39.2%. Among business schools XLRI Jamshedpur ranks 5th with 31.6%, Loyola Institute 16th with 13.7%, XIM Bhubaneswar 18th with 11% and Christ College Bangalore with 9%. *Recruiter's Choice: A Career Graph-Mode Survey*, Supplement to *The Telegraph* (Kolkata), March 2005, 31&47.

[60] For example, an advertisement in the classifieds asks for a lady/gent with convent background for various positions in a 5 Star hotel. In

the same newspaper the matrimonial classifieds describe the prospective bride as "convent-educated, slim and beautiful." *The Telegraph* (Kolkata), Classifieds February 13, 2005, 1 & 3.

[61] Makato Midzuno, "Liberation from Education and Uniformity - A Japanese View," in *An Encounter with Education for Liberation and Community*, ed. Toa Payoh (Singapore: Christian Conference of Asia, 1977), 14.

Bibliography

"Classifieds," *The Telegraph* (Kolkata), February 13, 2005.

Assembly of the Presbyterian Church in North East India, Golden Jubilee Souvenir (1926-76).

Balia, Daryl and Kirsteen Kim, eds. *Edinburgh 2010: Witnessing to Christ Today*. Oxford: Regnum Books International, 2010.

Edwards, David. "Reports of the North Lushai Hills 1936-37." In *Reports of the Foreign Mission of the Presbyterian Church of Wales on Mizoram 1894-1957*. Compiled by K. Thanzauva, 136-41. Aizawl: The Synod Literature and Publication Boards, 1997.

Hluna, J. V. *Education and Missionaries in Mizoram*. Guwahati, Delhi: Spectrum Publications, 1992.

Hminga, C. L. *The Life and Witness of the Churches in Mizoram*. Lunglei, Mizoram: The Literature Committee, Baptist Church of Mizoram, 1987.

Jones, D. E. "The Report of the Lushai Hills 1898-99." In *Reports of the Foreign Mission Missions of the Presbyterian Church of Wales on Mizoram 1894-1957*. Compiled by K. Thanzauva, 2-5. Aizawl: The Synod Literature and Publication Boards, 1997.

———. "The Report of The Lushai Hills 1900-1901." In *Reports of the Foreign Mission of the Presbyterian Church of Wales on Mizoram 1894-1957*. Compiled by K. Thanzauva, 9-11. Aizawl: The Synod Literature and Publication Boards, 1997.

Jones, D. E. and Edwin Rowlands. "The Report of the Lushai Hills 1902-1903." In *Reports of the Foreign Mission of the Presbyterian Church of Wales on Mizoram 1894-1957*. Compiled by K. Thanzauva, 16-19. Aizawl: The Synod Literature and Publication Boards, 1997.

Kane, J. Herbert. *Understanding Christian Missions*. Grand Rapids, Michigan: Baker Book House, 1974.

Lalchhinga. *Mizo Kristian Kohhran: A Chanchin Hmasa Lam Leh Presbytery Neih Hnulamte (1894-1939)*. Aizawl: L. M. Press, 1996.

Lalhmuaka, P. C. *Zoram- Thim Ata Engah*. Aizawl: Synod Publication Board, 1998.

Lalhmuaka, *Zoram Zirna Lam Chhinchiahna* (The Records of Zoram Education). Aizawl: Tribal Research Institute, 1981.

Llyod, L. Merion *History of the Church in Mizoram*. Aizawl: Synod Publication Board, 1991.

Lorrain, Reginald A. *Five Years in Unknown Jungle*. London: Lakher Pioneer Mission, 1912.

Mendus, E. L. "Report of the North Lushai Hills 1926-1927." In *Reports of the Foreign Mission of the Presbyterian Church of Wales on Mizoram 1894-1957*. Compiled by K. Thanzauva, 79-85. Aizawl: The Synod Literature and Publication Boards, 1997.

Mendus, Enoch Lewis. *The Diary of a Jungle Missionary*. 1956. Reprint. Aizawl: The Synod Publication Board, 1984.

Midzuno, Makato. "Liberation from Education and Uniformity - A Japanese View." In *An Encounter with Education for Liberation and Community*. Edited by Toa Payoh. Singapore: Christian Christian Conference of Asia, 1977.

Morris, John Hughes. *The Story of our Foreign Mission* (*Presbyterian Church of Wales*). Aizawl: Synod Publication Board, 1990.

Nair, C. N. S. "Mizoram." In *The Illustrated Weekly of India Annual*. Edited by Khuswant Singh, 182-184. Bombay: Times of India Press, 1973.

R. Lalsawmliana, *Rawngbawltu Ropui Rev Saiaithanga*. Aizawal: Lalthanliani Tuikhuah Tlang, 1993.

Ralte, Lalnghinglova *Zoram Nghahchan*. 2nd ed. Aizawl, Mizoram: The PresCom Production, 2000.

Recruiter's Choice: A Career Graph-Mode Survey, supplement to *The Telegraph* (Kolkata), March 2005.

Rowlands, Edwin. "The Report of the Lushai Hills 1902-1903." In *Report of the Foreign Mission of the Presbyterian Church of Wales on Mizoram 1894-1957*. Compiled by K. Thanzauva, 16-19. Aizawl: The Synod Literature and Publication Boards, 1997.

Ryngnga, Banrilang. *The Life and Work of Revd. William Williams*. Aizawl: Synod Publication Board, 1994.

Saiaithanga. *Mizo Kohhran Chanchin* (History of the Mizo Church). 3rd ed. Aizawl: Mizo Theological Literature Committee, 1993.

Sandy, F. J. "The Report of the Lushai Hills 1916-1917." In *Reports of the Foreign Mission of the Presbyterian Church of Wales on Mizoram 1894-1957*. Compiled by K. Thanzauva, 60-62. Aizawl: The Synod Literature and Publication Boards, 1997.

Strom, Donna. *Wind through the Bamboo: The Story of Transformed Mizos*. Madras: Evangelical Literature Service, 1983.

Williams, John. "Report of the North Lushai Hills 1923-1929." In *Report of the Foreign Mission of the Presbyterian Church of Wales on Mizoram 1894-1957*. Compiled by K. Thanzauva, 66-68. Aizawl: The Synod Literature and Publication Boards, 1997.

Zairema. *God's Miracle in Mizoram: A Glimpse of Christian Work among Head-Hunters*. Aizawl: Synod Press, 1978.

9
Missional Church in a Secular Age with Special Focus on the "Homo Areligiosus"

Martin Reppenhagen

Introduction

While being a guest student at Union Biblical Seminary I travelled extensively during the Christmas Break throughout India. Travelling alone and booking Sleeper Class Non-AC I found myself in the midst of Indian families, who were eager to get in contact with me. And there wasn't any problem to get in contact with each other e.g. on a train ride from Varanasi to Pune. We talked about my reasons for being in India, about my fiancée, who was still in Germany and wasn't with me – how astonishing, a Western young man without girlfriend travelling alone - about family and about religion. Nobody saw any difficulty to have a conversation with a stranger about such private things like family and religion. Religion was not just a private affair, but public truth. Even going to the Pharmacy in downtown Pune made that clear: Behind the counter everyone could see a picture of Christ witnessing to the fact, that the shop owner was a Christian.

Or just going to any of the shops downhill gives witness to the believes of the shop owner there. Mainly they worship Ganesh and I so often saw them celebrating a puja while a long line of customers were waiting with incredible patience outside the shop. No one complaint about the time spent for a religious undertaking in the world of business. No discussion at all.

Let us move some thousand kilometres westward to Europe. Let us board a train and spend a few hours on it. Most of the travellers will stick to their own. Just recently a little Indian girl, who was an a visit to Europe with her family, said to me: "They are all very serious on the train!" Usually you don't communicate with your fellow travellers. And even if you would, you start with the weather but usually don't come to family and religion. Family and religion are entities of the private sphere you hardly negotiate with others – especially not with strangers. Although you still find multitudes of church buildings from impressive medieval cathedrals to small village churches you won't find a business man or woman celebrating a short worship service while customers are waiting outside. That would just be unbelievable and unthinkable. Religion is for the private sphere and for the inside sphere of church buildings. In France, I was told, to ask your fellow worker a religious question, can be regarded as an offense and result in a dismissal by employer. Religion is private!

"The religious stance today is more internal than external, more individual than institutional, more experimental than cerebral, more private than public."[1] Of course the majority of Europeans still belong to either the Catholic or one of the major Protestant churches. But this says little about their religious practice and their believes.

> At the level of the individual, religion appears to be a multifaceted, often messy or even contradictory amalgam of beliefs and practices that no particular religious group that an individual belongs to necessarily considers acceptable or important. Individuals' lived religion is experienced and expressed in everyday practices (...). Religious socialization and ongoing interactions with others may inform, but cannot determine, each individual's personal practices and beliefs.[2]

And this happens usually in the publicly hidden rooms of privacy, which "means I leave my beliefs at home when I go to work or when I vote or run for public office."[3]

We shouldn't regard this development only as hostile to the Gospel. First of all we have to admit that from the discourse of modern societies you can't avoid the distinction between public and private. With these two spheres we have two distinct areas of accountability. Public offices and private roles of conduct are distinguished as well as public and private properties. This distinction is an important part of modern societies and modern legislation.[4] According to this differentiation religion belongs to the free space or shelter of the private room. Looking back to a medieval tradition in Europe, when religion was fixed by the ruler – *cuius regio, eius religio* – this achievement of Modern society has to be regarded as a positive development of religious freedom. And their can't be any doubt that even missionaries in the past were eager to promote the freedom of individuals to make decisions in religious matters.[5] For a religion focussing on conversion like the Christian faith does, religious freedom of the individual needs to be a major issue of mission.

Thus we may conclude that the privatization of religion is a result of religious freedom. Although it doesn't need to be a consequence. Did in the past the public religion rule the private, today we seem to have the opposite: religion is more

and more restrained to the private sphere having no significance
on the public market place, that religion "shall disappear
altogether except, possibly, in the private realm."[6] With the
words of Lesslie Newbigin we are confronted with "a system
of belief (…) which in principle denies the existence (…) of
realities other than those which can be measured by methods
of natural science."[7]

Secular Age

Speaking of "a secular age" as context for a missional church
we need to pause here for a while reflecting on secularization
and Charles Taylor. First of all we have to justify speaking
of secularization. 40 years ago there wouldn't have been the
need to justify the theory of secularization. The dynamics of
secularization in the Western world seemed to be obvious. Peter
L. Berger complaint in 1967 about the loss of religion in the
public sphere.[8] However 30 years later he withdrew his earlier
statement, that religions will disappear in modern societies and
speaks of a „desecularization of the world":

> My point is that the assumption that we live in a secularized world
> is false. The world today, with some exceptions (…) is as furiously
> religious as ever. This means that a whole body of literature by
> historians and social scientists loosely labelled 'secularization theory'
> is essentially mistaken. (…) The idea is simple: Modernization
> necessarily leads to a decline of religion, both in society and in
> the minds of individuals. And it is precisely this key idea that
> turned out to be wrong.[9]

Or in other words by the same Peter L. Berger: "Modernity
does not necessarily lead to a decline of religion. What it does
lead to, more or less necessarily, is religious pluralism."[10]

So what? Did religion survive secularization? Yes and no,
we may conclude. Religion still lives, but it changed extremely.
British sociologist Grace Davie coined it "believing without

belonging."[11] People still believe, but they don't believe in forms and terms of the traditional religions. Thus the term "spirituality" replaces more and more the term "religion."[12]

> In Europe as well as America, a new pattern is gradually emerging: that is a shift away from an understanding of religion as a form of obligation and towards an increasing emphasis on consumption or choice. (…) I go to church (or another religious organization) because I want to, maybe for a short period or maybe for longer, to fulfil a particular rather than a general need in my life and where I will continue my attachment so long as it provides what I want, but I have no *obligation* either to attend in the first place or to continue if I don't want to.[13]

Grace Davie focuses on a non-institutional religion saying that personal faith is experienced beneath the boundaries of institutional religions. Modern people don't look for institutions anymore to practice their personal believes; they look for "minimal religion" (Mikhail Epstein). Later Davie modified her understanding of "believing without belonging" speaking of a "vicarious religion" in Europe. With that she points to the fact, that only a minority of Europeans practice religion although they are not against religion, they just don't practice it.[14]

However this modern development leads to a kind of amnesia the French sociologist Danièle Hervieu-Léger pointed to:

> Modern societies seem to be more and more unfamiliar with religion; but it is not, as classical secularization theory claims, because they are more and more rational; it is because they are more and more amnesic, because they are less and less able to develop a living collective memory as a source of meaning for the present and orientations for the future.[15]

There isn't any more one religion or one ideology to take up the responsibility of being a collective memory of society. However people respond to religion, it "remains powerful in memory; but also as a kind of reverse fund of spiritual force or consolation."[16]

Despite all these different kinds of religious attitudes people live in a kind of immanent frame, which can't be questioned. According to Charles Taylor these closed world structures "function as unchallenged axioms." Thus living in an entirely immanent world one doesn't understand, why anybody can believe in a transcendent being – there is "no echo outside."[17] And he asks the simple question: "Why was it virtually impossible not to believe in God in, say, 1500 in our Western society, while in 2000 many of us find this not only easy, but even inescapable?"[18] And this is not just a question of creeds, of sentences of faith, but of experience and how we look at the world and ourselves.[19]

I am not going to focus now on Taylor's answers, how this development could happen from late Medieval difficulties with religious hierarchical systems or Reformation day until today. Just one glimpse here. One reason, Taylor argues, for renouncing the faith in a personal God being less mature for going for a materialist epistemology with clear general laws was not so much because of scientific proofs but that one system (science) replaced the other (religion).[20]

Again we should be hesitant to regard this only as a negative development. Referring to Charles Taylor we live in a disenchanted world and this for good reasons. We are no longer just vulnerable to external forces, we are free human beings. We are human agents and as such human beings "are rational, sociable agents who are meant to collaborate in peace to their mutual benefit.". This is a kind of new social order not depending on the "law of a people" or any hierarchy.[21] In modern societies "we have moved from a hierarchical order of personalized links to an impersonal egalitarian one, from a vertical world of mediated access to horizontal, direct-access societies."[22]

This ambivalent development, having positive and negative elements, in mind, we turn to the East German context. Here it is quite obvious, that we live in a world with "no echo outside". Even a "minimal religion" seems to be beyond reality. When Charles Taylor speaks of a "'post-secular' Europe" he may think of Russia, Poland and many other European countries, but not of the Czech Republic and East Germany. Here "the level of understanding of some of the great languages of transcendence" have almost completely disappeared and a "massive unlearning is taking place" or better: a massive unlearning is already completed.[23] In an interview a young man was asked: "What does God mean for you?", answer: "Nothing!", "And Jesus?", answer: "Also nothing!". He then added: "I am not superstitious!"[24] A manager was asked, whether he believes in God and he answered: "This question confuses me. I have asked such a question!" Around ¾ of the East German population don't belong to any Christian church or to any other religion.

Secularized Germany or "Homo Areligious"

At the end of the 19. Century German mission theologian Gustav Warneck could say at an international conference:

> Dear Brethern in England and America, I believe that I speak in the name of all my German fellow-believers, if I urge upon you to cease from looking upon Germany, the land of Luther and Melanchthon, Arndt and Spener, Francke and Zinzendorf, Tholuck, Fliedner and Wichern, as a half heathen and rationalistic country.[25]

However today we must say most of the places of Luther and Francke, Zinzendorf and Tholuck are mainly atheist. With "atheist" I mean here not, that the majority of people are against God. They just don't ask religious questions. To make it clear, they are no militant atheists, and even to call them atheists, would be a kind of rating far beyond their understanding. "Theos" is just beyond their understanding. They don't feel any deficit here. They don't miss anything. They are just normal!

Thus German sociologist Detlef Pollack challenged the theory of a non-institutionalized spirituality. According to his empirical data there is an ongoing decline of religious thoughts and practices. Only 7% of those in the West of Germany practice a kind of non-institutional spirituality. There is no evidence, that those leaving the church are now practicing their faith individually.[26] In the East of Germany it is even less. Thus the East of Germany is the least religious country of whole of Europe, where the majority is atheist.[27]

The reason for this development are manifold. It would be too easy to blame the Communist regime of the former GDR alone for that development. The roots of this massive development can be traced back to the 18th century and to church circles as well. However during the 40 years of communist regime major waves of decline in church membership took place. In 1952/53 the government started a new secular rite de passage, trying to replace the confirmation for youngsters at the age of 14 years. In 1956 the churches were called "legal positions of adversarial forces in the GDR."[28] Other waves of decline followed. Strange as it may be, although there was political pressure in the GDR especially upon those working in the field of administration, education and politics, only 20% of those who left the church said, that they felt political pressure fording them to leave the church.[29] The protestant majority church was on her move towards a minority church. And this process is still going on.[30] Even today a re-entry to the church seems to be beyond reach.[31]

East Germany seems to be along with the Czech Republic, Slovenia and Sweden the most successful part of the world in doing so. There is no religious quest at all! Even after the unification of the former Federal Republic of Germany and the German Democratic Republic East Germany has never experienced a return to church or a turning to alternative religious cults, neither to individualised religious practices nor to new forms of communal cults.[32] East Germany is as un- or areligious as Bavaria is catholic, catholic philosopher Eberhard Tiefensee says. East Germans even don't go to the Dalai Lama as their West German counterparts do. Referring to Max Weber we can say: East Germans are religiously "unmusical". However even that seems to be too much. In contrast to Max Weber, who was aware of religion, the majority of East Germans wouldn't call themselves "unreligious" or "religiously unmusical." Against Thomas Luckmann's thesis of an "invisible religion" he coins the term "homo areligiosus." However they just think they are normal. Only Christians call them "unreligious." Thus the religious quest will only be asked when Christians interact with them bringing with them the religious quest.[33] We may say that even the "spirituality of quest", Charles Taylor spoke of, is missing.[34]

But here we find Christians who actually have lost the language to articulate religious experience, to express their faith in ways the "homo areligious" can understand. Here we must say, that the loss of language is always a loss of reality.[35] Thus we need Christian communities as safe rooms to learn the language of faith while using the contacts the church still has with other organisations of society. For the East German context this actually means to add to the dialogue of religions the dialogue with the secularized or absolutely religion less people.

The Correspondence Between Faith and Church Membership

After "believing without belonging"[36] (Grace Davie) or "belonging without believing"[37] (Danièle Hervieu-Léger) or "belonging without even believing in belonging"[38] (Hans Raun Iversen) I would suggest "not-believing follows not-belonging" to describe the East German situation. You find very little evidence for spirituality or religiosity outside the church.[39]

The inner relationship between church membership and believe is supported by the research work done by Robin Gill. "Decline in Christian beliefs will follow rather than precede a decline in churchgoing and Sunday School attendance"[40] Detlef Pollack concludes the same for the East German situation. Although people in- and outside the church disputes it, there is an inner relationship between personal interaction with church and personal faith. People err about the conditions of faith.[41]

Thus there is a need to give as many opportunities for modern people to get in contact with church. Or to put it in the words of Michael Herbst: "We have to show that evangelism is a permanent dimension of a local church that is open and inviting, that loves to give a warm welcome to seekers, and that longs to give unchurched people as many opportunities as possible to experience the gospel."[42] And here we may refer again to Charles Taylor saying: "The fate of belief depends much more than before on powerful intuitions of individuals radiating out to others." Here Taylor points to the needed relations "between modes of quest and centres of traditional religious authority, between what Wuthnow calls dwellers and seekers."[43]

Looking for a Missional Church in a Secular Age

Looking at secularization with a special emphasis on East Germany we should now focus on a "missional church in a secular age." How can the church still be the church in a time of decline regarding church members and growth of those having no religion? I again cite Charles Taylor: "We shouldn't forget the spiritual costs of various kinds of forced conformity: hypocrisy, spiritual stultification, inner revolt against the Gospel, the confusion of faith and power, and even worse"[44] The solution can't be a call back to the traditional model of a Christendom church and society, which modelled Europe and North America for, let's say, 1600 years.

Here I would like to turn to the discussion of a "missional church" which can be traced back to the writings of late Lesslie Newbigin, formerly missionary and bishop of the Church of South India. Although "missional" is a British term, it only recently gained prominence in the North American discussion about a "missional church" actually started within the Gospel and Our Culture Network (GOCN) and here especially with "Missional Church: A Vision for the Sending of the Church in North America" edited by Darrell L. Guder in 1998. With the neologism "missional church" a paradigm shift is named, which breaks with the traditional understanding of mission as an church enterprise among others and focuses on mission as the *esse* not only *bene esse* of church. During the last 10 years "missional church" has become a buzz word in the North American context and beyond.[45] Among the contributors you find theologians from the mainline churches, Anabaptists and those more or less affiliated with the postmodern "emerging church" movement.

Despite many differences they share the opinion, that "mission needs to drive our understanding of ecclesiology."[46] And they may all be called "ecclesiologies at the margin" as the Dutch practical theologian Henk de Roest did.[47] One should look even beyond the term "missional" for missional ecclesiologies. Thus e.g. Jacques Matthey calls for a missiology, where the church as community of believers plays the major role in mission.[48]

According to those involved in the GOCN the term "missional" points to a paradigm shift:

> The church of Jesus Christ is not the purpose or goal of the gospel, but rather its instrument and witness. (...) It has taken us decades to realize that mission is not just a programme of the church. It defines the church as God's sent people. Either we are defined by mission, or we reduce the scope of the gospel and the mandate of the church. Thus our challenge today is to move from church with mission to missional church.[49]

For this Lois Barrett gives a very good definition of a "missional church" when she states:

> A missional church is a church that is shaped by participating in God's mission, which is to set things right in a broken, sinful world, to redeem it, and to restore it to what God has always intended for the world. Missional churches see themselves not so much sending, as being sent. A missional congregation lets God's mission permeate everything that the congregation does – from worship to witness to training members for discipleship. It bridges the gap between outreach and congregational life, since, in its life together, the church is to embody God's mission.[50]

The signal word pointing to the new situation respectively the need for an ecclesiological paradigm shift is "post-Christendom."

And Henk de Roest proposes to speak of "marginal or peripheral communities" with hint to the missional church.[51]

According to a missional ecclesiology the church is catholic or universal and contextual. For its sending into the world the church has a specific responsibility: "To be translators of the gospel today". With this task the church is pointed to every context and culture, in which the church stays. For that particular context or culture the gospel should be preached and translated. This is however not primarily a literal undertaking, but an incarnational process. It is the gospel witness "expressed by persons of the receiving culture." [52] The church's responsibility is to develop a kind of strategy on "how to be a contextually relevant church."[53] Within every specific cultural context is the need to develop a unique local theology, which according to Robert J. Schreiter has three roots: "The three principal roots beneath the growth of local theology are gospel, church, and culture."[54] And culture is shortly characterized by Louis J. Luzbetak as *"a society's design for living."*[55]

> Mission is to be a continuing process of translation and witness, whereby the evangelist and the mission community will discover again and again that they will be confronted by the gospel as it is translated, heard, and responded to, and will thus experience ongoing conversion while serving as witness.[56]

Starting point for that ongoing process of translation is the translability of the gospel. The gospel is "fundamentally missionary in nature, universal in scope, and, necessarily, translatable into the particular."[57] Here I just point briefly to the distinction of diffusion and incarnation as models of spreading the gospel resp. the distinction of "global Christianity" and "world Christianity."[58] Not western globalisation is the focus, but local involvement following God's universal but yet local working.[59] For a better understanding of a missional and incarnational approach I cite Lamin Sanneh, who speaks of an "indigenous discovery of Christianity rather than the Christian discovery of indigenous societies."[60] According to a missional approach the encounter between gospel and local culture should enable the local culture to understand the gospel as its own. This means "the fundamental missionary experience is to live on terms set by others."[61] German mission theologian Henning Wrogemann has coined the term "symbiotic evangelisation" to express this important dynamic relationship between gospel and culture resp. between evangelist and listener.[62] To be able allowing a "symbiotic evangelisation" there is the need for a "hermeneutic of intercultural understanding", which means, that the other is not just object of the message but in his otherness subject.[63]

To the church's public vocation belongs a "fundamental vocation of *not* belonging" to the powers and reigns of this world.[64] However I wonder whether a missional ecclesiology needs to follow the Anabaptist tradition with a very strict understanding of the church as social ethics and a tendency of having an anticultural approach keeping church and world in antithesis. Countercultural of course, but not anticultural. Then "if the church is to be the church, it must not only practice its beliefs within the community, it must show forth what they imply for the larger society (…),",[65] Robert N. Bellah can say. And Robert J. Schreiter means: "Good evangelization will also bring about culture change."[66] I would therefore suggest for the missional church to be a "public companion: as such, the emerging missional church acknowledges a *conviction* that it participates in the Triune God's ongoing creative work; in civil society the missional church exhibits a *compassionate commitment* to other institutions and their predicaments (…)

to *create* and *strengthen* the fabrics that fashion a life-giving and life-accountable world".[67] With the words of Lamin Sanneh "the gospel exists not to alienate but to invigorate and transform. It conflicts only and unavoidably with idolatries of race, nation, and power."[68]

However to be a transformed and transforming dynamic in this world the church needs to be reminded that she is

> a sign, pointing men to something that is beyond their present horizon but can give guidance and hope now; an instrument (not the only one) that God can use for his work of healing, liberating, and blessing; and a first fruit - a place where men and women can have a real taste now of the joy and freedom God intends for all.[69]

This we may call a church of authenticity. In such a church the dynamics of the church of faith radiates despite all shortcomings, dubieties and endangering through church of reality.[70]

I am suggesting that the only answer, the only hermeneutic of the gospel, is a congregation of men and women who believe it and live by it.[71] "The church displays the first fruits of the forgiven and forgiving people of God who are brought together across the rubble of dividing walls that have crumbled under the weight of the cross."[72] This focus on local expressions of church is not to be seen as an alternative to Taylor's focus on authentic believing individuals, but as an important Christian understanding focussing on the corporate nature of church and mission.

With regard to the East German situation one can say: We are in need of open minded but yet profiled Christian communities without any sect appearance being in contact with the people of their context. This includes the loving and diaconical care for the people in need witnessing to the

Christian faith as a gift of freedom – to be a public and at the same time authentic church.[73]

> It is the calling of the community, to which each Christian's vocation is integrally related, to be sent into the world, to participate in the course of human affairs and events as the evidence that God's redeeming work in Christ has happened, is in effect, and may be responded to and known.[74]

With that focus on missional church or mission minded Christian communities we have also to admit, that mission is again and again patchwork in regard to the kingdom of God.[75] But this patchwork is done not without promise. "But it is not therefore ineffectual – quite the contrary."[76] And this is true for the Eastern part of Germany as well.

Coming back to my train rides in India and Germany I may conclude, that speaking about religion is easier in India, but whether this means that mission or being a missional church is easier, I don't dare to conclude. Different contexts just need different answers and creative ideas, but nevertheless they all need Christian communities living by the Gospel.

Endnotes

[1] Wade Clark Roof, "God is in the Details: Reflections on Religion's Public Presence in the United States in the mid-1990s," *Sociology of Religion* 57 (1996): 153.

[2] Meredith B. Mcguire, *Lived Religion: Faith and Practice in Everyday Life* (Oxford/New York, 2008), 208.

[3] Robert Wuthnow, *American Mythos: Why Our Best Efforts to Be a Better Nation Fall Short* (Princeton, 2006), 157.

[4] Karl Gabriel, "Konzepte von öffentlichkeit und ihre theologischen Konsequenzen," in *Wieviel Theologie vertragt der Offentlichkeit*, eds. Edmund Arens and Helmut Hoping (Freiburg, 2000), 18.

[5] Andreas Feldtkeller, "Mission und Religionsfreiheit," *ZMiss* 3 (2002): 261-75. Cf. for the difficulties of conversion in Muslim countries or

even India Raj 1985; Lamin Sanneh, "The Church and its Missionary Vocation: The Islamic Frontline in a Post-Christian West," in *Mission in the 21ˢᵗ Century: Exploring the Five Marks of Global Mission*, eds. Andrew F. Walls and Cathy Ross (Maryknoll, 2008).

[6] C. Wright Mills, *The Sociological Imagination* (Oxford, 1959), 33.

[7] Lesslie Newbigin, *Honest Religion for Secular Man*, 2.ed. (London, 1966), 8.

[8] Peter L. Berger, *Zur Dialektik von Religion und Gesellschaft* (Frankfurt, 1973), 128.

[9] Peter L. Berger, ed., *The Desecularization of the World: Resurgent Religion and World Politics* (Washington, 1999), 2f & 9f.

[10] Peter L. Berger, "Pluralism, Protestantization, and the Voluntary Principle," in *Democracy and the New Religious Pluralism*, ed., Thomas Banchoff (Oxford, 2007), 21.

[11] Grace Davie, *Religion in Britain since 1945: Believing Without Belonging (Making Contemporary Britain)* (Oxford, 1994); also, "From Obligation to Consumption: Understanding the Patterns of Religion in Northern Europe," in *The Future of the Parish System: Shaping the Church of England for the 21st Century*, ed. Steven Croft (London, 2006), 33.

[12] Kieran Flanagan and Peter C. Jupp, eds. *A Sociology of Spirituality* (Aldershot, 2007).

[13] Grace Davie, *The Sociology of Religion* (Los Angeles, 2007), 96.

[14] Grace Davie, *Religion and Modern Europe: A Memory Mutates* (Oxford, 2000), 177ff.

[15] Danièle Hervieu-Leger, "Secularization, Tradition and New Forms of Religiosity: Some Theoretical Proposals," in *New Religions and New Religiosity*, eds. Eileen Barker and Margit Warburg (Aarhus, 1998), 31&38.

[16] Charles Taylor, *A Secular Age* (Cambridge, 2007), 522.

[17] Taylor, *A Secular Age*, 376 & 590.

[18] Taylor, *A Secular Age*, 25.

[19] Taylor, *A Secular Age*, 13f.

[20] Taylor, *A Secular Age*, 363ff.

[21] Taylor, *A Secular Age*, 159ff. Already Max Weber referred to secularization as development from an enchanted to a disenchanted world.

[22] Taylor, *A Secular Age*, 209.

[23] Taylor, *A Secular Age*, 534f & 727.

[24] Helmut Zeddies, "Konfessionslosigkeit im Osten Deutschlands: Merkmale und Deutungsversuche einer folgenschweren Entwicklung," *PTh* 91(2002): 150.

[25] Gustav Warneck auf der Missionskonferenz in London 1888; Cited in "Wilbert R Shenk, Contemporary Europe in Missiological Perspective," *Miss*. 35, no.2 (2007): 125.

[26] Detlef Pollack, "Religion und Moderne: Zur Gegenwart der Säkularisierung in Europa," in *Religion und Gesellschaft Europa im 20. Jahrhundert*, eds. Friedrich Wilhelm & Klaus GroBe Kracht (Graf Köln, 2007), 93ff.

[27] Jose Casanova, "Die religiöse Lage in Europa," in *Sakularisierung und die Weltreligionen*, eds., Hans Joas and Klaus Wiegandt (Frankfurt, 2007), 323f; Monika Wohlrab-Sahr, "Das stabile Drittel jenseits der Religiosität," in *Religionsmonitor 2008*, ed. Bertelsmannstiftung (Gütersloh, 2007), 100: The East of Germany was not only dechurched during the GDR, but also almost emptied of religiosity.

[28] Ehrhart Neubert, "Von der Volkskirche zur Minderheitskirche-Bilanz 1990," in *Rolle der Kirchen in der DDR - eine erste Bilanz*, ed. Horst Dähn (Munchen, 1993), 39.

[29] Detlef Pollack, *Kirche in der Organisationsgesellschaft: Zum Wandel der gesellschaflichen Lage der evangelischen Kirchen in der DDR* (Stuttgart Berlin Köln, 1994), 426.

[30] Neubert, "Von der Volkskirche zur Minderheitskirche-Bilanz 1990," 36.

[31] Detlef Pollack, *Sakularisierung-ein moderner Mythos?* (Tübingen, 2003), 129.

[32] Detlef Pollack, "Zur religiös-kirchlichen Lage in Deutschland nach der Wiedervereinigung," *ZThK* 93 (1996): 608.

[33] See Eberhard Tiefensee, "Chancen und Grenzen von 'Mission'-im Hinblick auf die konfessionelle Situation in den neuen Bundeslandern," in *Gemeindepflanzung-ein Modell fiuir die Kirche der Zukunft?* eds. Matthias Bartels and Martin Reppenhagen (Neukirchen-Vluyn, 2006), 69f & 77f.

[34] Taylor, *A Secular Age*, 530ff.

[35] Tiefensee, "Chancen und Grenzen von 'Mission'-im Hinblick auf die konfessionelle Situation in denneuen Bundesländern," 85.

[36] Davie, *Religion in Britain since 1945*.

[37] Hervieu-Leger, "Secularization, Tradition and New Forms of Religiosity," 34; also, Peter L. Berger, "Secularization and De-Secularization," in *Religions in the Modern World: Traditions and Transformations*, ed. Linda Woodhead (London, 2002), 295.

[38] Hans Raun Iversen, "Leaving the Distant Church: The Danish Experience," in *Leaving Religion and Religious Life*, eds. Mordechai Bar-Lev and William Shaffir (Greenwich, 1997), 157.

[39] See Pollack, "Religion und Moderne: Zur Gegenwart der Sakularisierung in Europa," 93ff; Casanova, "Die religiöse Lage in Europa," 323f; Wohlrab-Sahr, "Das stabile Drittel jenseits der Religiosität," 100.

[40] Robin Gill, *Churchgoing and Christian Ethics* (Cambridge, 1999), 66 & 129.

[41] Pollack, "Kommentar. Was tun? Ein paar Vorschlage trotz unübersichtlicher Lage," 132.

[42] Michael Herbst, "Evangelism in Theological Education," *IRM* 96, no. 382/283 (2007): 265f. A recent research about conversion done by the Research Institute for Evangelism and Church Development at Greifswald University com es to the conclusion, that people even without church upbringing com e to faith through personal contacts with Christians and through courses designed to welcome people into the Christian faith and the life of the Church (e.g. Emmaus, Alpha).

[43] Taylor, *A Secular Age*, 531ff.

[44] Taylor, *A Secular Age*, 512ff.

[45] See Darrell L. Guder, "Practical Theology in the Service of the Missional Church," in *Theology in Service of the Church: Essays in Honor of Joseph D. Small 3rd*, ed. Charles A. Wiley (Louisville, 2008), 15. It is quite interesting to see, that the term "missional" has just recently entered the Anglican-Methodist approach of "fresh expressions of church" or "mission-shaped church." See Steven Croft, ed., *Mission-shaped Questions: Defining Issues for Today's Church*, 2.ed. (London, 2009), 19ff & 43ff. On page 24 is a very compromised but helpful list of "contributories" for a missional ecclesiology.

[46] Richard Bliese, "The Mission Matrix: Mapping Out the Complexities of a Missional Ecclesiology," *Word and World* 26, no. 3 (2006): 239. See the shift from "church-shaped mission" to "mission-shaped ecclesiology," in Craig Van Gelder, "Some Further Reflections on Church and World Worship and Evangelism," *CTJ* 27, no. 2 (1992): 374ff.

[47] See Henk De Roest, "Ecclesiologies at the Margin," in *The Routledge Companion to the Christian Church*, eds. Gerald Mannion and Lewis Seymour Mudge (New York, 2008).

[48] See Jacques Matthey, "Mission als anstöBiges Wesensmerkm al der Kirche," *ZMiss* 3 (2002): 226.

[49] Darrell L Guder, ed., *Missional Church: A Vision for the Sending of the Church in North America*, The Gospel and Our Culture Series (Grand Rapids, 1998), 5f.

[50] Lois Y. Barrett, ed., *Treasure in Clay Jars: Patterns in Missional Faithfulness*, The Gospel and Our Culture Series (Grand Rapids, 2004), x.

[51] See De Roest, "Ecclesiologies at the Margin," 254.

[52] Darrell L. Guder, *The Continuing Conversion of the Church*, The Gospel and Our Culture Series (Grand Rapids, 2000), 71 & 83.

[53] H. Jurgens Hendriks, "Missional Theology and Social Development," *HTS* 63, no. 3 (2007): 1002.

[54] Robert J. Schreiter, *Constructing Local Theologies*, 15th ed. (Maryknoll, 2008), 20.

[55] Louis J. Luzbetak, *The Church and Cultures: New Perspectives in Missiological Anthropology*, American Society of Missiology Series No. 12 (Maryknoll, 1988), 139.

[56] Guder, *The Continuing Conversion of the Church*, 73.

[57] Guder, *The Continuing Conversion of the Church*, 81.

[58] See Harriet Hill, "The Vernacular Treasures: A Century of Mother-Tongue Bible Translation," *IBMR* 30, no. 2 (2006): 86; Lamin Sanneh, *Whose Religion is Christianity? The Gospel beyond the West* (Grand Rapids, 2003), 22f; Lamin Sanneh, *Disciples of All Nations: Pillars of World Christianity* (Oxford, 2008), 217f.

[59] Theo Sundermeier, *Mission - Geschenk der Freiheit. Bausteine fur eine Theologie der Mission* (Frankfurt, 2005), 111.

[60] Sanneh, *Whose Religion is Christianity?*, 10.

[61] Andrew F. Walls, *The Cross-Cultural Process in Christian History* (Maryknoll, 2002), 41.

[62] See Henning Wrogemann, "Wer betreibt Inkulturation? Evangelium und Kulturen im Spannungsfeld von Machtkonstellationen, Anerkennung und kritischem Dialog," *ZMiss* 32, no. 3 (2006): 246ff.

[63] See Theo Sundermeier, "Begegnung mit dem Fremden.Pladoyer für eine verstehende Missionswissenschaft," in *Konvivenz und Diferenz.Studien*

zu einer verstehenden Missionswissenschaft, ed. Volker Küister (Erlangen, 1995), 81ff; Sundermeier, *Mission- Geschenk der Freiheit.Bausteine für eine Theologie der Mission*, 38; also, David J. Bosch, *Transforming Mission: Paradigm Shifts in Theology of Mission* (Maryknoll, 1991), 368 & 375.

[64] See Rowan Williams, *On Christian Theology: Challenges in Contemporary Theology* (Oxford, 2000), 228 & 233.

[65] Robert N. Bellah, "Cultural Barriers to the Understanding of the Church and Its Public Role," *Miss.* 19, no. 4 (1991): 473.

[66] Schreiter, *Constructing Local Theologies*, 157.

[67] Simpson, *A Reformation Is a Terrible Thing to Waste*, 93. Background of the understanding of a missional church being a "public companion" is the understanding of a civil society and discourse by Jüirgen Habermas.

[68] Sanneh, *Disciples of All Nations*, 56.

[69] Lesslie Newbigin, *A Word in Season: Perspectives on Christian World Mission* (Grand Rapid, 1994), 33.

[70] Heinrich Bedford-Strohm, "Kirche-Ethik-Öffentlichkeit.Zur ethischen Dimension der Ekklesiologie," *VuF* 51, no. 2 (2006):19.

[71] Lesslie Newbigin, *The Gospel in a Pluralist Society* (Grand Rapids, 1989), 227.

[72] Guder, ed. *Missional Church*, 103.

[73] See Sundermeier, *Mission-Geschenk der Freiheit.Bausteine fir eine Theologie der Mission*.

[74] Guder, "Practical Theology in the Service of the Missional Church," 19; Herbst, "Evangelism in Theological Education," 266ff.

[75] Sundermeier, *Mission - Geschenk der Freiheit.Bausteine für eine Theologie der Mission*, 111.

[76] Lesslie Newbigin, *The Light has Come: An Exposition of the Fourth Gospel* (Grand Rapids, 1982), 20.

Bibliography

Barrett, Lois Y., ed. *Treasure in Clay Jars: Patterns in Missional Faithfulness.* The Gospel and Our Culture Series. Grand Rapids, 2004.

Bedford-Strohm, Heinrich. "Kirche - Ethik - Öffentlichkeit. Zur ethischen Dimension der Ekklesiologie." *VuF* 51, no. 2 (2006): 4-19.

Bellah, Robert N. "Cultural Barriers to the Understanding of the Church and Its Public Role." *Miss.* 19, no. 4 (1991): 461-73.

Berger, Peter L. *Zur Dialektik von Religion und Gesellschaft.* Frankfurt, 1973.

————. "Secularization and De-Secularization. In *Religions in the Modern World: Traditions and Transformations.* Edited by Linda Woodhead, 291-98. London, 2002.

————. "Pluralism, Protestantization, and the Voluntary Principle." In *Democracy and the New Religious* Pluralism. Edited by Thomas Banchoff, 19-29. Oxford, 2007.

———— ed. *The Desecularization of the World: Resurgent Religion and World Politics.* Washington, 1999.

Bliese, Richard. "The Mission Matrix: Mapping Out the Complexites of a Missional Ecclesiology." *Word and World* 26, no. 3 (2006): 237-48.

Bosch, David J. *Transforming Mission: Paradigm Shifts in Theology of Mission.* Maryknoll 1991.

Casanova, José. "Die religiöse Lage in Europa." In *Säkularisierung und die Weltreligionen*, 322-57. Edited by Hans Joas and Klaus Wiegandt. Frankfurt, 2007.

Croft, Steven ed. *Mission-shaped Questions. Defining Issues for Today's Church.* 2. ed. London, 2009.

Davie, Grace. *Religion in Britain since 1945: Believing Without Belonging (Making Contemporary Britain).* Oxford,1994.

————. *Religion and Modern Europe: A Memory Mutates.* Oxford, 2000.

————. "From Obligation to Consumption: Understanding the Patterns of Religion in Northern Europe." In *The Future of the Parish System: Shaping the Church of England for the 21st Century*, 33-45. Edited by Steven Croft. London, 2006.

————. *The Sociology of Religion.* Los Angeles, 2007.

De Roest, Henk. "Ecclesiologies at the Margin." In *The Routledge Companion to the Christian Church*, 251-272. Edited by Gerald Mannion and Lewis Seymour Mudge. New York, 2008.

Feldtkeller, Andreas. "Mission und Religionsfreiheit." *ZMiss* 3 (2002): 261-75.

Flanagan, Kieran and Peter C. Jupp, eds. *A Sociology of Spirituality.* Aldershot, 2007.

Gabriel, Karl. "Konzepte von Öffentlichkeit und ihre theologischen Konsequenzen." In *Wieviel Theologie verträgt der Öffentlichkeit.* Edited by Edmund Arens and Helmut Hoping, 16-37. Freiburg 2000.

Gill, Robin. *Churchgoing and Christian Ethics.* Cambridge, 1999.

Guder, Darrell L. *The Continuing Conversion of the Church*. The Gospel and Our Culture Series. Grand Rapids, 2000.

————. "Practical Theology in the Service of the Missional Church." In *Theology in Service of the Church: Essays in Honor of Joseph D. Small 3rd*. Edited by Charles A. Wiley, 13-22. Louisville, 2008.

———— ed. *Missional Church: A Vision for the Sending of the Church in North America*. The Gospel and Our Culture Series. Grand Rapids, 1998.

Hendriks, H Jurgens. "Missional Theology and Social Development." *HTS* 63, no. 3 (2007): 999-1016.

Herbst, Michael. "Evangelism in Theological Education." *IRM* 96, no. 382/283 (2007): 263-76.

Hervieu-Léger, Danièle. "Secularization, Tradition and New Forms of Religiosity: Some Theoretical Proposals." In *New Religions and New Religiosity*. Edited by Eileen Barker and Margit Warburg, 28-44. Aarhus 1998.

————. *Pilger und Konvertiten. Religion in Bewegung*. Würzburg, 2004.

Hill, Harriet. "The Vernacular Treasures: A Century of Mother-Tongue Bible Translation." *IBMR* 30, no. 2 (2006): 86.

Iversen, Hans Raun. "Leaving the Distant Church: The Danish Experience." In *Leaving Religion and Religious Life*. Edited by Mordechai Bar-Lev and William Shaffir, 139-58. Greenwich, 1997.

Luzbetak, Louis J. *The Church and Cultures: New Perspectives in Missiological Anthropology*. American Society of Missiology Series No. 12. Maryknoll, 1988.

Matthey, Jacques. "Mission als anstößiges Wesensmerkmal der Kirche." *ZMiss* 3 (2002): 221-39.

Mcguire, Meredith B. *Lived Religion: Faith and Practice in Everyday Life*. Oxford/New York, 2008.

Mills, C. Wright. *The Sociological Imagination*. Oxford, 1959.

Neubert, Ehrhart. "Von der Volkskirche zur Minderheitskirche - Bilanz 1990." In *Rolle der Kirchen in der DDR - eine erste Bilanz*. Edited by Horst Dähn, 36-55. München, 1993.

Newbigin, Lesslie. *Honest Religion for Secular Man*. 2. ed. London, 1966.

————. *The Light has Come: An Exposition of the Fourth Gospel*. Grand Rapids, 1982.

—————. *The Gospel in a Pluralist Society*. Grand Rapids, 1989.

—————. *A Word in Season: Perspectives on Christian World Missions*. Grand Rapid, 1994.

Pollack, Detlef. *Kirche in der Organisationsgesellschaft. Zum Wandel der gesellschaftlichen Lage der evangelischen Kirchen in der DDR*. Stuttgart Berlin Köln, 1994.

—————. "Zur religiös-kirchlichen Lage in Deutschland nach der Wiedervereinigung." *ZThK* 93 (1996): 586-614.

—————. *Säkularisierung - ein moderner Mythos?* Tübingen, 2003.

—————. "Kommentar. Was tun? Ein paar Vorschläge trotz unübersichtlicher Lage." In *Kirche in der Vielfalt der Lebensbezüge*. Edited by Wolfgang Huber, 129-33. Hannover, 2006.

—————. "Religion und Moderne. Zur Gegenwart der Säkularisierung in Europa." In *Religion und Gesellschaft Europa im 20. Jahrhundert*. Edited by Friedrich Wilhelm and Klaus Große Kracht, 73-103. Graf Köln, 2007.

Raj, Sunder. *The Confusion Called Conversion*. New Delhi, 1985.

Roof, Wade Clark. "God is in the Details: Reflections on Religion's Public Presence in the United States in the mid-1990s." *Sociology of Religion* 57 (1996): 149-62.

Sanneh, Lamin. *Whose Religion is Christianity? The Gospel beyond the West*. Grand Rapids, 2003.

—————. "The Church and its Missionary Vocation: The Islamic Frontline in a Post-Christian West." In *Mission in the 21st Century: Exploring the Five Marks of Global Mission*. Edited by Andrew F. Walls and Cathy Ross, 130-47. Maryknoll, 2008.

—————. *Disciples of All Nations: Pillars of World Christianity*. Oxford, 2008.

Schreiter, Robert J. *Constructing Local Theologies*. 15th ed. Maryknoll, 2008.

Shenk, Wilbert R. *Contemporary Europe in Missiological Perspective, Miss.* 35, no. 2 (2007): 125-40.

Simpson, Gary M. "A Reformation Is a Terrible Thing to Waste: A Promising Theology for an Emerging Missional Church." In *The Missional Church in Context. Helping Congregations Develop Contextual Ministry*. Edited by Craig Van Gelder, 65-93. Grand Rapids, 2007.

Sundermeier, Theo. "Begegnung mit dem Fremden. Plädoyer für eine verstehende Missionswissenschaft." In *Konvivenz und Differenz. Studien zu einer verstehenden Missionswissenschaft*. Edited by Volker Küster, 76-86. Erlangen, 1995.

————. *Mission - Geschenk der Freiheit. Bausteine für eine Theologie der Mission*. Frankfurt, 2005.

Taylor, Charles. *A Secular Age*. Cambridge, 2007.

Tiefensee, Eberhard. "Chancen und Grenzen von 'Mission' - im Hinblick auf die konfessionelle Situation in den neuen Bundesländern." In *Gemeindepflanzung - ein Modell für die Kirche der Zukunft?* Edited by Matthias Bartels and Martin Reppenhagen, 68-85. Neukirchen-Vluyn, 2006.

Van Gelder, Craig. "Some 'Further' Reflections on Church and World, Worship and Evangelism." *CTJ* 27, no. 2 (1992): 372-76.

Walls, Andrew F. *The Cross-Cultural Process in Christian History*. Maryknoll, 2002.

Williams, Rowan. *On Christian Theology*. Challenges in Contemporary Theology. Oxford, 2000.

Wohlrab-Sahr, Monika. "Das stabile Drittel jenseits der Religiosität." In *Religionsmonitor 2008*. Edited by Bertelsmannstiftung, 95-103. Gütersloh 2007.

Wrogemann, Henning. "Wer betreibt Inkulturation? Evangelium und Kulturen im Spannungsfeld von Machtkonstellationen, Anerkennung und kritischem Dialog." *ZMiss* 32, no. 3 (2006): 234-52.

Wuthnow, Robert. *American Mythos: Why Our Best Efforts to Be a Better Nation Fall Short*. Princeton, 2006.

Zeddies, Helmut. "Konfessionslosigkeit im Osten Deutschlands: Merkmale und Deutungsversuche einer folgenschweren Entwicklung." *PTh* 91 (2002): 150-67.

10
Mission to the Digital World

J. N. Manokaran

Introduction

The Internet media provides daily dose of Wiki leaks (250 000 plus documents), its interpretation and its imaginary impact. For the print and television media, it is sensational and hot selling. Overnight, Julian Assange an Australian journalist and an Internet activist becomes a global celebrity. For the past five years or so, he was providing a variety of information for the global Internet audience. Later on, he started leaking cables of diplomats sent to White House. When he challenged the might of 'Goliath' America, Assange became the 'David' the hero for Postmodern youngsters who lack role models and heroes. Attacking institutions, questioning authorities, and challenging establishment are their favourite pastime of the Digital Generation. Julian Assange's *modus operandi*, intention or motives is a suspect but not questioned by the gullible sensation hungry audience.

Information Explosion

'Information Explosion'; 'Information Paralysis'; and 'Information Overload' are some of the common terms in today's vocabulary.

The humanity has moved from Hunting Era to Agriculture Era to Industrial Era to Information Era. There is 'flooding' of information from all directions. The information available today has exponentially grown and it overwhelms people.

Bible and Information Era

Bible speaks of this era very vividly. In the last days, people could be called 'Global Nomad' and there would be information explosion as Prophet Daniel foresaw: "Many will go here and there to increase knowledge."[1] Knowledge available today has its depth in content, micro details, multi-dimensional and from multiple sources.

Prophet Habakkuk declared that the stones could speak and even beams of woodwork would echo it. "The stones of the wall will cry out, and the beams of the woodwork will echo it."[2] It is amazing to see how God spoke about 'micro-chips' through Habakkuk in 7th century B.C. On the Palm Sunday, Pharisees wanted the disciples to be quiet; however Lord replied that stones would cry out if they keep quiet. "Teacher, rebuke your disciples!" "I tell you," he replied, "if they keep quiet, the stones will cry out."[3] In fact, 'micro-chips' would cry out, if people quit praising and worshiping Him.

Prophet Isaiah wrote that God has engraved his children in his palms[4] which was beyond human comprehension, until we go the palm top computers. Now, even mobile phones could store thousands of images and profiles.

Jesse Rice reflects: "You and I were made to participate in a divine ordering of management of affairs and events in the world – a dispensation. We were made to have a small piece of the world over which we have creative influence. The appeal behind owning and operating our own island – even behind creating and maintaining a Facebook profile-is a truth embedded deeply in our hearts. It is our nature to rule and to do so in partnership with God and in partnership with others."[5]

Micro-chips

To put in simple terms: "Microchips are basically bits of sand that can think."[6] Sand is available in plenty. "There are few things in the world as simple as sand, and perhaps none as complex as computer chips. Yet the simple element silicon in sand is the starting point for making the integrated circuits that power everything today, from supercomputers to cell phones to microwave ovens."[7]

Indeed the sand in the mortar of walls, stones that are broken to be sand and silt are God's microchips. At last human beings have discovered one of the scientific truths and that has transformed the world in many ways. Micro chips have changed the form of governance, communication, culture, connections, vocabulary, work place, travel, education, lifestyle, medical world, entertainment...etc. The imprint of the impact of micro chips is almost on all aspects of life.

Great Commission has been entrusted to the Global church. The Holy Spirit has been given for the Church to be a bold witness in the world. "But you will receive power when the Holy Spirit comes on you; and you will be my witnesses in Jerusalem, and in all Judea and Samaria, and to the ends of the earth."[8] If our Lord would have made the statement today, he would have added 'cyber world or digital world' along with the ends of the earth.

Global and Indian Context

Internet is beyond geographical boundaries. Digital or Cyber community seems to be transnational. Let us take the example of the social networking website called Facebook. If Facebook membership is taken into consideration, it could be the third largest nation in the world next to China and India. And this happened over a period of just six years.

Social networking site Facebook officially has 500 million users, the company announced on 21 July 2010. The milestone means that the six-year old website now reaches eight percent of the planet's population, just 18 months after it passed the 150 million user mark. Facebook marked the milestone with the launch of a special section in which users are encouraged to post their personal stories about how Facebook has affected them. "Half a billion is a nice number but the number isn't what really matters here. What matters are all of the stories we hear from all of you about the impact your connections have had on your lives," Zuckerberg (CEO) said in a video message. "Instead of focusing on numbers, we want to help people around the world hear about these stories for themselves, and we want to let you tell your own story."[9]

Here is a condensed version of Dilip Bobb's article in *India Today*. Today's teenagers are causing concern because of the hours they spend multi-tasking with their gadgets, TV and the Net. M-Generation is the first wave of wired teenagers who are media-obsessed, tech-savvy, are current focus of research around the world because they do media multi-tasking, a majority between four and eight hours a day. Those between the age of 12 and 21 are the first generation to feel that technology is an integral part of their lives and not just a nice thing to own. Today's switched-on teens stoutly defend multi-tasking and brag about listening to the iPod, messaging, watching TV and surfing the Net all at the same time. Perhaps young minds can handle all the stimuli simultaneously. The question that rises is whether they could retain that is important and ignore that are non-essential. Can media meet their emotional needs? Some teenagers have become dependent on these gadgets and get irritated when they are not there. Technological trappings could cause health problems and a weak physical constitution. These electronic gadgets disconnect the M-Generation from peers and family. Internet is used by teenagers to download tutorials, doing research work or project works and music that are stress buster. Gadgets tend to become their lives instead of being part of their lives. 70% of parents surveyed agreed that their teenage children influence in choosing brand for purchasing items like computers. Students think that Internet as necessity and not as indulgence. A survey done by Cartoon Network in 2004 revealed that 40 per cent of Indian children are computer literate and use computers. Long time spent by teenagers before computers means lack of development of soft skills. They are poor in interacting with others, developing healthy interpersonal relationships and sense of identity. Indian Academy of Paediatrics found an average Indian child spends more hours in front of TV in a week – 30 hours than in school – 25 hours in school. Parents could not withhold these gadgets as more and more children own it. When there is overall exposure of gadgets, the generation tends to become smarter. Teenagers who are multi-tasking are also good in problem solving but they have serious problem of attention span. In the long run multi-tasking affect the ability to maintain concentration and focus. Teenagers without cell phone means being with a missing limb. This new generation is smarter, confident and is more tuned to global trends. Teenagers could conquer wired world, but same technology could crash and burn them also.[10]

According to a new study compiled by Techzone (a Value Added Service (VAS) company. Even mobile phones have become handy tool to surf Internet. Here is an example from the city of Chennai: There are more than one crore mobile phone users in Chennai and nearly four lakh of them surf the net from their phones, of these, 80,000 are high school students. There are nearly two lakh high school students in the city. Nearly 20% of high school students use the net from their cell phones. School students access social networking sites, download songs and other entertainment content from various websites. Students also visit reference sites. High school children prefer surfing on cellphones as they can do so without their parents' knowledge.[11] 84% of Chennai's children, 83% of Bangalore, 86% of Delhi and Mumbai are online with access to computers; many are not legally eligible to be on line; according to Tata Consultancy Service that surveyed 10,000 children in the age group of 12- 18 in 11 cities across India.[12]

The summary of a news report: According to a survey done by Indiabiz News Research Services (INRS)in major cities – Delhi, Mumbai, Kolkata, Chennai and Bengaluru, youths prefer Facebook as the favourite website and Linkendin is the second. Tech savvy Indian youths are spending at least two hours a day online to network to connect with others. 45 percent of users are reading or writing blogs and express opinions. 70% of bloggers spend 30 minutes – mostly for gaining information. 30 percent of youth use mobile phones to access networking sites. Another survey by Neilson claims that 70% of users prefer Orkut.[13]

Communication is Redefined by Technology

Technology brings changes in the communication. As human history evolved, communication also has evolved. The changes were through the technological inventions. In fact, technology redefines communication.

I have divided the history of humanity into five eras. This is a simple classification that would help us to understand the fifth era, which is our focus in this article/paper.

Oral Communication Culture

In the beginning oral communication was dominant. Without tools and technological development, oral communication was the only possibility. Speech, poetry, folk songs, rhythm and music were the common modes of communication. These were developed to store the words or information in the minds. There was no external storage. Later external storage was possible, like writing in clay tablets, skins...etc. However, they were expensive and occupied huge storage space. Face to face communications, sending a person with message to the recipients, or proclaiming orally in market places were means of communication.

Print Communication Culture

The invention of printing press by Gutenberg in 1450s transformed the world. The ideas that were once communicated only through oral means and stored in certain places could be reduced to writing and printing in small, portable books. Even these books could be mass produced for wider distribution and circulation. Now information was not just stored in one central place, like king's palaces, but could be taken to any place.

Printing of books was not favoured by the elite, because it gives power to masses. They understood knowledge as power. With the printing press, novels, religious books, text books became common. Later newspapers, magazines, journals and pamphlets were developed.

Though reading and writing became an important skill, only developed nation provided this to the whole population. Even today, many nations have huge number of illiterates.

Audio Broadcast Communication Culture

Radio was another innovation that changed the communication in the world. In the 1900s it started in US and other Western countries. In 1927 radio was introduced in India. The information could travel faster than print. Radio needed a receiver to get the information. However, people depended more on print mass media than the radio. They would hear the news over radio broadcast and would like to verify the next day in the newspaper.

Radio also brought multi-tasking a possibility. Women could hear radio as they cooked. Men could hear radio as they drove. Radio became a tool for information sharing, advertisement and entertainment.

This media had its own innovations of audio cassettes later the digital format of MP3 and even FM radio.

Television Telecast Communication Culture

The next progress of media is 'audio-visual' communication. Cinema was a mass media but was a public media and not a private media. However, television became a mass media that could be view privately at homes. Initially, it was audio with some pictures. But, it developed well on its own. Television started occupying the central places in homes all over the world.

The innovation of telecast media was the VCDs and its digital cousins are DVDs.

Digital Communication Culture

With micro-chips invention, computers invasion, the digital communication became a pervasive influence around the world. Digital communication was exponential and impacted the world profoundly.

In the year 1996, Sabeer Bhatia introduced Email to the world. Within 14 years (2010) E-mail has invaded many parts of the world. The impact of Print Media took 500 years to reach all corners of the world. (There are many who are still illiterate).

Technology Changes Fast

For eighteen year olds like my son, email is outdated. For them Instant Messenger is the latest communication tool, so is the SMS and MMS. The technology changes so fast, that only young people are capable of handling new technologies. Jesse Rice writes: "In the dark ages of digital technology, cell phones were used for calling people. Now we use them to play music, plan events, check and respond to emails, text until our thumbs bleed, help us find the nearest takeout pizza, and check our investment portfolio."[14]

Distance and Time Conquered

Digital media has overcome the distance and time barrier. Now it is possible to transfer documents within second to any part of the world. It is not only information, photos, videos and even money transaction could happen in seconds.

Mark Penn writes: "Internet-users tend to believe they have control over their lives. New Luddites don't. In fact some New Luddites reject technology because they hope it will help them to take control. From their point of view, the technology that was supposed to make our lives easier has only made them busier and more stressed. Whatever time we saved with instant communication seems to have been filled up with more communication."[15]

Video phone calls, skype conference calls have helped people to communicate in real time surpassing long distances.

Digital Natives and Digital Immigrants

Digital technology has divided the people into two groups: Digital Natives and Immigrants.

> A digital native is a person, mainly a young person, who was born during or after the general introduction of digital technology, and through interacting with digital technology from an early age, has a greater understanding of its concepts. A digital immigrant is an individual who was born before the existence of digital technology and adopted it to some extent later in their life. Alternatively, this term can describe people born in the latter 1970s or later, as the Digital Age began at that time; but in most cases the term focuses on people who grew up with 21st century modern technology. This term has been used in several different contexts, such as education (Bennett, Maton & Kervin 2008) (in association with the term New Millennium Learners (OECD 2008)).[16]

In Urban India, it could be considered as people born in the year 1985 or later. The impact of Information technology and invasion of PCs happened later than in the Western nations.

The digital natives in US have this background in digital world. "Today's average college grads have spent less than 5,000 hours of their lives reading, but over 10,000 hours playing video games (not to mention 20,000 hours watching TV. Computer games, email, the Internet, cell phones and instant messaging are integral parts of their lives."[17] Students in US today are digital natives - "native speakers" of the digital language of computers, video games and the Internet. [18]

So what does that make the rest of us? "Those of us who were not born into the digital world but have, at some later point in our lives, become fascinated by and adopted many or most aspects of the new technology are, and always will be compared to them, *Digital Immigrants*."[19] In fact, Digital immigrants are also ignorant or least exposed to technology. Their behavior betrays their immigrant status.

"There are hundreds of examples of the digital immigrant accent. They include printing out your email (or having your secretary print it out for you - an even "thicker" accent); needing to print out a document written on the computer in order to edit it (rather than just editing on the screen); and bringing people physically into your office to see an interesting web site (rather than just sending them the URL). I'm sure you can think of one or two examples of your own without much effort. My own favorite example is the "Did you get my email?" phone call. Those of us who are Digital Immigrants can, and should, laugh at ourselves and our "accent.""[20]

The distinction is clear. Digital natives are comfortable in their digital culture, while the digital immigrants struggle to adapt to that culture.

Convergence of Media

Internet has converged all predecessor media into one stream. Now, newspapers have an online edition. Newspapers could be read as hard copy or as soft copy in the digital format. There are e-books apart from printed copies. FM could be broad cast through Internet. Hence, the audio media has been integrated to Internet. You Tube is the integration of audio-video media in the Internet. "The roots of network convergence can be traced to the advent of digital communications, which reduced information into discrete, identifiable and thus, more easily transferable pieces of information. It also efficiently maximizes the transfer of information by allowing more signals to move through a single communication path."[21]

Today, voice, video, and data converges in one interactive media called Internet. "The Gutenberg era is over. A new digital communications technology has emerged. An electronic superhighway is beginning to girdle the globe as voice, video and data converge, bringing in their wake a new basket of digital, multimedia and interactive communication technologies."[22]

Adapted Fast

Internet has been adapted all over the world in pretty quick time. It took decades for new technologies to reach under developed nations. With digital communication, even under developed nations are able to integrate with the global communication system. Young people from all over the world aspire to be globally connected. "In a matter of very few years, the Internet has consolidated itself as a very powerful platform that has changed the way we do business, and the way we communicate. The Internet, as no other communication medium, has given an International or, if you prefer, a "Globalized" dimension to the world. Internet has become the Universal source of information for millions of people, at home, at school, and at work."[23]

Cyber World and Real World

Is there a distinction between the Real World and Virtual world or Cyber World? Virtual world has become virtual reality for many youngsters. The following newsreport provides ample evidence for this confusion. Smitha Namboothiri writes: 'Manju (name changed) is a programmer in a reputed IT firm in Kochi. Her parents are busy looking for a good partner for her. Little do they know that their daughter is into her third marriage through a website providing 'virtual marriage' services, having divorced' two of her 'partners' for adjustment problems. Move over, match-making websites and internet dating. The world of virtual marriage is the latest craze among the Gen-X. Many teenagers, who are active in the cyber world, are virtually married. Virtual marriage, now an online game in the West, has triggered serious debates among parents and educationists. The game, challenging traditional ethics and family values, will definitely weaken family relations, feel experts. What's interesting is married people 'marry' again in the virtual world! The process is simple: Create a user name and a password to register. Having done that, propose to other registered users and marry them. Want to marry your friend? Register, click the mouse...and you're man and wife! Before finalising a proposal, both the persons can exchange live visuals of their naked body parts through webcams. Unfortunately, many such visuals are cleverly used to blackmail or tarnish the girl when she gets proposals from the real world. <www. bored.com> <www.virtualweddingonline.com> are some of the popular websites offering virtual marriage services. What's interesting is that not a single virtual marriage has translated to 'real world' marriage. However, some privately admit that they live like 'real life couples.' The website will issue marriage certificates online. A printed certificate costs Rs1,500. Though the website clearly indicates that such marriages are part of an online game and are not legally valid, most 'married couples' are serious about it.[24]

One Place Solution

Internet offers one place solution. It is not only sharing of information, tasks could be accomplished, and games could be played. It is possible to pay utility bills, order daily needs of home through Internet. Teenagers sitting in different places could play a game watching through their respective monitors. It is possible to get things done from the Government also. Filing Income Tax, getting birth certificates, applying for Passport, even for college admissions, Internet is a viable tool.

Empowering Media

Internet also empowers 'lay' people with information. Professionals in any area of work cannot conceal any information. For example, detailed information about various ailments and sickness is readily available in the Internet. A medical doctor cannot conceal vital information. Citizen Journalists upload information before professional journalist could reach the spot from where the story originates.

Internet is considered as democratic media, even though the cost of acquiring accessibility is high. "Internet can be regarded as any-to-any connectivity, irrespective of geographical location or cultural difference. What is ignored here, is that any-to-any connectivity can only occur when the machines that define the internet are acquired."[25] However, Internet Cafes in cities have made it possible for any person to have access to a media with a global audience.

Pull Media

Generally media has to be 'pushed'. For example, a printed book has to be 'pushed' through book shops. Television viewers have to be 'pushed' to switch on the television sets and tune on to a particular channel. But, people flock to Internet without being pushed. So, it is called as Pull media. "We became high-tech turtles with mobile technology for a shell; we can now take 'home' with us wherever we go."[26]

Interactive Media

Digital Internet media is an interactive media. News could be read in an online newspaper and responded immediately. Instant Messenger brings immediate response from another person in another part of the world. "Forums are the Internet at its liveliest, where people meet, millions of them, every day and all the time. Forums are fun, they're useful, and there are lots of them, hundreds of thousands in fact, and more each day."[27]

Impact of Digital Culture

The impact of digital culture over youngsters are for good as well as not good.

Control Over Lives

Digital culture gives a sense of having control over our lives. That provides optimism and hope. "Control is key to our sense of well-being. When we believe we have a reasonable amount of control over our lives, then we feel optimistic and hopeful."[28]

Growth and Relationships

"As we develop through adolescence, living for what psychologists call an 'imaginary audience' is part of how we organize our inner worlds."[29] Now the imaginary audience become cyber world audience. This would impact inter-personal relationships. "In effect the hyperconnection of Facebook changes the nature of our relationships by turning our friends into audience and us into performers."[30] The face to face relationship is not easy becomes strained. This is because authenticity is not there, only hypocrisy. "Facebook is indeed reinventing and tearing at traditional boundaries, stirring up a hornet's nest of new issues related to privacy as employers befriend employees, teachers 'add' students, and parents friend request their children."[31]

Past Haunts

"One of the most interesting things about cyberspace is that it doesn't forget. If you've downloaded it, posted it, searched for it, or looked at it, there is probably a record of the event floating 'out there' somewhere."[32] What is posted as fun could be interpreted as lack of judgment by someone who does ot understand the context.

Multi-tasking

Jerome Burne writes about his daughter, a typical digital native who seems to be expert in multi-tasking: Like millions of othere teenagers my 14-year old daughter Kitty is often to be found on the sofa, laptop on her knees, checking facts for the essay she's writing. The TV is on and occasionally she scrolls through Facebook. She sends SMS's, makes calls on her mobile and take her iPod headset on and off. To me-and most other parents – this seems an impossible way to work. "How can you think with all that noise?" we yell. Homework used to be something to be done in silence with all distractions firmly removed. Yet for Kitty and her peers this is normal.[33] Multi-tasking is essential skill for survival in digital culture.

There are two kinds of intelligence: Fluid intelligence and Crystalline intelligence. Fluid intelligence is used to make connections, allows to spot patterns and solve problems. Crystalline intelligence relies on long-term memory that stores everything from phone numbers, sports scores, dates, how to ride a bike and it does not usually start declining until we attain 60 years of age. Digital culture has radically changed all that. Much of the crystalline intelligence is outsourced today through Internet.[34]

Jerome concludes: "At the moment I can just about keep up with Kitty because I've got more stuff stacked away in my crystalline intelligence, but she's definitely starting to overtake me in the fluid department."[35]

Restless

The online youngsters like to be online 24/7. Here is a summary of research done in US: Thirty-four per cent of the women aged 18 to 34 surveyed by Lightspeed Research for Oxygen Media said checking Facebook was the first thing they did in the morning, even before washing their face or brushing their teeth. Twenty-per cent admitted they sneak a peek at Facebook during the night while 26 per cent said they get up in the middle of the night to read text messages. Thirty-nine per cent of the 1,605 social media users aged 18 to 54 surveyed for Oxygen Media, a service of entertainment giant NBC Universal, in May and June described themselves as "Facebook addicts." Fifty-seven per cent of the women aged 18 to 34 said they talk to people online more than face-to-face and 31 per cent feel more confident about their online persona than their real life one. Sixty-three per cent of the young women use Facebook as a career networking tool, but 42 per cent said they did not think there was anything wrong with posting photos of themselves visibly intoxicated. Forty-eight per cent of the young women said they find out about news through Facebook while 41 per cent said they use Twitter to keep up to date. Fifty per cent of single women aged 18 to 34 said it's okay to meet and date other singles they meet through Facebook compared with 65 per cent of single men. Six per cent of the young single women use it as a way to "hook up" as opposed to 20 per cent of men. Men aged 18 to 34 are also more likely than female counterparts to break up using Facebook — 24 per cent for men compared with nine percent for women, the survey found. InsideFacebook.com, a site dedicated to the social network, said meanwhile that Facebook's growth slowed in the United States in June as it picked up only 320,800 new monthly active users last month compared with 7.8 million in May. Inside Facebook said the slowdown in growth could "simply be a blip."[36]

Vulnerable Children

About 77% Indian kids face negative situations online and only 27% parents control the cyber activities of their kids, says a global family survey on children's online lives and safety issues released. On an average, an Indian child has 46.17 online friends; only 46% kids can claim to have met all their online friends; 14% have met few.[37]

Overfed and Too Many Choices

Certainly, digital media provides multiple options, a variety of solutions and many times available free. "At the digital all-you-can-eat buffet, we don't have to stuff ourselves until we throw up."[38] So young people are overfed with information and have too many choices to choose from.

Porn Games and Sex Toys

"There's a sexual revolution happening in computer games. Porn games and sex toys are flooding the market. These games also take care of parental control. If someone walks in while you are at it, there is a panic button. Press it; the game pauses and some other document opens up. So you are saved. Maria and Sexual Fantasy are chartbusters in the 10-18 age group. These games give the players a feeling of virtual sex with the help of superb sound effects and detailed body parts. And there's something for everyone - spanking, bondage, rape, hentai, gay, lesbians, underwater, super models and several of types of girls like Asian, American, African and Australian. Games like Kamasutra, Larry Sexy game, Pamela Anderson and Strip Poker are the rage. The famous Tetris game is already out with an avatar carrying a downloadable nude picture of a supermodel."[39]

Value System

The digital community has its own values and social normas. Four principles of Wikinomics are:[40] 1) Openness 2) Peering 3) Sharing and 4) Acting globally.

Misled Youngsters: Premarital Sex and Divorces

Even dating has become digital. "Internet dating is increasingly viewed as fun way to meet more potential dates, while also efficiently weeding out the Totally Undesirable."[41]

There is also ill effect of the digital culture. The Synod Social Front of the Mizoram Presbyterian Church recently carried out a survey among the residents, mostly youngsters, of Aizawl and other district headquarters and observed that invasion of the media, especially cellphones, in everyday life has "undermined the social values of the Mizos and increased pre-marital sex among the youth".[42] Here is a case study of teenagers misled through Internet: 'A teenager, she thought she was in love. But this changed when she learnt that her boyfriend had made an MMS clip while having sex with her. The accused, Devendra Goel (25), a Borivli resident, has been arrested for allegedly having a physical relationship with his 17-year-old college-going neighbour for the last couple of years, the police said. About a month back, the girl, Rita Shah (name changed), learnt from Goel's friends that he had made the MMS clip, but scared it would tarnish her name, she chose to keep mum, said police sources. Later she confided in her maternal aunt. Accompanied by her aunt, the Std XII student lodged a complaint at Kasturba Marg police station. He has been arrested for having physical relations with a minor.[43]

According to the survey by the American Academy of Matrimonial Lawyers; one in five divorces in the US now involve the popular social networking sites; a staggering 80 per cent of divorce lawyers have also reported a spike in the number of cases that use social media for evidence of cheating. Flirty messages and photographs found on Facebook are increasingly being cited as proof of unreasonable behavior or irreconcilable differences. Many cases revolve around social media users who get back in touch with old flames they hadn't heard from in many years, the 'Daily Mail' reported. Facebook was by far the biggest offender, with 66 per cent of lawyers citing it as the primary source of evidence in a divorce case. My Space followed with 15 per cent, Twitter at 5 per cent and other choices lumped together at 14 per cent, the survey found. The survey reflects the findings of a UK law firm last year showing that 20 per cent of its divorce petitions blamed Facebook flings.[44]

New Addiction

New kinds of diseases are affecting the digital natives. Here is a news report: Textaphrenia, textiety or post-traumatic text disorder are some of serious mental and physical disorders that teenaged Australian "text addicts" are suffering from. The research into youth communication habits identified the risks teens face from texting excessively every day, and the symptoms included anxiety, insecurity, depression, low self-esteem and "repetitive thumb syndrome". According to figures released by Boost Mobile, a reseller of the Optus network, text messaging has increased by 89% in the last two years. Jennie Carroll, a technology researcher from RMIT University in Melbourne, has studied of the effects of modern communication since 2001 and said the mobile phone had become meshed into teenagers' lives. Her study identified four distinct disorders — textaphrenia, textiety, post-traumatic text disorder and binge texting. Textaphrenia is thinking a message had arrived when it hadn't, while textiety is the anxious feeling of not receiving or sending text messages. "With textaphrenia and textiety there's a feeling no one loves me, no one's contacted me," the Daily Telegraph quoted her as saying. Post-traumatic stress disorder involved physical and mental injuries from texting, like walking into things while texting and even crossing a road without looking. There were reports from Japan of 'repetitive thumb syndrome' and thumbs growing because of texting leading to 'Monster Thumbs'. Binge texting is when teens send multiple texts to feel good about themselves and try to attract responses. This is the reverse of the anxiety — you think you've been left out of the loop so you send a lot of texts and wait for responses.[45]

Church and Internet

The church was in the forefront to communications, especially in the beginning of printing era. As we know, Bible was the first book to be printed in many languages. However, in Internet media, the Indian Christian presence seems to be minimal or it could be stated as 'nil.'

"But the world is changing and so are the rules. With the proliferation of desktop computers, desktop publishing and lower cost printing, there are ways to self-publish a book that completely circumvent the world of traditional publishing. If you have a good idea, the ability to write, access to a decent editor, a creative graphic designer and a few thousand dollars to spend for printing, you can produce your own book whether the publishing world wants you to or not. If you are willing to go print on demand, you don't even need the few thousand dollars."[46]

T.V. Mahalingam writes: Suddenly, the market for Indian mythology has boomed with the estimated market share of Rs. 1000 crore. Ganesha, Hanuman, Buddha and Krishna are some of the mythological animation films that are hitting the market. The gods are likely to grace the silver screen, television, comics and merchandise like T-Shirts, coffee mugs and key chains.[47] However, similar innovations are not seen in the Christian world.

Internet as Evangelism Tool

Internet could be used for evangelism, helping people in the digital world to find Lord Jesus Christ as their personal savior. "Internet evangelism is a form of evangelism where the gospel is presented on the internet. This may include a website defending the accuracy of the Bible, someone discussing their faith in a chat room, evangelical messages or advertisements on the home pages of Christian organizations, or other methods of using the internet to spread Christianity."[48]

Websites

Christian websites have to be developed to present the gospel for those of other religious persuasions. It could be a website that simply presents the truth. There could be websites that need not explicitly share the gospel, but offers life solutions for various problems. However, when analyzing the problems, the Christian worldview of man, sin and salvation is clearly presented. The local churches should have their own website that provides a platform for sharing the gospel with other people.

Blogs

Blogs are short articles that fit in a single computer screen (about 250 words). The content of these articles are generally experiential. "A blog (a blend of the term *web log*) is a type of website or part of a website. Blogs are usually maintained by an individual with regular entries of commentary, descriptions of events, or other material such as graphics or video. Entries are commonly displayed in reverse-chronological order. Most blogs are interactive, allowing visitors to leave comments and even message each other via widgets on the blogs and it is this interactivity that distinguishes them from other static websites."[49]

Christians have experienced the goodness of our Lord through answered prayers, miracles, specific guidance, and victory in adverse circumstances. These experiences could be inspiration for others and also help them to come nearer to Lord Jesus Christ.

Social Networking

"A social network is a social structure made up of individuals (or organizations) called "nodes", which are tied (connected) by one or more specific types of interdependency, such as friendship, kinship, common interest, financial exchange, dislike, sexual relationships, or relationships of beliefs, knowledge or prestige."[50]

Social networking has become influential in the lives of youngsters who are digital natives. "Social networking establishes interconnected Internet communities (sometimes known as personal networks) that help people make contacts that would be good for them to know, but that they would be unlikely to have met otherwise. In general, here's how it works: you join one of the sites and invite people you know to join as well. Those people invite their contacts to join, who in turn invite *their* contacts to join, and the process repeats for each person. In theory, any individual can make contact through anyone they have a connection to, to any of the people *that* person has a connection to, and so on."[51]

Chats

Chats is another area where Christians could be proactively involved in helping people spiritually. "Internet chatting is when two or more online individuals come together to talk inside a chatroom, virtual software, or instant messenger. Chatting is a popular way in which people stay connected-whether it be for business or for family who live many miles apart. While chatting can be fun and entertaining, you must take protective measures against yourself as well to avoid internet stalkers and predators."[52]

Youtube

"YouTube is one of the most popular website on the internet which allow you to watch and upload videos for free. These are uploaded by YouTube members on this video sharing platform. One more thing YouTube membership is free so anyone can join, however membership is not required for watching videos. So you can either watch videos or upload your own videos in order to share with your friends, family and other YouTube members. Once you get addicted at watching video, you can call yourself a YouTuber!"[53]

Internet as Edification and Training Tool

Internet could be used as edification tool for believers and training believers so that they are equipped for effective ministry.

Internet as Mission Mobilization Tool

Internet could be used as effective tool for mobilizing young people for missions. Keeping with the attitude and trends of the postmodern generation, many digital natives develop their own missions. Steve Moore writes: "If we don't figure out how to collaborate creatively—if we use all of our metaphorical bandwidth for downloading—our constituents will increasingly pursue 'punk missions' that circumvent entirely the old school structures. Perhaps they will rewrite the punk music ad: "Here's a cell phone, here's a computer, now launch your own mission."[54]

It is essential to harness the power and connection of Interwork the inject contagious mission fever. "Only in an upload world can you engage, or could we say 'infect,' hundreds of thousands of people in a matter of days for free. By leveraging twitter, youtube, facebook and other social networking sites it is possible to communicate and mobilize large groups without traditional systems or structures. That's what makes it so scary. That's what makes it so powerful."[55]

Challenge

The digital world has opened up new opportunities and open doors for innovative mission. The digital natives could not be reached out through traditional methods and strategies. It is essential for the Church to look at this as new mission frontier and allot resources for reaching this world effectively. "When he saw the crowds, he had compassion on them, because they were harassed and helpless, like sheep without a shepherd. Then he said to his disciples, "The harvest is plentiful but the workers are few. Ask the Lord of the harvest, therefore, to send out workers into his harvest field."[56] There is a huge crowd in the Digital World. They are like sheep without a personal shepherd. The Global Church as congregation of shepherds should reach out to this digital community with diligence. The challenge is to evangelize, disciple, develop disciple makers and leaders from among the digital natives using digital tools.

Dominic Crossan captures the postmodern or Digital Natives predicament in the following lines:

There is no lighthouse keeper,
There is no lighthouse,
There is no dry land,
There is only people living on rafts made from their own imaginations.
And there is the sea.[57]

The digital world citizens need lighthouse, light and certainly hope of the gospel. Will the Global Church respond?

Endnotes

[1] Dan 12:4 NIV.

[2] Hab 2:11 NIV.

[3] Luk 19:39-41 NIV.

[4] Isa 49:16 NIV.

[5] Jesse Rice, *The Church of Facebook: How the Hyperconnected are Redefining Community* (Colorado Springs, David C. Cook, 2009), 117.

[6] "Microchip," accessed December 30, 2010, http://mirror.uncyc.org/wiki/Microchip.

[7] Gary Anthes, "Quickstudy: Making Microchips," accessed December 30, 2010, http://www.computerworld.com/s/article/72461/Making_Microchips.

[8] Ac 1:8 NIV.

[9] "Facebook Reaches 500mn User," accessed July 22, 2010, http://www.hindustantimes.com/Facebook-reaches-500-mn-users/H1-Article1-575913.aspx.

[10] Dilip Bobb, "Wired Generation," *India Today*, November 20, 2006, 48-60.

[11] "Rise in Students Using Net on Mobile Phones in Chennai," accessed December 20, 2010, http://timesofindia.indiatimes.com/india/indiaarticlelist/-2128936835.cms.

[12] "84% of Chennai Kids are on Online Social Networking," accessed November 20, 2010, http://timesofindia.indiatimes.com/city/chennai/84-of-Chennai-kids-are-on-online-social-networking/articleshow/6961949.cms.

[13] "Gen-X Needs 2 Hours a Day Online to Network," *The New Indian Express*, July 21, 2010, 9.

[14] Rice, *The Church of Facebook*, 141.

[15] Mark J. Penn and E. Kinney Zalesne, *Microtrends: The Small Forces Behind Tomorrow's Big Changes* (New York: Twelve, 2007), 259.

[16] "Digital Native," accessed December 30, 2010, http://en.wikipedia.org/wiki/Digital_native.

[17] Marc Prensky, "Digital Natives, Digital Immigrants," accessed December 30, 2010, http://www.twitchspeed.com/site/Prensky%20-%20Digital%20Natives,%20Digital%20Immigrants%20-%20Part1.htm.

[18] Marc Prensky, "Digital Natives."

[19] Marc Prensky, "Digital Natives."

[20] Marc Prensky, "Digital Natives."

[21] Marc Prensky, "Digital Natives."

[22] Ravi, "Media Convergence," accessed January 2, 2011, http://rrtd. nic.in/MEDIA%20CONVERGENCE.htm.

[23] "Internet World Stats: Usage and Population Statistics," accessed January 2, 2011, http://www.internetworldstats.com/emarketing.htm.

[24] Smitha Namboothiri, "Will you be My Virtual Wife?" accessed August 8, 2010, http://expressbuzz.com/states/kerala/will-you-be-my-virtual-wife/196338.html.

[25] Joanne Jacobs, "Internet Democracy," accessed January 2, 2011, http://www.abc.net.au/ola/citizen/interdemoc/democ.htm.

[26] Rice, *The Church of Facebook*, 141.

[27] "Internet Interactions," accessed January 2, 2011, http://journeytoforever.org/internet_how.html.

[28] Rice, *The Church of Facebook*, 99.

[29] Rice, *The Church of Facebook*, 111.

[30] Rice, *The Church of Facebook*, 112.

[31] Rice, *The Church of Facebook*, 131.

[32] Rice, *The Church of Facebook*, 131.

[33] Jerome Burne, "How to Change Your Mind," *Readers Digest*, March 2010, 75-80.

[34] Burne, "How to Change Your Mind."

[35] Burne, "How to Change Your Mind."

[36] "Wake Up America; Check Facebook," accessed July 8, 2010, http://timesofindia.indiatimes.com/world/us/Wake-up-America-check-Facebook/articleshow/6141566.cms.

[37] Shreya Roy Chowdhury, "Only 27% Parents Control Online Activities of Their Children: Survey," *Sunday Times of India*, June 27, 2010, 8.

[38] Rice, *The Church of Facebook*, 193.

[39] Vivek Seal, "Sex Games Kids Play," accessed August 14, 2005, http://www.dailypioneer.com/indexn12.asp?main_variable=front%5Fpage&file_name=story3%2Etxt&counter_img=3?headline=Sex-games-kids-play.

[40] Don Tapscott and Anthony D. Williams, *Wikinomics: How Mass Collaboration Changes Everything* (London: Atlantic Books, 2008), 270.

[41] Penn and Zalesne, *Microtrends*, 21.

[42] "Mizo Church Body Blames Cellphones for Pre-marital Sex," *The Times of India*, December 21, 2010, 12.

[43] Shiva Devnath, "Rape, MMS Clip and Betrayal," accessed June 17, 2010, http://www.mid-day.com/news/2010/jun/170610-borivli-resident-arrest-mms-clip-sex-with-minor.htm.

[44] "Facebook Causes One in Five Divorces: Survey," accessed December 1, 2010, http://ibnlive.in.com/news/facebook-causes-one-in-five-divorces-survey/136246-19-93.html?from=tn.

[45] "Textaphrenia & Textiety: Message Conveys Disorder," *The Times of India*, July 1, 2010, 13.

[46] Steve Moore, *While You Were Micro-sleeping: Fresh Insights on the Changing Face of North American Missions* (The Mission Exchange, 2009), 2.

[47] T. V. Mahalingam, "May Gods Be with You," *Business Today*, November 19, 2006, 197-201.

[48] Approaches to Evangelism," accessed January 2, 2011, http://en.wikipedia.org/wiki/Approaches_to_evangelism#Internet_evangelism.

[49] "Blog," accessed January 3, 2011, http://en.wikipedia.org/wiki/Blog.

[50] "Social Network," accessed January 3, 2011, http://en.wikipedia.org/wiki/Social_network.

[51] "Social Networking," accessed January 3, 2011, http://whatis.techtarget.com/definition/0,,sid9_gci942884,00.html.

[52] Anana Cherry-Shearer, "How to Chat in Internet," accessed January 3, 2011, http://www.ehow.com/how_4824204_chat-internet.html.

[53] Yasim Ikram, "YouTube Explained for Novice Internet Users and How to Use YouTube to Upload and Watch Videos," accessed January 3, 2011, http://ezinearticles.com/?YouTube-Explained-for-Novice-Internet-Users-and-How-to-Use-YouTube-to-Upload-and-Watch-Videos&id=5547986.

[54] Moore, *While You Were Micro-sleeping*, 25.

[55] Moore, *While You Were Micro-sleeping*, 29.

[56] Mat 9:36-38 NIV.

[57] J. N. Manokaran, *Christ and New Generation Youth* (Chennai: Mission Educational Books, 2010), 123-124.

Bibliography

"84% of Chennai Kids are on Online Social Networking." Accessed November 21, 2010. http://timesofindia.indiatimes.com/city/chennai/84-of-Chennai-kids-are-on-online-social-networking/articleshow/6961949.cms.

"Digital Native." Accessed December 1, 2010. http://en.wikipedia.org/wiki/Digital_native.

"Facebook Causes One in Five Divorces: Survey." Accessed December 1, 2010. http://ibnlive.in.com/news/facebook-causes-one-in-five-divorces-survey/136246-19-93.html?from=tn.

"Facebook Reaches 500mn User." Accessed on 22 July 2010. http://www.hindustantimes.com/Facebook-reaches-500-mn-users/H1-Article1-575913.aspx.

"Gen-X Needs 2 Hours a Day Online to Network." *The New Indian Express*. Bhuvaneswar. July 21, 2010, 9.

"Internet Interactions." Accessed January 2, 2011.http://journeytoforever.org/internet_how.html.

"Mizo Church Body Blames Cellphones for Pre-marital Sex." *The Times of India*. December 21, 2010.

"Rise in Students Using Net on Mobile Phones in Chennai." Accessed December 20, 2010. http://timesofindia.indiatimes.com/india/indiaarticlelist/-2128936835.cms,

"Textaphrenia & Textiety: Message Conveys Disorder." *The Times of India*. July 1, 2010.

"Wake Up America; Check Facebook." Accessed July 8, 2010. http://timesofindia.indiatimes.com/world/us/Wake-up-America-check-Facebook/articleshow/6141566.cms.

Ac 1:8 NIV.

Anthes, Gary. "Quick Study: Making Microchips." Accessed December 30, 2010. http://www.computerworld.com/s/article/72461/Making_Microchips.

Bobb, Dilip. "Wired Generation." *India Today*. November 20, 2006.

Burne, Jerome. "How to Change Your Mind." *Readers Digest*. March 2010.

Chowdhury, Shreya Roy. "Only 27% Parents Control Online Activities of Their Children: Survey." *Sunday Times of India*. June 27, 2010. Dan 12:4 NIV.

Devnath, Shiva. "Rape, MMS Clip and Betrayal." Accessed June 17, 2010. http://www.mid-day.com/news/2010/jun/170610-borivli-resident-arrest-mms-clip-sex-with-minor.htm.

Hab 2:11 NIV.

"Approaches to Evangelism." Accessed January 2, 2011. http://en.wikipedia.org/wiki/Approaches_to_evangelism#Internet_evangelism.

"Blog." Accessed January 3, 2011. http://en.wikipedia.org/wiki/Blog.

"Social Network." Accessed January 3, 2011. http://en.wikipedia.org/wiki/Social_network.

"Microchip." Accessed December 30, 2010. http://mirror.uncyc.org/wiki/Microchip.

"Media Convergence." Accessed January 2, 2011. http://rrtd.nic.in/MEDIA%20CONVERGENCE.htm.

"Social Networking." Accessed January 3, 2011. http://whatis.techtarget.com/definition/0,,sid9_gci942884,00.html.

"Internet World Stats: Usage and Population Statistics." Accessed January 2, 2011. http://www.internetworldstats.com/emarketing.htm.

Ikram, Yasim. "YouTube Explained for Novice Internet Users and How to Use YouTube to Upload and Watch Videos." Accessed January 3, 2011. http://ezinearticles.com/?YouTube-Explained-for-Novice-Internet-Users-and-How-to-Use-YouTube-to-Upload-and-Watch-Videos&id=5547986.

Isa 49:16 NIV.

Jacobs, Joanne. "Internet Democracy." Accessed January 2, 2011. http://www.abc.net.au/ola/citizen/interdemoc/democ.htm.

Luk 19:39-41 NIV.

Mahalingam, T.V. "May Gods Be with You." *Business Today*. November 19, 2006.

Manokaran, J. N. *Christ and New Generation Youth*. Chennai: Mission Educational Books, 2010.

Mat 9:36-38 NIV.

Moore, Steve. *While You Were Micro-sleeping: Fresh Insights on the Changing Face of North American Missions*. The Mission Exchange, 2009.

Namboothiri, Smitha. "Will You be My Virtual Wife?" Accessed August 8, 2010. http://expressbuzz.com/states/kerala/will-you-be-my-virtual-wife/196338.html.

Penn, Mark J. and E. Kinney Zalesne. *Microtrends: The Small Forces Behind Tomorrow's Big Changes*. New York: Twelve, 2007.

Prensky, Marc. "Digital Natives, Digital Immigrants." Accessed December 30, 2010. http://www.twitchspeed.com/site/Prensky%20-%20 Digital%20Natives,%20Digital%20Immigrants%20-%20Part1.htm.

Rice, Jesse. *The Church of Facebook: How the Hyperconnected are Redefining Community*. Colorado Springs, David C. Cook, 2009.

Seal, Vivek. "Sex Games Kids Play." Accessed August 14, 2005. http://www.dailypioneer.com/indexn12.asp?main_ variable=front%5Fpage&file_name=story3%2Etxt&counter_ img=3?headline=Sex-games-kids-play.

Shearer, Anana Cherry. "How to Chat in Internet." Accessed January 3, 2011. http://www.ehow.com/how_4824204_chat-internet.html.

Tapscott, Don and Anthony D. Williams. *Wikinomics: How Mass Collaboration Changes Everything*. London: Atlantic Books, 2008.

Questions and Concluding Remarks by Paper Presenters and Participants in the Final Session held on 14th of January 2011

Sungjemmeren Kijong Imchen

Here below is a compilation of questions and comments made by the paper presenters and the participants, and a final remark on the theme, the consultation, and the aftermath, which was made by the former principal of Union Biblical Seminary.

Peniel Jesudason Rufus Rajkumar

Witness today, I think, one of the questions that we are dealing with today is with regards to the issue of diversity that India is facing today. Wither that can be a challenge for Christian witness? How do we respond to the facts of diversity?

Matt Friedman

I think the question that resounds loudly in my mind is the issue of secularism in relation to postmodernism. One of the things that keep coming to my mind is that; How much of the negative side of secularism is taking hold in some of the Christian communities especially in Urban North India?

Joshua Iyadurai

The Spirit of God has a role to play and it would be good to have a model of witnessing which encompasses this line of thought.

Joshua Kalapati

What is the model of witnessing that balances between evangelization and socio-politico-economic action? What is the motive in our witnessing? We need to identify the challenges to witnessing to Christ. We need to understand the context to which we are witnessing. We need to understand the audience to whom we are witnessing. We need to evaluate the strength and weaknesses of our own model of witnessing.

Mariana Ngursanzeli Behera

We should emphasize more on the holistic way of witnessing. We should emphasize more on the issue of partnership and networking in terms of us living in a globalized world where it is possible to interact and network together which brings us to a point where we realize that as Christians we are all one in Christ.

Martin Reppenhagen

To Dr. Echols – Should we focus more and more on the Old Testament to get advice on mission?

To Dr. Friedman- How are the concepts of *theosis*-sanctification related to "party spirituality" in India? (Love your God and Love your neighbour)

To Dr. Marina – What is the influence of education on society? Is there a process of secularization in Christian schools in India?

Ajit Hazra

How can the ideals and models (information) discussed here be helpful to those actively engaging in witness in the grass-root level so that it can be used in the daily context? In other words how do we practicalize it?

P.S. Jacob

How do we go to the context and apply what we have learned from this consultation? Secularization has different format in different countries. In India *Sarvodharma* holds strong which says, "Equal respect for all religion". How do we witness in this context?

Jagat Santra

I have the desire to see the evangelicals open up to ideas from others. How do we go main stream and impact as the history tells that Christians have impacted much with education, health care and community development? How can we think more boldly and radically to make more impact?

The polarization of the ecumenical and evangelical divide is no longer relevant to us in witnessing. To be evangelical is not the concern but rather to be Indian and to be Christian is the concern. It is not only preaching gospel but to live the gospel is very important. Mission consultation must be more of a practical experience, sharing and solution to the questions that arises.

V.V. Thomas

Is it more important to put our emphasis on conversion or permeating India with Christian values?

Jesus asked to go and to preach. He never said go and build my church. He said I will build my church. Unfortunately, we put more emphasis on building churches today. We are to be witnesses and do what we are asked to do.

Beom Cho

How to keep and strengthen our Christian identity? How to approach the people with effectiveness?

Johnson Thomaskutty

Be open to ideas; Be open to praxis; But not to over contextualize. We must develop a more biblical mission theory. Let Christ go through the roads of India.

Asish Thomas Koshy

Our challenge in witnessing is to live out the gospel the message of liberation and all its other aspects. But we are reminded of the fact that living out the gospel will also result in taking up suffering as a consequence.

David Muthukumar

Witnessing Christ has an aspect of selling Christ as one of the products. But witnessing Christ can be representing Christ in contrast to selling Christ.

Catholic representation missing.

Sunil Kumar

How can our theological writings appeal to mission practitioners or Christians living in witnessing conditions?

Praveen Paul

Diversity within the church – theologies of mission/ motives of mission/ evangelical and ecumenical divides – should be addressed. Western domination in the understanding of mission should be balanced by Indian understanding of mission by having more of such consultations.

Sanjay Singh

Please be a witness!

Shekar Singh (Principal UBS when this Consultation took place)

The context in which we live in India is truly diverse. No one can single handedly define what the context is because it is very diverse. Within every context our task is to witness Christ. I know there are many challenges; be it religious fundamentalism or it could be caste barriers, it could be socio-economic injustices, or it could be other areas.

There was another colloquium on "Indian Pluralism and Solidarity for More Just Humanity". Father Augustine was making this particular comment on "Changing Context" or "Diverse Context". He said,

> Nearly 2000 years, Asia was the most challenging and most difficult of every ancient and sophisticated civilization and religion. Excluding the Philippines the Christian population is less than three percent. In spite of great missionary enthusiasm hard work and even aggressive method of innumerable western missionaries particularly during the past 500 years 97 percent of the Asians are finding salvation through their own religion. Their basic belief and attitude is that all religions with their strength and weakness are more or less the same in all the essence and are adequate to salvation in God's plan.

How do we make our witness known in the world, is, I would say a challenge for us. Even when we go to some of the villages or the rural contexts of India (because in urban areas people know what Christianity is and what Christianity has to offer) we will find people who do not know about Christ. When you talk about the gospel they do not know. So, I think, although Christianity did come 2000 years ago to India witness is still a challenge.

Through the various paper presentations we know what are the diverse contexts and how can we make an impact on those diverse context more effectively. But it should not remain within the four walls. It must reach out to the people who are there, out there in the field.

We have taken note of some of the suggestions in terms bringing mission practitioners or missionaries to such consultations and also bringing people from diverse context whereby representativeness in such consultation becomes more visible.

Let me say to all the paper presenters that you have done excellently well. I think all of us have been enriched by it. And I hope that you will be going with the questions which have been raised and I hope it will help you to revise your paper and send back to us. We would like to see that in book form.

It will not only be available in our libraries or in book stores, but I would like to see the wider publicity and people having them in their hands so that these materials can be used in their given realities in which they live.

Contributors

A. Selvaraj, IRCO, Trivandrum

Charles Echols, Union Biblical Seminary, Pune

J.N. Manokaran, TOPIC, Chennai

Joshua Iyadurai, Mylapore Institute, Chennai

Joshua Kalapati, Madras Christian College, Chennai

Matt Friedman, Asbury Theological Seminary, USA

Marina Ngursangzeli, United Theological College, Bangalore

Martin Reppenhagen, Griefswald, Germany

Rufus Peniel, United Theological College, Bangalore

V.J. John, Bishops College, Kolkata